Praise for the novels of
***New York Times* bestselling author**

HEATHER GRAHAM

writing as Shannon Drake

"Drake constructs a well-drawn plot and provides plenty of sexual tension and romantic encounters as well as exotic scenery."
—*Publishers Weekly* on *The Pirate Bride*

"Bestselling author Drake...keeps Ally's relationship with her aunts and godparents playful, forming an intriguing contrast with the grim progress of the murder probe, while satisfying romantic progress and rising suspense keep the book running on all cylinders."
—*Publishers Weekly* on *Beguiled*

"Drake is an expert storyteller who keeps the reader enthralled with a fast-paced story peopled with wonderful characters."
—*RT Book Reviews* on *Reckless*

"[Shannon Drake] captures readers' hearts with her own special brand of magic."
—*Affaire de Coeur* on *No Other Woman*

"Bringing back the terrific heroes and heroines from her previous titles, Drake gives *The Awakening* an extra-special touch. Her expert craftsmanship and true mastery of the eerie shine through!"
—*RT Book Reviews*

"Well-researched and thoroughly entertaining."
—*Publishers Weekly* on *Knight Triumphant*

Also available from

HEATHER GRAHAM

Night of the Wolves

And writing as

Shannon Drake

The Pirate Bride
The Queen's Lady
Beguiled
Reckless
Wicked

HEATHER GRAHAM

NIGHT OF THE VAMPIRES

HQN™

ISBN-13: 978-1-61664-970-8

NIGHT OF THE VAMPIRES

Printed in U.S.A.

With lots of love and all best wishes to an extraordinary group of up-and-coming authors—Jodine Turner, Tabitha Bird, Karisa Hatfield, Autumn Dawson, Lynn Brown, Sharon Duncan and Leslie Bard. My "girls" from New Orleans!

NIGHT OF THE VAMPIRES

PROLOGUE

THERE WAS JUST something about the man.

Kim knew it from the moment she first laid eyes on him.

It was just turning from summer to fall, and the day was beginning to die. Dust dazzled in the streaks of color that still formed the sky as the sun sank, while, already, the bountiful full moon was starting to peek out and rise into what would become a velvet and star-studded night.

He was the most unusual man. Even motionless, he compelled attention—she had simply known he was there the minute he had come to stand beneath the gnarled oaks. His stature was impressive, his very stillness somehow provocative.

There was a sadness about him, a melancholy, really, that drew Kim Forrester in despite the amazing bounty of handsome, wealthy and eligible bachelors in the room. He was tall—certainly a plus—extremely fine in physical appearance and with the requisite broad shoulders offsetting a lean waist. His hair was smooth and dark, his face clean shaven. He wore an elegant gray evening frock coat with a crimson brocade vest and a fine, matching stovepipe hat.

Something undeniable informed his movement. Sleek, like a great cat. Fluid, as if he were filled with confidence. This was strange, because Kim did not know him, and she knew most of the young bucks here, the sons of the most affluent men in the affluent community of exceptionally fine houses along the battery of Charleston, South Carolina.

"I do declare!" Marybelle Claiborne said, whisking her fan a thousand miles an hour. "That gentleman, why, he is just scrumptious! So darkly dangerous, mysterious, and—downright alluring!"

"He's not from here," Alice Payne said, sniffing, her nose in the air. "I've heard there's something quite scandalous and horrible in his past!"

Alice Payne was known for her darling and elegant button nose. In Kim's silent opinion, it gave her the appearance of a little piglet. Adorable, but a piglet all the same.

Kim forced a smile. She'd promised there would be no scenes here. In her mind, the balls were mindless endeavors where parents tried to sell off their daughters like chattel, hoping for the highest prices and the very best family alliances. Ah, and alas, so much for the pride of America, the people who would not bow down before kings! Here, there was a new king, and it didn't even have a soul: cotton. Sugar, of course, was in the royal court, and land meant everything. It provided a palace for the king.

"So seductive, yes, and scandalous. *Why?* We don't know, do we? And that's part of what makes him scandalous! They say that he's from Texas, that he's wealthy beyond measure," Julia Lee chimed in. She winked. "He's given the other fellows a run for their money. I believe he's come here with Lieutenant Weston, and I believe that the lieutenant befriended him at a cattle sale. Business has brought him to Charleston. And we are, of course, my darlings, known for our *Southern hospitality!*" She rolled her large blue eyes.

As they watched the distant figure, Benton McTavish strode out to where the young ladies stood, sheltered by the leaves of a giant oak. He greeted them all with a swaggering bow and the tilt of his hat. "Afternoon, ladies. If you're gathered here in number for fear of the newcomers amidst our group, let me assure you. We of your community—"

He meant social rank, Kim was certain!

"—will absolutely assure that no harm will come to the damsels of Charleston!"

Kim looked away, teeth gritting. Benton McTavish never lifted a finger to do an honest moment's work. He rode to the hounds, drank brandy and smoked cigars and pretended to know about his father's business. Proud as a peacock over his sexual prowess, it was rumored he had already sired several children with one of the beautiful young slaves on his father's plantation. She wondered how the poor thing bore his attentions, but she knew as well that the woman had no choice. She hoped that at least she received lighter household duties in exchange for those she was forced to perform upon her back.

"Why, Benton, we'd never be afraid, not with big, strong fellows like you around," Alice said, slipping her arm through his.

Kim turned around, pretending great interest in the golden color of an oak leaf, lest she look straight at Benton and gag.

"Shall we, ladies? A true pleasure to escort you all in! I do believe that our supper is about to be served."

Kim hung back. She watched them go, wondering

if, when they noticed that she wasn't with them, they would then discuss her as freely and maliciously as they had the stranger. As hard as her mother might try—as successful as she'd been in seducing Kim's very rich stepfather—Kim would never be among these elite. She was from the Caribbean, not Charleston, and her beauty seemed a curse, a cautionary tale about the seduction of good men, and nothing more.

It was thus that she was standing when the man came to her at last.

He smiled ruefully, and seemed to realize that she was here and yet far away, and among the crowd yet not of it.

"Miss, you seem at a loss. May I escort you in?"

His voice was rich, deep, cultured and bore an accent of the Deep South. The sound of it was like a sweep of honey into her bones. His eyes were darker than ebony and yet seemed to have a glow brighter than hell's fire.

"Forgive me. My name is Fox. I'm here at the urging of a Lieutenant Weston. I don't mean to be rude or impertinent in any way."

Kim found herself smiling. *Of course not—not with that accent. He had been born and bred to play the game.*

Her smile faded, and she frowned. A chill, and then a rush of heat flashed through her.

Fear.

She knew.

She knew because of her mother. Her mother, who had been raised in the Caribbean, who had been the grandchild of—

To her surprise, the sensation that had overcome her disappeared just as quickly. Her smile returned to her features. There was something so tragically sad about his eyes.

Looking at her, he somehow knew that she knew. The melancholy air about him deepened. "I would never hurt you," he said simply. He opened his mouth, as if there might be more explanation, but he repeated, "I would never hurt you."

She nodded. She thought about her mother, and the change that had come over her after the death of her father—her increased obsession with wealth and social prominence. She thought about her high-and-mighty—and quickly acquired!—stepfather, and the less-than-honorable way he looked at her when her mother wasn't watching.

She thought about the way her mother had spoken to her this very morning.

We will see you married off, young lady, betrothed today, and that is that. And if you don't choose among those who are proper, I will choose for you, and you will do as you are told!

"Miss?"

"My name is Kimberly Forrester," she told him. "Kim."

"Miss Forrester."

"Kim, please," she whispered.

"Hardly proper." And his crooked smile was beautiful; he made her feel as if she were melting into the earth.

"Neither is this." She came closer to him.

Not proper at all. But her life was a sham of obedience, and she loathed the life she had been intended to lead. Women were well-groomed puppets. They followed ridiculous rules. They turned away while "men were men" and lived with the shame and, in time—as she had seen too often—the bitterness and hatred.

She knew that she wanted something different.

She wanted life, passion, something real—if only for a moment.

"Careful," he warned, looking down at her where she stood, so close. Those eyes of his were pure fire. "I'm not…I'm not the one to give you what you need."

"You will never understand what I need, Mr. Fox," she assured him.

"Escape," he said flatly.

"And can you help me escape?" she whispered.

"That…but little else. You don't understand—I can't, I won't, I haven't ever been able to stay near those…those I have loved, or those who touch my soul."

She lowered her head for a moment. *Loved. Once upon a time, he had loved someone. And he knew what he was. Just like those playing this game here tonight, this game of charm, this charade of decency, he knew how to play the game he must.*

She stared into his eyes. "I want you to help me. Take me away. Get me away from this awful place now."

"It's not so awful," he told her. "There is a certain honor here, as well. There is loyalty, and many a man here is a good man."

"Not one who might be intended for me," she assured him. "Please. I'll never look back. And I'll expect nothing in return."

He wanted to stop her. She thought that he might be nearly as seduced as she, perhaps by her appearance, more likely by her boldness.

Or maybe it was just bloodlust for a willing victim.

And still, he wanted to stop her.

"Before the barbecue?" he inquired, his tone light and teasing, and again, she felt that she was desperately in love with just the sound of his voice.

"Now." Her voice trembled; so did she.

He stared back at her.

"Do you really know what it could mean?"

"Yes."

They were alone. Alone in the late day when the sun had fallen completely at last and the moon was riding high in the sky, and the echo of words and laughter and conversation had faded away.

He took her suddenly by the shoulders, and his hands were powerful, almost rough.

"Do you really know what it means?" he demanded.

"Yes!" she cried.

He shook his head, angry with her, angry with himself.

"Don't you understand? I can't be there to pick up the pieces. I can't…I can't stay. I can never stay. I can never stay long in one place. Don't ask me this— Go. Go into your ball and marry the proper young fellow and bear fine young sons and—"

"Live with a man who will despise me in time as I despise him, and fade into the woodwork behind the fabric of charade?" she demanded softly.

"But you would trade it all—"

"Yes."

Now he wasn't melancholy. He was tortured, angry… and still beautiful. He seemed to sigh, his eyes meeting hers. He touched her hair, stroking, cradled her skull in his hand and drew her to him. “You may trade your very life,” he told her.

His lips touched hers.

And she didn’t care.

CHAPTER ONE

Washington, D.C.

"LET'S DO IT—let's do this thing now," Cole Granger's voice was low and filled with grim conviction as he spoke to his three comrades.

They had quietly skimmed the stone wall surrounding the prison yard. Earlier in the night, a perimeter had been formed by able-bodied soldiers in the blocks surrounding the area, troops badly needed elsewhere holding the streets around this fortress. But now there were no guards left to stop anyone from entering, those who had been on duty having fled inside amid bullets and blades.

Not that it would help them.

This wasn't a holding cell for the hardened criminal awaiting execution, or even for a pack of murderous madmen. Those incarcerated were guilty only of bowing before a different, Southern power, and they were being held only until the war's end.

For several seconds, Cole Granger, Cody Fox and Brendan Vincent remained frozen in place, listening. Strange noises, soft cries, sucking sounds, eerie laughter—punctuated by bone-chilling shrieks and screams—issued forth from within the massive brick facade they faced.

"Truly, the situation is only becoming worse by the second, gentlemen," Cole noted.

Brendan Vincent, veteran of many a battle and even many a war, nodded severely, his handsome and distinguished face set like a rock.

"Yes. Time to move," Cody agreed. Cody—who knew exactly what they were up against, who had brought Cole into this strange, other battle that had nothing to do with North or South, blue or gray.

"Indeed—*now.*" Cole couldn't believe he was saying the words, or that they were entering the main prison, that he was holding his breath and about to go into action against a horde of bizarre demons.

Again.

Hell.

Victory, Texas. Things had been going well there—so damned well that maybe they'd let down their guard a bit. But this wasn't Victory, and Cole still wasn't entirely sure what he was doing here, except that he'd seen the results of what was commonly known as "the plague." It had come to the West, and, back then, Cole hadn't believed what he now *knew to be true.* There was one thing that caused the bizarre deaths, the madness, the murder and bloodlust of man tearing apart fellow man and woman.

One thing.

Vampires.

They'd come to his hometown and nearly annihilated the population, his people. They'd massacred almost everyone in Hollow Tree, too. But, thanks to the arrival of Cody Fox, they'd gotten things under control. So, improbably, now here he was, a Texas sheriff, called into the hallowed halls of a beleaguered nation, to help solve a plague again. A Texan, a Rebel, fighting monsters in the heart of the Union.

The key word in his strange situation was actually *Texas.* Out in the frontier of far west Texas, there were still folks who didn't even know that a war was taking place. They were too busy trying to feed cattle and sheep or grow subsistence from a lot of dry and rocky land. Most such hardy folk got along with their neighbors, including the Indians, but it was also an area where the different Apache or Comanche clans might go on the warpath. Civil war was something happening far, far away, to someone else.

Cole himself had wanted no part of it. Hard to say who was right and who was wrong when the abolitionist John Brown had flat out murdered slave owners in Kansas, and when the guerilla retaliation had been flat out murder, as well. John Brown had hanged at Harpers Ferry, and Robert E. Lee, sent out to apprehend the man, was now head of the Confederate Army. It was a mess of tangled loyalties all around, and among men who used to be brothers.

It was death. The death of the youth of one country, torn asunder; and it was mothers crying over the loss of their sons, little more than babes, because war always killed the fit, just as it killed the beauty of youth. Confederates were ripping it up as amazing cavalrymen and sharpshooters, naturally, because they mostly lived off the land, while their Northern brethren were simply whopping down hard on the South because they had numbers—numbers of men, numbers of weapons, numbers of financiers, numbers all the damned way around.

So many dead now.

The war was over States' Rights, and the main right

that many of the states wanted had to do with slavery, while half the boys fighting on the Southern side couldn't afford a good horse, much less a slave. They weren't really fighting for themselves but someone richer. Always someone richer.

It was a mess to begin with. It was horrible; it was ugly, it was heartbreaking.

Death, horror and bloodshed.

Then throw in a few vampires.

But, then, you could go on forever and not even know about the vampires. Most didn't. The creatures had to slake a bloodlust, but they worked around the whole killing and draining human being thing by feasting on cattle—just like man himself feasted on beef. Then again, Cole knew a few folks who didn't eat much meat at all—they lived on the land, consuming mass quantities of vegetables and beans and the like.

There were no vegetarian vampires, he thought wryly. Not that he knew about, anyway, but some were better than others, some had to be.

Cody, for instance. Well, half of Cody.

"Cole, five o'clock!" Cody Fox whispered to him.

He turned; the shadow was just slipping up behind them. He saw it, and quickly assessed his supply of weapons. He wanted to keep it quiet—didn't want the creature screaming and alerting others.

A stake.

Quick and hard, straight through the heart...his aim needed to be good—

The shadow pounced, becoming substance, the flesh and blood of something that had once been human. It started to snarl, gnashing its teeth, but Cole moved swiftly, his stake honed, his aim true. He rammed the creature through the heart, pinning it to the wooden door marked Warden. Unless it was the leader, an old vampire, it wouldn't turn to ash. No, this one wouldn't. It was wearing the tattered remnants of a uniform, butternut and gray—a recent soldier. The fellow had been a prisoner here. Already beaten and bested at war, he was now dying in truth, pinned by the stake. The thing's eyes widened and seemed to dampen with sorrow; its jaw continued to work. It—*he*—looked at Cole with a split second of humanity, and there seemed to be gratitude in the eyes.

Cole felt his heart squeeze. The thing twitched and went still.

Brendan stepped forward, a bowie knife in hand. A second later, the head fell to the floor. Brendan jerked the stake from the creature, returning it to Cole with a nod.

Once the rush began, there wouldn't be time for such thoroughness, neither in the killing nor in the covering up of their deeds. Brendan, a Unionist to the core, could manage the Union authorities and make their actions disappear if need be.

After all, it was Brendan who had gotten them here tonight. Cody Fox, who had come to Victory in a time of need and become a damned good friend. He had been military with Brendan, but Brendan had been in the service his whole life—right up to and into this War of Northern Aggression, as Texans called it. Not that that stopped him from coaxing Cody Fox out to Victory, Texas, to stop the infestation that had killed so many Southerners out there. Nonprejudicial infestation—the damned vampires didn't care much if you were free, slave, white, black, red, yellow, old, young, man or woman.

The bastards and their plague could certainly get around—here they were now, in D.C.

Hell. Ah, hell.

Maybe a Texas sheriff shouldn't be in Washington, D.C.

Maybe he was even a traitor, in a way. There was a sad irony to this. Here he was, a Texas sheriff, with a ragtag band in a Federal POW camp, having to put down not just the Union guards, but his Southern brethren, as well.

But Cole knew himself, when he'd heard about the madness, it wasn't going to matter to him any if the new bloodshed was occurring in the North, the South or Timbuktu, he was in on stopping it. Humans were humans, and that was that. He'd seen what the vampires could do, and he'd fight them with his fellow man, no matter what label anybody wanted to put on anyone.

God knew where they'd really come from, the whole damned war was so crazy, brothers choosing different sides, Lincoln's wife's family all in the South, fathers finding their own sons dead on the battlefield.

And now—this. No matter who was what and what uniform went on what man, there was no going around this.

"They're going to be coming en masse any second now," Cody said quietly. He looked at the others; they nodded to one another and stepped forward.

"Best we can, let's pick them off before the numbers flood in," Cole said.

"Oh, yes, yessir. As quiet as can be until…" Brendan said.

They all knew what he meant.

It started slowly. A few of them sensing—or smelling—fresh blood. They came slinking out along the walls, unorganized, instinct and bloodlust guiding them. Cole picked off another two, and Cody caught a couple while Brendan kept his keen eyes out, giving the warnings.

Then Brendan shouted, *"They're coming in force!"*

And they did. Confederate and Union soldier, prisoner and guard, old and young. They arrived without further warning.

The first wave were all young vampires, or so it seemed. They weren't turning to mist, weren't moving at the speed of lightning. They were awkward, untutored. They hadn't been diseased slowly, properly; they had been taken in a frenzy and, in turn, they were more like a sad and ragtag pack of stumbling, hungry corpses than creatures of wit and malice and true evil.

Vampires thrived in times of war and chaos. They could gorge themselves, and no one would really know what was going on—nobody could distinguish what was part of the war and what was part of an evil hunger. Vampires could be very clever, naturally keeping their numbers down by disposing of their food properly. Unless they were attacking an isolated people and had some luxury of time—such as with Hollow Tree or Victory—most vampires refrained from turning others. Mostly because they couldn't always control them, and they didn't like the competition. They could be restrained and clever, sliding right into society.

But vampires could also be like rabbits. Throw in a *reckless, vicious few* who didn't seem to care about competition, and suddenly they'd be coming out of the woodwork…and wild. The feeding here had been a careless one like that.

A Union guard staggered toward Cole, his head cast to the side. His face was gray, his throat a raw and bleeding mass where something had ripped it away. The three men were at a set distance from one another; they had learned how to watch one another's backs. Cole moved straight forward, Brendan and Cody flanking him.

The creature went down easily with a single strong slash of Cole's sword.

A boy came next. A drummer boy, perhaps. He couldn't have been more than thirteen or fourteen.

Some distant mother's child, not dead by canon fire, or the enemy's intent, but dead when he should have lived to go home one day, and tell his children and grandchildren tales of the great conflagration, and how it had ended in time, when people became reasonable again. What would come, he would never know.

There was no choice: the boy suddenly hurled himself at Brendan, fangs dripping, an eerie cry tearing from his throat.

Cole pinned him but inches from his companion's face. Brendan shuddered and quickly flashed Cole a nod of acknowledgment and gratitude.

More.

Older soldiers.

Even younger soldiers.

Emaciated, but no longer needing the bandages that had covered their wounds, the splints that held together shattered bones.

They came.

And they went down.

At one point Cole grew particularly tense: at least ten of the maniacal beings flooded into the fray at once. There was so little room in the corridors and offices of the prison, and with this battle different from standard warfare in that the enemy must always be kept at arm's length, at times he doubted they'd make it out alive.

In a fury of motion and intent, the three fought together, closing their circle at times, stepping out when it was necessary to repel the attacks before the creatures came too close. Cody could best withstand a slash of the fangs, but it was critical that even he be constantly aware of an assault from any direction.

It had been worse than this, though, Cole thought, back in Victory, Texas. His thoughts always returned to his decimated hometown. There, the vampires had risen and sheltered, had gained strength and learned how best to survive their new existence. They could be shadow and wings against the umber light of the moon, and they could suddenly be behind a man and everywhere around him with no warning.

And in Victory there had been those infected who could still be saved. Sometimes vampires retained a certain amount of humanity—call it a soul—that bred a desperate, choking kind of hope when one fought them.

This prison had been...this had been a massacre. A changing with no guidance. A certainty that all infected would become monsters.

Out of the corner of his eye, Cole saw a flash of darkness—a shadow, a form. Instantly, he knew that this being was older. Clever—bent on survival.

There was always a head, king or leader in a pack of vampires. Once he was taken down, the rest fell far more easily. An idiot in life was an idiot as a vampire. Pure and simple. Murdering idiots were easy to kill in life, and they were easy to kill off again in death.

Thing was, sometimes, once a leader was killed,

another picked up the reins. Or those who survived an out-and-out fight with human counterparts moved on and subtly started up again until they had power once more. Power in numbers. The right numbers.

It was a slippery slope for a would-be king. You needed enough followers to perform all your dangerous dirty work, but not so many that people began to realize that a real plague had been unleashed.

He spun around, certain that the creature was coming to lunge upon his back and sink his fangs into Cole's neck.

No. There was nothing there.

He spun around again, moving swiftly and with maximum speed.

"Cole!"

Cody shouted the warning. There was one to the front of him, one to the right. Think quick, double time on movement. Holy water to the left, his sword to the front with a massive slash.

Again, he felt it. Something…something at his rear. He could feel the hair rising at his nape.

Still there was that thing…behind him…no things! *Two—*

He spun as Brendan shouted a warning. There were two. They seemed to be in concentrated battle with each other. Cole snapped open a vial of the holy water and tossed it, then drew back with his sword, ready to strike.

The first of the creatures burst into dust, ash and a clattering of bones. The second turned—at his mercy.

He heard a shriek, a cry. There was a blur before his eyes and he spun again—it was in front of him.

"No!"

He slashed the air, and the form pitted downward, rolling to make an escape.

It registered in his mind that the voice was feminine.

Well, they held women prisoners here sometimes. Women they suspected of spying. The Union had always threatened that women would be executed for spying right along with their male counterparts, though that had yet to happen.

But this one…

Yes, she appeared to be a shadow form because she was wearing men's black breeches and a black cotton shirt. She had blond hair that glistened in the light of the moon and the few torches that still burned in the yard.

He saw her face.

Aquiline, sculpted, the face of an angel. Huge eyes, which glittered like gold, stared up at him. In contrast, her skin was as delicate and pale as porcelain.

He couldn't hesitate!

He strode forward, intending to finish her off. Straddling over her form, he raised his stake high in the air.

"Damn you, what are you, an idiot cowboy?" she demanded, scuttling a little away from him.

She was whole; she didn't seem maddened, *diseased,* in any way.

He had to hesitate; she might be among the living. Untainted.

"Who the hell are you, and why the hell shouldn't I kill you?" he demanded.

"Strike Cole, strike! It's deception, it's always deception!" Brendan cried.

He lifted his stake again.

"Please, for the love of God! I don't want to hurt you!"

she cried. She glanced toward the others, then back at him.

"What?"

"Cole!" Cody shouted in warning.

At his back!

He twisted, just in time to spear the man wearing a preacher's collar who was about to rip apart his back. He didn't dare take more than seconds to shake the fellow from his stake, not with the woman beneath his feet.

The body fell near her and she shuddered, but her eyes never left Cole's.

"Cole!" Brendan warned—there were two of them circling him.

"Give me a reason not to kill you!" Cole shouted to the woman at his feet.

She continued staring straight up at him.

"Cole!" Cody shouted at him this time; he could see that Cody was involved in helping Brendan—there were three around him, and now one had gained a certain power and speed, probably one of the first to be infected in the prison.

It sickened him. It had always sickened him. Self-survival had allowed him to learn to kill the creatures, just as the need for law and order and justice had always helped him out when a firm hand was needed in Victory.

But too often this felt like…

Murder.

He didn't want to do it; God help him, he didn't want to do it. Neither did he want to be seduced into a dreaded death, granting mercy, and finding that a harpy suddenly flew from the face and shape of the angel, and dragged sharp, wicked fangs into his neck.

Tension riddled his frame.

Time. Time could be everything.

His fingers wound more tightly around the stake.

"Damn you! Prove it, prove you're not one of them. For the love of God, then, give me a reason not to kill you!" he shouted above the fray to the woman beneath his feet.

She looked straight at Cole. "One can prove nothing in this world."

He raised the stake with purpose.

"Wait, *damn you,*" she cried. "I'll give you a very good reason not to kill me."

"And that is?"

"Fool! I've been fighting with you, not against you."

What?

"I'm Megan Fox. Don't you understand, cowboy? I'm Megan Fox, Cody's long-lost sister," she said with a dry and weary drawl that shook him, even in the middle of the melee.

CHAPTER TWO

MRS. GRAYBOW'S ROOMING House on the edge of the mall was a pleasant place. Until the war it had just been the home of Mr. and Mrs. Arnold Graybow.

But Arnie Graybow had been among the first to die at Manassas, and so now Martha Graybow, a thirty-two-year-old widow with two little mouths to feed, ran a boardinghouse. Mrs. Graybow and her brood, Artie and Marni, twelve and seven respectively, resided in the carriage house in back and to the left of the main house, otherwise empty now with the carriage and horses having long ago been sold. The main house itself consisted of five bedrooms upstairs, a lovely dining room, parlor, kitchen, pantry and music room downstairs. It was a fine and private temporary residence for vampire hunters.

As fortune would have it, Megan Fox was friends with Martha Graybow. They both hailed from Richmond. Once upon a time, Martha would babysit her when her mother had business at the bank, or would sometimes allow her to "help out" at the boardinghouse, though she'd been too young to be of any real assistance.

But, of course, Martha had no idea what Megan was up to nowadays. Martha, bless her, thought that Megan was just a fiery young woman, the kind that didn't swoon, that was happiest standing up against injustice. And indeed, Megan had faith, but she was pretty sure the world had a long way to go. One day there would be justice, and equality would exist. But not this way, not with the North decimating the South. Instead of shaming their brethren, the industrial North should have been figuring out ways to educate those in the South. But maybe she was wrong. Maybe half the planters were just greedy, and they didn't see anything equal in their darker brothers. Nothing about the war—despite the bloodshed, death and devastation—was cut-and-dried, or black-and-white. It was all gray and red—the color of the blood of all the Americans dying in the war, Yankee, Rebel, black man, white man, yellow, pink, dark or tan.

But she knew that a different war was also being waged. One that most of the world knew little about. Sometimes, she really wanted the entire world to know about it. Maybe they would stop fighting one another and face the true threat if they knew, but the words she had spoken to Cole were true: it was hard to prove the existence of the evil creatures to a large, disorganized populace to a satisfactory degree. The world wasn't ready to understand that the myths actually represented a very real part of the world.

And a part of her.

Cole Granger, the tall, sturdy, striking fellow who had nearly staked her, paced the room. His eyes were more than suspicious. He was thinking that he should have staked her.

Select—*very* select—Union troops had been called in for the cleanup of the prison fight. And so, now, there were four of them at the boardinghouse, and she sat on a chair in the center of the music room—the music room, rather than the parlor, which faced the street and afforded less privacy—seated very much as any prisoner of war might have been.

She was being questioned.

Cole kept pacing, trying to keep silent, and let Cody Fox take charge. She was attempting to explain to them all that she was Cody's sister. And it was interesting, of course, because she knew that Cody would certainly have told them all that he'd grown up *without* a sister, which would have been, in his mind, correct. They didn't know what she knew, of course, because she was Cody's *younger* sister—and she knew everything that their father had told their mother long after Cody had left. Still, she hadn't thought that it was going to be this difficult to explain.

But none of them had actually managed to sit quiet long enough for a nuanced discussion. She tried to remember the barrage of questions they had last voiced—in the order they had voiced them.

"No. Yes. No. And yes, and yes, I believe," she said, staring from one man to the next. Brendan Vincent first, older than the other two men and straight as a ramrod—a military man, possibly retired. His eyes showed age and knowledge; the hollow structure of his face betrayed pain even as the mobility of his mouth hinted at a kindness remaining despite the lessons of the world. Then there was Cody Fox. Her brother. He should easily believe her—apparently, the wheaten color of their hair had been their father's, along with the strange hazel-and-gold hue of their eyes. He had sharp eyes, ever watchful. And shouldn't he be able to sense their mutually *other* nature? And Cole Granger. Rock solid, with piercing blue eyes of a shade deep and dark blue, enigmatic. In contrast to the others, his hair was almost jet-black. Each of his limbs seemed muscled and toned, as did the breadth of his chest. He was evidently a physical man, one accustomed to constant movement—the look of a frontiersman, someone who met every challenge. His mouth was grim and one that had apparently forgotten all about trust or kindness. Maybe that wasn't true. He seemed to trust Cody Fox and Brendan Vincent.

"She's got a sarcastic mouth on her, that's for sure," Cole said.

"Yeah. That could mean some proof that she's Cody's sister," Brendan commented.

Cody's gaze turned on Brendan, ever so slightly dry and indignant.

Cole Granger was suddenly hunched down in front of her. "Who are you *really,* and what were you doing there?" he demanded quietly. But even when his words were soft, they felt deep enough to fill any room.

She inhaled deeply, refusing to be intimidated by the man.

"I'm Cody Fox's sister, Megan Fox. You can ask me a million times, and I will give you the same answer. There is none other to give," she said, staring back at him.

"I don't have a sister," Cody said harshly.

"Well, yes, you do, and it's me. Oh—and there might be others out there, too. Our father is out there, still, I believe. I know about you, and I'm sorry you know nothing about me. My mother actually looked for you for many years and discovered that you were in New Orleans. But you were gone by the time I managed to get there."

Cody glanced at his friends, a glance that assured her that he might be starting to believe her.

"Anyone might have researched Cody Fox," Cole Granger said. He was still directly in front of her, and his proximity was unnerving. The man seemed to have iron in his jaw, and she wasn't sure that he'd yet blinked since the interrogation began. If she didn't have a certain inner sense that she'd developed as a child, she might have thought he was one of…whatever she and Cody were.

A unique kind of "half-breed."

"And you just *happened* to be at the prison tonight?" Brendan Vincent asked, his words filled with doubt.

"Nothing just *happens.* I knew Cody was there. And if a Texas sheriff can be found in Washington, D.C., right now, there's obviously something going on. Of course, absent even those indicators, I knew already. I was sent by the government," Megan explained.

Brendan Vincent snorted—very rudely—she thought. "*We* were sent by the government—I know that. And I know that you weren't."

She stared at him coldly. "There are two governments in this country right now, sir. I realize that you prefer not to recognize the second, but it does exist."

She thought that he would pull his gun then and there. He refrained because Cody had lifted a hand. "Brendan, come on, we all know that we don't take sides in this."

"She's taking a side!" Brendan protested.

Cole continued to stare at her.

The whole thing was bizarre. Cole Granger was a Texas sheriff. Her half brother had hailed from New Orleans. From the research she had done, she was pretty sure that Brendan Vincent hailed from Texas himself, though he was clearly U.S. military through and through. But, then again, Lincoln had asked the South's major asset—General Robert E. Lee—to lead the Union troops. Lee had suffered long and hard while making his decision, but in the end he had thought himself a Virginian above all else. The war was a horrible tangle of loyalties, with half the boys on the bloody fields not sure of exactly what it was that they fought for.

With a pang, she remembered her mother's words.

The war itself is wrong. Doesn't matter, we're all losers in this debacle. Time, talk and the legislature should have taken precedence over the use of arms, and now...well, we have dead boys everywhere.

She'd loved her mother. Loved her so much. Her look at the world around her, and her ability to discover the truth, no matter how many layers of opinion and variation were piled upon it.

"No. I'm not taking a side. Any more than you are," Megan told Brendan.

"So, then...?"

Megan hesitated again. "All right. I'm from Virginia. I grew up in Richmond."

"The capital of the Confederacy," he said, nodding, as if that immediately meant she had fallen in from the skies.

"Brendan," Cody protested. "I was in New Orleans, and you came after me. And you're not even on active duty these days."

Ah! So the man who seemed to think of himself as the *Stars and Stripes wasn't even official.*

"Please, I don't know who is right and who is wrong anymore, really," Megan said. "And I can't do a damned thing about the fact that the two sides are just going to continue to shred one another to pieces until the agony becomes too great and someone on high is brought down into the dust and realizes that it has to end. I am here with the...consult of a government, but it has nothing to do with which government has the right to which piece of land. And if I'm touchy on the subject, well, I *am* from Virginia. But I wasn't asked to come here because of that—or because the South wishes to cause any harm to guards, prisoners, soldiers, nurses, visitors.… It's not to stage a mass escape. It's not for any reason of warfare." She looked at the three men, and then softly added, "Accepted warfare, that is."

Cole remained hunkered down in front of her.

"So, who sent you?" he asked.

She paused. She wasn't at all sure he was going to believe her. "It doesn't matter. I was sent by a Confederate general, one who's seen what an outbreak can do," she said at last.

"And how are you so familiar with outbreaks?" Cole asked.

She inhaled. "The Battle of Fredericksburg."

"What about it? You were there? You're in the army, of course," Cole said drily.

She stood, angry, and glad to see that she nearly knocked him down. He was quick, though, and regained his balance to stand, as well. She turned away from him, talking to Cody Fox and Brendan Vincent. "There was a time when I was a conveyor of information."

"A spy?" Cody asked.

She shrugged. "All of us are caught in this."

"There was a time—no more?" Brendan asked. The older man was perplexed. A loyal Unionist, he had apparently come to terms with his need for Cody; he would come to terms with her as well, eventually.

She shook her head. "This is—this is something that goes beyond war."

"Go on," Cody said.

"The Battle of Fredericksburg was horrible, truly devastating—"

"A complete route of the Union," Brendan interrupted. "And yet you say 'horrible.'"

"A Southern soldier was so agonized by Union losses that he brought water to the wounded Federal soldiers on the field," she said. "Sergeant Richard Kirkland, from South Carolina, didn't even bother with a flag of truce—he had to alleviate the suffering. The men whispered that Lee, watching from the heights, commented, 'It is well that war was so terrible, or we should grow too fond of it.' The point I am making is that the battle itself and the aftermath were so strewn with blood, it was difficult to notice one man's agony or death.... Or even that of several men."

Cole, now with his arms crossed over his chest, was frowning and seemed to understand what was going on. Completely.

"When was the vampire attack?" he asked.

She didn't mean to do so, but she shivered, remembering. "It was cold," she began. "December, and cold. And the men on the field screamed and cried. Many of us then went out to see what we could do. I was with a fellow who'd had his leg destroyed by shrapnel. That's when I heard the first scream—a scream so different.... I turned, and I saw the...the man. Darkness was falling, dusk was all around and at first I was confused. I thought it merely someone in a greatcoat who had come to help the wounded, as well. But that scream came again. More chilling than anything before...and I heard quick movement and then the sucking sound...and I looked around. One of our medics—a man who had not been wounded—

protested, demanding to know what was going on. And then one of them fell upon him, and he screamed...."

Megan paused. Cole's expression had not changed during any of this. "I knew then. But there were several of them, and the men on the field weren't really listening to me. I'm sure they thought I was crazy and that whenever they delivered pistol shots into the chest of one of the creatures, it would stay down. But I knew. And I was armed. I was able to take down three of the four I counted. But it was insane on the field! Those who witnessed the event and survived were certain that the opposing troops had somehow risen to fight one another again."

"The Battle of Fredericksburg was a while back," Cody said.

"We've been chasing this for a long time," Megan said. "Through many battles. But the thing is—now it's all come here. For me, Fredericksburg was the beginning. We think we have the situation under control, and then...there's a new outbreak. Recently, after the Battle of the Wilderness, things grew worse." She drew a deep breath. "There were dead and wounded from both Rebel and Union armies, and we know that some of ours were taken...and that a few of the officers were taken to the prisoner-of-war facility where we met tonight. I'd already been sent North when word came that there were 'riots' going on at the prison. And so I...I came. I'd heard as well, of course, that I might at last find my long-lost brother among those sent in."

"How did you hear that?" Cody asked, frowning.

She laughed. "No major feat of intelligence. People are whispering about it on the streets. And, I believe, it will remain nothing more than whispering. Most people mock the idea of anything outside the ordinary. Cody, you're simply known as an excellent man at taking down a horde of unruly men, and Cole Granger—" she paused, turning to stare at the man, hoping that she had all her dignity about her as she did so "—Cole Granger is famous, or infamous, for being the best man to maintain law in a wild frontier town. And, naturally, Brendan Vincent, it's long known that you're a staunch Unionist—despite being a Southerner from one of the Texas towns recently annihilated...by 'outlaws,' of course, they say."

All three men were quiet, staring at her. She hadn't really lied; people were whispering on the streets. She hadn't explained just how far up in the Southern echelon it was known that something beyond the absolute horror of warfare was going on. She didn't want to—certainly not now. She wasn't trusted as it was. Cody was trusted; she was not. They surely knew what he was. And Cody had been with the Southern army—until his wounds had sent him home to New Orleans, held firmly in Union hands. All this, and still they trusted him but not her.

Cole set a hand on her upper arm, spinning her around to look at him, still the skeptic. She stared at the hand. He stared back at her; he didn't let go.

"What?" she asked icily.

"Why didn't you try to contact us first?"

A knock at the back door stalled any answer she might have been able to dream up.

"Keep her here—I'll get it," Cody said.

"Well?" Cole asked as Cody walked to the door.

"Well, what?"

"Why didn't you contact us?" he asked. "Why did you chance going into that prison alone? *How* did you get into that prison alone?"

"I think Cody can answer that for you."

"I think *you* should answer the question for me, right now."

But before she could pretend to answer, she was suddenly swung about and pulled hard against his chest; he had a large, long-fingered hand clamped over her mouth.

She heard Martha Graybow speaking. "Cody, is everything all right? I saw you all come in, and then I noticed that you still have lights on. It's so late, and you fellows never came for your supper, so I was worried."

Martha. She should call out to Martha, and Martha could vouch for her. But then again, what good would that do? None—it could only do harm! Brendan Vincent was a diehard—if he knew that she knew Martha, he might decide that Martha was a Southern spy!

She held still and waited, tempted to bite Cole Granger's hand.

She somehow refrained.

If she were to bite him…

"Everything is fine, Martha, thank you. We did have a late night—you heard about the trouble at the prison. Well, it's all over now and we're just sitting with a bit of whiskey and winding down," Cody said.

"Oh, thank goodness. I do worry about you boys."

Martha, beautiful, sweet Martha. She hadn't wanted her husband to go off. She had known she would become a widow.

"Boys?" Cody said with a laugh. "I'll have to tell Brendan. He'd appreciate that."

"You young men!" Martha corrected.

"Thank you for your concern. We're fine. And we won't forget breakfast, Martha, I promise you."

The door closed. Megan gave a good hard kick backward, getting Cole Granger in the shin. He tensed but didn't let go.

"I don't think I like your *sister* much, Cody," he said, easing his hold then and pressing her firmly away.

She turned and stared at him, it was becoming increasingly difficult to remain calm in the face of this irritating man. "You don't know how lucky you are that I'm a temperate and reasonable woman," she said pleasantly.

"Oh, you can get worse than this?" Cole inquired.

Patience...

But her temper had flared. She drew back her lips and let out a hissing sound, displaying the fangs she could summon within seconds. She felt they were really quite beautiful...not that that was the effect she was going for here.

"Holy, Jesus!" Brendan Vincent cried, jumping back.

Cole Granger held his ground.

"Don't make a move!" Cody warned.

She smiled sweetly, retracting her fangs. "If I'd wanted to hurt anyone here, Cody Fox, I could have bitten off the ever-so-charming Sheriff Granger's fingers just moments ago. Don't you get it? What is the matter with you? Why don't you believe me? I'm your sister—your half sister, your father's daughter!" she said, praying again for patience and control.

Brendan Vincent stared at Cody. "She could be any bloodsucking monster out there," he cautioned. "She could have found out things about you. God knows—there is a war going on. She could be here to kill us all in our sleep. I say we stake her right now."

"Now, now, hold up," Cole said, arms crossed over his chest as he walked around her. "She did fight with us at the prison. And look close. She and Cody have the same eyes."

"I'm not getting *that* close," Brendan said.

Cole smiled at that. "She could have killed us a few times already, if that had been her intent. Well, maybe she couldn't have killed *Cody*."

"Well, maybe you should have just staked her at the prison," Brendan muttered.

Cody had moved closer. Megan stood very still, watching him as he resurveyed her, head to toe. Admittedly, she wasn't particularly well dressed. One didn't pick one's finest ball gown for a romp with ravenous killing machines in a prison yard. She wore a simple tailored blouse, vest, form-hugging, knee-length jacket, men's breeches and boots.

But he wasn't looking at her attire, she knew.

His gaze rose at last so that his eyes met hers. Fire and ice. They were the same hazel and green color of his own, a color that seemed like gold. She wore it well. Her eyes were fascinating, compelling—mesmerizing. Or so her admirers had told her.

Cody touched her hair, drawing his fingers through it. Suddenly, he smiled. "Let me see those fangs again."

She flushed, looking at the others. "Cody, it makes your friends uncomfortable."

"My friends know exactly what I am. They just want you to be the same, and nothing worse."

She allowed her fangs to show once again.

Yes, she was half vampire. Go figure. Her father seemed to have a steady ability to propagate. It wasn't like all the things that she'd read about vampires, but then again, who really knew anything about them?

"What else did your mother say about my father?" Cody asked.

"It's really a long story...."

"A *long story,* Cody," Cole Granger spoke up from behind her brother, coming forward. "I personally find long stories wonderfully intriguing." To her astonishment, he paused, gripped her chin and looked into her mouth—at her receding fangs. He looked at her mouth and studied her teeth and fangs as if he were looking at the quality of a horse he was considering for purchase.

Oh, she was tempted to bite.

Oh, so tempted.

She restrained. He was pushing her. He knew that a bite wouldn't turn him into an uncontrolled maniac. Nor would a single bite kill him.

He was trying to see if she would snap—if she was capable of control.

She pretended boredom. And strangely, surprisingly, she discovered that she liked something about him....

It was his scent, she realized. He smelled of leather and musky soap, of the night air and of something more subtle and deep and alluring. Horses, whiskey...and himself.

Bathed.

God, she loved the smell of a man who had bathed. These days, it didn't seem there were many of those. God knew that many a man's uniform, worn day in and day out as the war dragged on, reeked to high heaven. Well, this fellow wasn't a soldier. He was a sheriff, in a town, with a house most likely.

"We are always ready to be entertained by a story, and yet I find myself wondering not about any story, but rather what thoughts are prowling through that little mind," Cole said.

She blinked. There was certainly no chance she intended to have a deep and philosophical discussion with this man.

No matter how delicious he smelled.

She smiled. "I was actually thinking, sir, that you smell quite good."

Cody burst out with a laugh.

Brendan even grinned. "Good thing you do enjoy lathering away in a tub, Cole."

She couldn't help herself. She allowed her smile to deepen. "Good enough to eat," she said sweetly.

She was surprised when Cody came to her defense, though he spoke too coldly. "Give it up. You're not going to bite anyone, rip anyone's throat out or devour their blood. Gentlemen, please do say hello to *my sister*. Oh, and please do return the use of her jaw back to her."

"How have you come to that determination?" Brendan asked. Cole hadn't even looked at Cody. He'd released her jaw, of course, but he was still studying her with those eyes of his, pure blue ice.

She almost flinched when Cody reached out to touch her, lifting a small strand of hair away from her neck. She had a tiny mark there. Not dark, but rather a light, tiny, almost heart-shaped birthmark.

"I bear the same mark," he said quietly.

"You do? Really? I never noticed it," Brendan said, frowning. "But then, I'd not have noticed it on the young lady if you hadn't pointed it out, and you wear your hair long around your ears, Cody, and—oh, my. Well. If you say you both have the same mark…" he finished lamely.

Cody had pulled his own hair back to prove the point.

Cole walked across the room, taking a seat at the piano bench. He folded his hands prayer fashion, in thought.

"Cole," Brendan said. "It appears the young lady is telling the truth."

"Yep."

Cody turned to look at him. "That's all?"

"Congratulations. You have a sister," Cole said. "That really solves nothing at all."

Cody grinned. "And that means…?"

"It means," he said with his long, deep drawl, "that we know she's your sister. Whether or not we can trust her? Well, that remains to be seen."

CHAPTER THREE

COLE DIDN'T SLEEP well during the night. He lay down to rest with a stake in his hands and his bowie knife beneath his pillow.

He knew that Brendan Vincent would be doing the same in his room.

But morning arrived without incident, and when he came downstairs, he discovered that Cody's newfound *sister* was in the kitchen with their hostess, Martha, setting out utensils for their breakfast, something Martha Graybow prepared wonderfully. Apparently Cody thought it a good idea to introduce them, lest Megan's presence in their rooms seem somehow untoward.

He instantly wanted to protect the woman—stand between her and Megan Fox and make sure that the young half-breed vampire wasn't about to pounce. Martha Graybow was a mature woman, but she had a beautiful, kind face, and Cody had a feeling that she wouldn't be a widow long, once the war was over.

If there were any men left.

Martha had apparently loaned their surprise guest clothing; that morning, Megan Fox was wearing a demure cotton day dress that displayed the sleekness of her slender, shapely form to perfection. Actually, she'd worn men's clothing well, too, but, this morning, she appeared as pure, sweet and innocent as a newborn angel. Her hair was quite gold, gold like her eyes.

So much like Cody's.

And yet so different. So sultry, even when she was looking innocent. Somehow.

You smell good. Good enough to eat.

He found it hard to admit even to himself, but her fangs were equally stunning. He didn't think he'd ever been able to say that before.

"Good morning, Sheriff," Martha said, her voice bright, her smile sincere.

"I'm only a sheriff in Texas, ma'am," he reminded her with a smile of his own. "Cole will do just fine, thank you."

"Well, then, Cole it is," Martha said, flushing. "And I'm Martha to my friends. We'll be dispensing with the 'Mrs. Graybow,' when you speak to me, young man, if you please."

"As you wish, Martha," Cole said.

He was standing close enough to Megan to hear her mutter beneath her breath. "Charming. Oh, so, charming."

He ignored her. Ignored her—while keeping a wary eye on her. Last night, Cody had suddenly seemed to embrace the young woman. Of course, Cody was happy. He had just married a beautiful woman, and now he was finding that he had a sister. He'd been alone in the world for years, and now he had a family.

Thing was, though it seemed Megan Fox was his sister, they had grown up far apart. She seemed like a loose cannon—an unknown quality in a world filled with many kinds of dangers.

"Is there anything I can do to help?" he asked Martha.

"Everything is all set to go." She used a handwoven pot holder to lift the heavy coffeepot from the stove and began to pour the brew into the cups at the table. Cole noted that there were settings for six, and he frowned. Martha always joined them, on the days when her children were off to school, at least, but he didn't know who the sixth setting was for. Then he heard a commotion out in the drive and hurried out the back door.

Cody was already standing at the edge of the drive that led to the renovated old carriage house. A carriage had just arrived.

"Alex!" Cody cried out with pleasure. He opened the carriage door and held out his arms. His wife leaped into them and Cody spun her around for a minute before drawing her to him in a warm embrace. They kissed, and Cody let her slide down to put her feet on the ground. He went to pay the driver, but the man tipped his hat.

"Taken care of, sir!" the driver said, delivering Alex's portmanteaus to the walk. "Where would you like these taken?"

"We'll get them, my good fellow," Cole said, stepping forward.

"Cole!"

Alex smiled with delight and came to give him an enveloping hug, as well. He'd known Alex long before Cody had. Somehow, strangely, he'd forgotten that Alexandra was due that day. Chalk that one up to vampire-sister.

"So!" she said happily. Her brows knit suddenly as she looked around. "So?" she said again, a question in her eyes.

He turned. Megan Fox was there.

He cocked his head to the side. "Oh. Ah, Alex. That's Megan Fox. Your sister-in-law," he said mundanely.

Stunned, Alex stared at the girl, and then at Cody.

"We've just met," Cody said.

"Oh?" Alex inquired politely.

Cole bent slightly to whisper audibly to Alex, "Yes. She's just like Cody."

"I think we should go inside," Cody said.

"Martha's inside," Cole said pleasantly, getting Alex's bags. "But, by all means, let's."

He led the way, then carried Alex's bags upstairs while she hugged the hostess. Alex knew Martha from when she'd lived in D.C., right at the outbreak of the war. She'd been engaged once before, prior to meeting Cody; her fiancé had perished at the first route at Manassas, a battle for which people had actually taken carriages out to the fields to witness the *entertainment*—until they had seen how bloody and devastating that *entertainment* would become.

When Cole came back downstairs, Brendan, Cody and Alex were at the table. Martha was still fussing over Alex, and Megan was busy setting large platters of fluffy scrambled eggs, bread and heated dried beef with gravy on the table.

"My journey was fine, and without incident," Alex was saying as Cole took a seat on the other side of the table. "Long, of course, but you all know how long it can be. My papers were in order, and though we passed through different checkpoints, with soldiers on both sides stopping us for identification, I wasn't detained at any point."

"Dear, dear, it's only going to get worse," Martha said.

"They say that Lee is planning another invasion into the North."

"He's the world's finest general!" Megan said, her adoration for the man evident.

Cole himself admired Lee. Still, he'd never been sure that the general's determination to invade the North had been a wise choice and he'd been right—the Battle of Gettysburg had been a massive boon to the North and a horror for the South. But he figured the general had been weary of the battles being fought on Southern soil. Every battle cost the people of a region—it devastated the land, and it meant feeding tens of thousands of soldiers with the South's own stores, which couldn't last forever.

He noted then that Martha looked at Megan and gave her a knowing nod.

It occurred to him then that their hostess had known their surprise guest even before Cody had brought them together. For the time he'd keep his silence—and a careful watch on both women. There had been as many young women swept up with the war effort as there had been young men, and he knew that loyalties in war could be passionate, sometimes out of control. But his team's work wasn't about the known war, and he didn't want anyone's loyalties getting in the way of what had to be done.

"You two are looking mighty suspicious," Brendan said, voicing Cole's thoughts out loud.

"Suspicious? Regarding breakfast?" Megan asked.

"You're just looking mighty suspicious," Brendan told her. "And it's time to take heed to the truth of what has happened. The South will lose. General Lee was beaten back bad at Gettysburg, and the knots around the Confederacy are drawing tighter all the time."

"But that hasn't been the way of the entire war," Megan pointed out. "The South has won many—"

"Antietam Creek cannot be considered a *win* by anyone," Cole heard himself say, though he had meant to stay out of the argument. "Fifty-thousand Americans dead. That's not a win for anyone in my book."

Megan looked at him, quiet.

"Now, now, please!" Martha said, drawing out a chair to join them at last. Cole, Cody and Brendan stood quickly to assist her, but she raised a hand and slid into her own seat. "We're trying to have a nice civil breakfast here, and there's going to be no talk of the war, if you all don't mind. Not one of us here can solve it, that's the simple truth, and it's the arguing that got us all into it from the get-go, so… My, my! Cole, have you been in Washington before? Can you see how it's changed? My, my, from sleepy little place to giant industrial city in just a matter of a few years. And the construction going on! Why, President Lincoln has seen to it that the work on the Capitol Building continues. It will go up—he is determined."

Brendan Vincent was quite taken with Martha Graybow. "Indeed, dear lady. The city grew by nearly sixty-thousand souls in just a few years, so it did. Imagine this marshland becoming such a cultural center."

They were still in the process of finishing the meal when a knock sounded from the front door. Cody nodded at Cole and they both excused themselves, Cody holding back while Cole stepped to the door.

"Cole Granger, are you asking me in? Or leaving a lady on the steps?" said a mischievous voice on the other side.

And Lisette Annalise, actress by trade and newly

minted agent of the Pinkerton National Detective Agency, had arrived.

Cole opened the door with a smile on his face. "Why, Miss Annalise, no man in his right mind would leave you waiting anywhere," he replied, inviting her in with a flourish. Cole had met her briefly years earlier when she had been performing in *Faint Heart Never Won Fair Ladies* on the Western circuit. She was a young Jenny Lind, a stunning, petite woman with the voice of an angel. Lisette had most recently telegraphed Cole, having heard about the success his town of Victory, Texas, had in fighting off a ruthless gang of outlaws.

Some loathed her fellow "Pinks," as they were called. Some thought that they were a viable private enterprise. But there was no denying that war changed everything, and the Pinkertons were becoming a true power. The Pinkerton National Detective Agency had been founded in Chicago by Allan Pinkerton as a private security agency for rich and important businessmen and their interests. As president-elect, Lincoln himself had hired them, which tended to mean that Lisette would mention, almost right from the beginning of any encounter, that she'd met the man and admired him greatly, both of them enjoying the theater.

Cole liked Lisette, and he admired her. But she sometimes frightened him, as well. Her passion verged on fanaticism, and he'd never met a fanatic who could think with a straight head.

Overjoyed to see his old friend, Cole stepped out and quickly caught up with her about Victory, some common acquaintances and their business in the capitol.

"This is our contact?" Cody asked, suddenly appearing in the doorway, barring the way to the rear of the house.

"Yes, I'm sorry, forgive me," Cole said, making the introductions.

Cody and Lisette exchanged greetings cordially but with some tension about them. "Did you tell her about Megan?" Cody asked Cole.

"Not yet," Cole said.

"Ah," Cody said, expressing what seemed to be the key sentiment of the moment.

Lisette had dark brown eyes and auburn hair, and flyaway eyebrows that rose in question.

"Cody discovered a long-lost sister just last night," Cole explained.

"Megan," Cody said.

"A sister?" Lisette said, her lips pursing into a bow. "Does that mean…?"

"Yes," Cole said simply.

"Come along in, we'll be suspicious out here," Cole said, and gestured all into the house.

"Oh, of course. But I'm *suspicious* of this sudden sister already," Lisette said, which Cole couldn't help but smile at.

In the kitchen, introductions and greetings went around again. Martha was thrilled to meet Lisette. She had seen her perform onstage long ago in Richmond. Lisette was charming and said that she'd be performing in Washington soon.

"I find it so difficult these days, with so many soldiers out dying on the fields," Lisette said.

"Oh, but you entertain those left behind at home. You help them bear the hours while their loved ones are away!" Martha said enthusiastically.

"Just how is it that you know each other?" Megan asked sweetly. Her eyes glittered gold, though she smiled as she asked the question.

"Well, Cole and I go back a long way," Lisette said. She cast Cole a warm glance and lingered over the words, inviting all types of speculation as to what that exactly meant. "He wrote that he'd be here. May I ask you the same, Miss Fox? I'm always surprised that so many Southerners are enjoying a Union capital."

"I had word that Cody would be in Washington. I was anxious to meet my brother."

"Ah, yes, nothing like a little teasing sibling rivalry!" Lisette said.

Maybe it was natural that Lisette should subtly suggest that Megan Fox wasn't here with the noblest of intentions, to insinuate to those who understood the undertone that Megan might possibly hold an agenda that involved infesting the capital with the plague—and thus getting the Union to capitulate to the South.

To her credit, Megan was composed. "Rivalry? Oh, Miss Annalise, I wouldn't dream of attempting any form of rivalry with my brother. I've been hoping to meet him for so long! No, miss, I assure you, I shall do nothing but follow in my brother's wake, and hope to be so fine a—being."

"How utterly charming," Lisette said. She rose from her position at the table, smiling graciously. "Would you please forgive us? In these dreadful times of war, we never know when we will meet. Cole and I would like to take a bit of a walk." She smiled at him, blinking, as if she were about to burst into tears—as if there were far more between them than there had ever been. She was the ultimate actress.

Megan quickly and awkwardly rose, as well. "How nice! How very lovely. Yes, yes, the two of you must up and away for a lovely stroll. Pity the streets are little but mud and the dust flying about is terrible, but I'm sure you'll have a charming walk, so sweet when time is precious and two people are together."

One woman wanted his company, another was evidently more than anxious to get rid of him. He needed to see the one, and he was afraid to take his eyes off the other.

Megan was Cody's sister. And Cody certainly knew the score.

"Of course, Lisette," Cole said. "The streets are not so bad here—the house is not on a direct march line for the troops coming and going into and out of town. Let's do stroll."

"You will excuse us?" Lisette asked Martha, her beautiful smile all encompassing as she looked around the room.

They left by way of the rear door, the carriage entrance.

When they came around the front, Cole saw a sad-looking young woman standing on the front walk, an envelope and a clipboard in her hands. He started toward her.

"Cole, just walk, she'll come," Lisette said, taking his arm.

"She'll come? Who is she?"

"It's just Trudy."

"Who is *just Trudy* and why is she standing there?" he demanded.

Lisette sighed. "She's my assistant. The agency seems to think I need one, but I loathe being followed around.

Luckily, she's a little mouse and stands wherever I tell her."

"You had her just standing outside while you came into the house?" Cole asked.

"Well, outside and around the corner. I wanted some time alone with you. Besides, it's her job. She serves me. And she's paid to do it," Lisette said, waving a hand dismissively in the air.

She might be a mouse—a paid mouse—but Cole didn't intend to be that rude. He walked over to the woman, extending his hand. "How do you do, Trudy? I'm Cole Granger."

The young woman flushed and nervously shook his hand. "I'm fine, thank you, sir. How do you do?"

"Well enough, thank you. It's a pleasure to meet you."

Lisette slipped her arm through his. "Come. I have things to discuss with you." She moved ahead. Trudy waited, then followed them at a distance.

Lisette didn't speak at first as they walked from the house toward the mall, all manner of men and women moving past them, many of them soldiers. Though it had grown immensely and was a bevy of storage, manufacturing, industry and all things associated with war, there was still something inviting about the Union capital. The president spoke daily with his constituents—and his enemies—in the White House. He took his carriage out daily, often with his Mary, and despite the fact that there were those who despised him for the war, Lincoln was a man of the people. Cole had only seen him at a distance and heard him speak to crowds; Alexandra Fox knew him. She had been arrested for knowing what she shouldn't have known once because Alex had her own special gift. Her dreams could be prophetic. And she had tried to stop a battle, which had meant that she had found herself arrested for espionage. Lincoln had stepped in. They were friends.

Alex was no form of monster, as Cody sometimes called himself. But she was a different person. She had those dreams, or dream-visions. Alex often said that it might just be intuition, her senses warning her of what was to come.

She had never—she had assured Cole once—ever seen what the war would become.

"This is extremely distressing," Lisette said, when they had come to the Mall at last, looking to make sure that Trudy was still a good distance behind them. The great expanse divided the streets and had been designed as park area—though it was now most often muddy terrain where troops drilled—and it finally seemed to afford Lisette some sense that they were isolated enough to speak freely. They stood in front of the Castle, the first building of the Smithsonian Institution, where even now, in the midst of the war, the work of scientists went on. James Smithson had never set foot in the United States, but the country's dream of democracy had appealed to him, and he'd bequeathed the funds to an ideal. While troops drilled, business went on, and so the museum and the Mall were dreams and ideals loved by the people, constants amid chaos.

"This?" Cole asked.

"Megan Fox," Lisette said.

"We didn't bring her. She found us last night at the prison."

"Convenient. Are you certain that she hadn't been *in* the prison?"

"She had several chances to inflict damage on us and she didn't," Cole said. "She seemed to be fighting *with* us."

"Seemed!" Lisette said.

Cole listened to the sounds of the street, children still being children, playing on doorsteps and in patches of grass, carriage wheels running over potholes, line riders avoiding those potholes and even the rustle of fabric as ladies picked up their cumbersome skirts to cross the streets.

"Seemed?" Lisette repeated sharply.

"Look," Cole said. "I'm here with Cody and Brendan on a mission. I'm not here as part of a war. Cody says that she's his sister, and that's that in my book. I don't believe she's here on a sinister quest to rid the country of Union forces by setting forth a league of vampires. Take the war out of this when you're speaking to me, or I'm done."

Lisette had her hands on her hips as she stared at him; no one would mistake them for lovers at that point.

"I forget. You're one of them," she said. *"Texas!"* She nearly spit out the word.

"Humanity," he said flatly. "Look, are you going to tell me where we stand and what's needed, or are you going to spout political rhetoric?"

"The South will lose!"

He lowered his head for a minute. "Yes. Eventually. The blockades grow tighter, and for every Federal killed, another steps off a ship from another country, barely speaking English, ready to die like a canary sent into the coal mine of freedom. I'm done talking, Lisette. Tell me what you want, but, please, make no more references to the evil of Texas and my brethren. Just tell me where we are with the trauma at hand."

She pursed her lips with displeasure. "You did well last night. Extremely well. But we know that a number of the creatures escaped."

"How?"

"Have you seen the paper this morning?"

He shook his head. "No."

She reached into her bag and produced the morning's newspaper, unfolding it so that he could see the headline—Murder on Florida Avenue.

He took it from her hands and read the article. A Joshua Brandt, his wife, mother and two servants had been found dead. The bodies, white as sheets, had been discovered strewn about the house.

BREAKFAST HAD LONG been cleared away. Martha had gone to be with her children. Alex had tactfully taken Brendan for a "constitutional" walk. And Megan sat with Cody in the parlor, sensing what was coming next.

"You knew about me all your life?" he asked her.

She shook her head. "No, not all my life. But I knew about my father. Well, when I was young, my mother would tell me that he'd been a wonderful man, but that he didn't stay long in one place. That he…that he had a quest in life, and that his quest was important and undertaken for the sake of all humanity. I never saw our father. I was born in North Carolina, where my mother had friends. I would tell the children that I played with at parties and so on that my father was a great man, but when I was about six, I think, one of the older boys told me that my father was a drifter and I was a bastard. Shortly after, we moved to Richmond, my mother married a fine man named Andrew Jennison and my life went on from there."

She had barely finished speaking when the door opened and Cole stepped in. The woman, *Lisette Annalise,* was not with him. Megan had to admit she was glad. She didn't like Cole Granger and she liked him less alongside the actress who seemed to think she *was* the Army of the Potomac.

Cole looked at them then closed the door carefully. He walked over to Cody, placing a newspaper on his lap.

Cody groaned.

"What is it?" she asked.

"The plague at the prison might have been stopped, but we didn't get them all," he replied.

Megan stood and hurried over to Cody's side, brushing past the solid granite that was Cole Granger, and looked down at the giant headline on the newspaper.

"At least it's not—Battlefield at Antietam, at Gettysburg, the Wilderness…Tens of Thousands Dead," she said weakly, looking for something positive to say.

"How many do you think made it out?" Cody asked Cole.

"Can't be many. But even one is enough."

Cody exhaled. "Well, hopefully, the ones who escaped were new, young vampires that will need rest by daylight. But where?" he asked softly, frowning.

"St. Paul's, Rock Creek—Prospect Hill?" Megan suggested. The former, a Colonial church, had quite an impressive burial ground. The latter was a large expanse, fairly new, but with many plots sold. "Oak Hill Cemetery? And beyond. The law stipulated not so long ago that new interments had to be outside the city line… but there are crypts and vaults in the oldest churches, as well. Most likely new vampires would find rest in a cemetery—I don't think they'd be able to endure the burn of trying to sleep within an actual house of worship."

"My bet is on Prospect Hill," Cody said. "It is all hallowed ground, but many who would have been buried there perished on battlefields far away, and their remains were never returned."

"Though Prospect Hill is German-American," Cole noted, "I remembered reading a small article on it the day it was consecrated."

"Yes, but many bought plots there," Megan said.

Cody stood and looked at them with determination. "We'll flag down a carriage," he said. "It's not walking distance." He was thoughtful and then shook his head wearily. "Oak Hill is possible, too—its natural landscape lends itself to many places where a vampire might find enclosures in which to rest."

"And if one of the older, seasoned vampires survived, he might have a place already set up...*anywhere,*" Megan said.

"We'll just keep searching. We'll start with Prospect Hill, move on to Oak Hill...and go from there."

Cole nodded in agreement. "The surviving attackers must be found, but we also must get into the hospital morgue where the remains of the deceased were taken. Quickly. I don't want to wait for nightfall—better that we handle the situation now."

"All right," Cody began. "Brendan will come with me. We'll start on the cemeteries. You can bring Megan—"

"What? Oh, no," Cole said.

"You know, cowboy," Megan said, irritated, "one day, you'll be grateful to have me at your side, when your weakness is shown to be great next to those you choose to pursue."

"I know my business. You ask your brother. I learned to hold my own the hard way," Cole said. "Why, I nearly killed *you* last night."

"Oh, no, you did not," Megan corrected him. "I could have killed you, but instead, I saved your skin. You were with Cody. And then I offered you my services."

"You were at my mercy," Cole said softly.

"I—"

"All right, stop!" Cody said. "Cole, you come with me, and I'll send Megan and Brendan—"

"No! I know she's technically on our side, but you're not going to risk Brendan going with her," Cole said.

"It's early enough," Megan said. "And, Cody, you're a trained medical doctor. It will make sense if we both go to the hospital. Then, we'll go to the cemeteries together. We are talking vast tasks at each location. The hospitals are huge, and—"

"Even the morgue area will house many," Cole interrupted quietly.

"I think, since resources are limited, the murdered family might be kept separately," Megan concluded. "In the morgue area, but separate from those who have died of their battle wounds, or of disease."

"All right. We go together. Cole—Megan *is* my sister," Cody said.

"One you've known for less than twenty-four hours," Cole pointed out.

Megan moved toward the door. "Sheriff Granger, we need to leave. You may come—or not. As you see fit. But I am going."

She wasn't sure what he said; it was beneath his

breath. She didn't think that it was good. She didn't much care.

"I need my coat," he said. "You'll wait."

"I'll get Brendan and my medical bag," Cody said.

Cole was heading to the rear, for the hooks by the kitchen door, to retrieve his railway frock coat.

It was a long coat. Megan thought that it was also probably well supplied—with stakes, a mallet and a number of sharp knives. With his height and the length of the coat, his heavy supply of armor might not be noted beneath its folds.

She made it out the door first, walking purposely for the street and seeking a carriage to hail. Cole was right behind her, towering over her and lifting his hand high as he hurried her along. Just as Cody and Brendan caught up to them, a carriage for hire pulled alongside them and Cole asked that they be delivered to the Lincoln General Hospital. The four of them climbed in, Brendan being the one to first appear the gentleman and hand her up the footstep so that she might take a seat.

In short time, they reached the hospital. It was immense, founded in 1862 because of the staggering number of war injuries and diseases that plagued the soldiers. When they set foot at the emergency arrivals area, it seemed that the place was nothing but chaos, which was good for their purposes. Cole had a letter of authority from the Pinkertons—who were ostensibly investigating the mysterious murders—and a grim medic, hurrying from one tent to another, directed them to the far rear of the encampment.

"Did we really need all four of us for such a task?" Brendan grumbled, wincing as they walked past a pile of amputated limbs. "My dear!" he added, pulling Megan close to him. "These are not sights really fit for a lady."

"How kind, sir. But I've been on many a battlefield."

"I'm sure you have," Cole said.

"Where is your actress–Amazon warrior friend, Sheriff?" Megan asked sweetly. "Wouldn't she have better directed us on this mission?"

"Miss Annalise is a superb actress and songstress, in the city to warm the hearts of the injured and those working on the home front, and even those just waiting, raising their children," Cole said pleasantly. "She is otherwise occupied by her very important work."

Megan tried to restrain from an unladylike snort. She did manage to suppress the sound to a barely audible sniff.

She didn't like Lisette Annalise. She was sure that the woman would happily propel enough bombs to obliterate the entire South, heedless that it would kill countless innocents and take out half the Northern troops, all in her determination to exterminate her enemies. Did Cole realize that? she wondered. It hadn't taken any great intellectual mind to realize that the woman was a Northern spy, working with the Pinkertons. Though Cody had not told her so directly during Cole's absence, he hadn't denied her query about the woman, either.

A soldier suddenly barred their way. "What business have you here?" the man demanded. "If you're seeking the body of your kin, you've passed the tent where the latest casualties lie."

"I'm here under a matter of government concern," Cody said, and Cole produced their letter of authority.

The soldier nodded, looking a little white. "Dr. Mansfield examined the bodies earlier. I shall conduct you and remain with you throughout your own examination, sir."

Megan knew that her part in the charade was at hand.

"Oh!" she whispered suddenly.

Making sure that she was far enough from the men, she brought the back of her hand to her eyes and pretended to waver.

"Miss!" the soldier cried, rushing forward to catch her before she could fall.

"Oh, thank you!" she cried, circling her arms around him. "I don't know what's come over me! I've nursed men on the fields.... I just need...perhaps a bit of water."

"My poor dear sister!" Cody said, starting forward.

Cole caught him by the shoulder. "Dr. Fox, we've been asked to make a report as soon as possible on the condition of the poor family!"

"Indeed," Cody said, distressed.

"I have the young lady," the soldier said, now staring at Megan with something like puppy love in his eyes. "Be brief, please. I am ordered to watch over the corpses—God knows why. They are certainly not going to rise and fight the Union. And who would seek to steal a corpse—and besides there are thousands on the battlefields. There are sons in the family, but they are in the field. Oh, just hurry, sir, and do what examining it is that is necessary. I will see to the young lady. My officer's tent is just there...." He pointed.

"Oh!" Megan said again, clinging to him.

"Dear girl! Dear girl!" he said. And barely aware of the others, he helped her as she leaned hard against him, and they walked to the officer's tent. She glanced back over her shoulder just once, smiling at the trio of men. She noticed Cole looking back at her, appearing amused.

THE OBVIOUS FACTOR regarding the corpses was their color.

Or lack thereof.

"White" was the term used, and yet they weren't really white at all. They appeared to be a pale, opaque shade of yellow-pearl, and they seemed hollow, as if they had never been human at all.

Cole noted immediately that in addition to the massive trauma apparent on their necks, their throats had been neatly slit as well, though long after the blood had been drained. The perpetrators had been savage, making no tiny pinprick point in the throats of their victims, but tearing at them like rabid dogs. Young vampires, yes. And maybe an older one, hastily trying to cover their tracks.

Cody looked at the victims, laid out on the ground, covered in poor, unbleached cotton sheets, bearing the muddy look of the ground where they lay.

Cots would have been saved for the living.

Joshua Brandt had been a man of perhaps fifty or sixty years; even in death, he had a furrowed brow. His wife was thin, probably pale in life as well, her face portraying the wrinkled countenance of a life that had been long lived. Brandt's mother was long, excruciatingly thin, and probably soon for death even without the vampire's kiss. The servant girl was young and had been pretty; her hands were callused. There had been a male servant as well, an older man, bearing signs of stooped shoulders from a long life of labor. The bodies had only received cursory inspections and thus remained fully clothed.

"The heads, or stakes?" Cole asked Cody with sadness in his voice.

"Stakes, beneath the shirts and bodices," Cody said.

Cole hunkered down and reached into his coat for a long, narrow, honed stake and his mallet. He paused before looking down then discovered that he was poised above the body of the young servant girl. She looked peaceful, young and lovely.

To his surprise, her eyes opened. She looked at him and smiled, and he paused again. Then he saw that something in her eyes was registering cunning and evil intent.

He hammered the stake into her heart just as her lips drew back and saliva dripped off her fangs. He sat back, trembling slightly. She had changed quickly. And in daylight.

Cody had already dispatched Joshua Brandt and his mother; Brendan had made a quick, clean disposal of Mrs. Brandt. They both looked at him without words.

We all know that you never hesitate, their silent glances seemed to say.

And, yes, he knew. But he also knew that in Victory, Texas, they had let some of the *changed* retain their strange new existences. But they *knew* those they had allowed this for. It might have been possible that someone as young as this girl would awaken and search for a way to appease her hunger without attacking humans, but that would have been an amazing rarity.

He nodded, and though he felt tremendous pain again, he pulled down on the worn shirt of the older male servant and made quick work with his stake and mallet. A slight shudder seemed to escape the man.

There was no blood.

Cole pulled the man's shirt back into position.

They had completed their task.

The three of them rose, carefully seeing that the dead were covered again in their poor shrouds, and left them in peace. They headed for the helpful officer's tent. Orderlies, nurses, doctors and civilians who had come to see what comfort and aid they could possibly give patients were hurrying about in different directions bearing water, medical bags, alcohol, bandages and surgical instruments. As they walked, despite the stream of humanity, Cole heard someone crying out pathetically for help. He found himself pausing despite himself and the mission that still lay before them.

"Go on," Cody said. "We'll get Megan."

He followed the sound of the cries. They were coming from a tent that must have held at least thirty cots. There were four nurses or attendants, but they were all moving as quickly as possible. Men lay about in bloody bandages. Some had stumps for legs. Some were covered with sheets that quickly soaked blood from wounds that refused to completely mend.

He heard the cry again and passed by a wounded soldier who did nothing but stare blankly ahead. And then he found the victim crying so pitiably.

He looked about for a makeshift camp table and found a pitcher of water and a glass, poured some from the first to the latter and came down on one knee by the soldier's cot. He noted the man was still in uniform, a strange one at that.

"Where are you wounded, sir?" Cole asked, moving to lift the man's head.

The fellow's eyes took on a strange light. He smiled suddenly.

And opened his mouth.

Cole had never moved so quickly in his life, reaching into his coat, finding a stake. He couldn't bother with the mallet but had to depend upon his own strength and positioning between the ribs.

He laid himself hard against the man, trying to hide his deed with the mass of his shoulders and back.

The man's jaw locked in an open position. The eyes glazed slowly. The fangs retracted even more so.

Almost shaking, Cole withdrew slowly, secreting the stake back into the inner pockets of his coat. He realized he was still gripping the water in his free hand.

"Sir! What is happening there?" An orderly or doctor, standing behind him now, demanded.

He drew back, shaking his head. "I'm afraid I came too late, Doctor. This man is gone."

Cole stood, rising to his full height, meeting the doctor's gaze. For a moment, he was afraid the man might to challenge him.

But the doctor just shook his head. "Cover the poor boy then. God knows, we can't save them all, try as we will."

The doctor was too busy to tarry long. Cole hurried from the tent, scouring the faces and bodies of the others in the tent ward as he did so.

The "plague" here was bad.

Very bad.

No one else was crying out in the same way, though, and Cole moved on.

He should have known. He should have known from the sound of the cry that it had been a moan of an unnatural hunger.

He'd heard the cry often enough before.

And he had fallen for the plea of the hungry, thirsty, desperate new vampire despite all that he knew.

They needed to be doubly wary now.

He found Cody, Brendan and Megan still with the officer who had been charged to deal with the current, imminent danger.

He found himself looking at Megan, who was politely thanking the officer and apologizing for the time she had taken. The man was smitten, of course. The officer was young, and the war had probably taken him far from those he loved. Having a pretty young woman like Megan needing his attention was probably something he would remember and dream about in the long days and nights to come.

Poor boy. He didn't know.

Megan turned to look at Cole as he arrived among them. He felt a slight trembling in his length, a heat, a tension in his body.

She was a stunning woman with her perfect face and mesmerizing golden eyes. And she, perhaps more so than even Lisette Annalise, was quite an amazing actress.

That, he told himself, was something he was going to have to remember at all times. Especially now that she seemed to be doing such a superb job of joining in with them.

Especially now that it seemed Cody had accepted her, and even Brendan seemed to be falling for the beauty and sweetness of her spirit and…

Facade.

CHAPTER FOUR

MEGAN STOOD IN the middle of the cemetery, feeling the faint stirring of the breeze and looking around, wondering where to begin. The cemetery was relatively new. And yet, it was new at a time when the death toll was staggering. Across the country—or both countries—women waited at railroad stations for the post to come in, to read the lists of newly fallen, and pray that their beloved husbands, sons and brothers were not on those lists.

Many injured returned home. And died.

Disease was rampant.

Prospect Hill had been created when the law had stated that new burials must take place beyond city boundaries for such reasons. Technically, it was owned by the Men's Evangelical Society of Concordia Church; it had been consecrated in 1858, and it officially opened the following year. It wasn't a soldier's cemetery, but since Washington had been the staging ground for the First Battle of Bull Run, as the Union called it, the First Manassas, as the Confederates called it, many local sons had died very early on.

Now graves were dug in expectation, but those who had been destined to reside within them might never do so. Exigencies meant that far too many men had to be buried where they fell. Some remains would be retrieved at later dates; some would remain where they had fallen forever.

She was alone with Cole on the mission; the day was not long enough for their small party to cover the many places that came to mind after they had attended to the victims who had been murdered during the night. It had been Cole himself who finally realized that they needed to split up, and since it seemed most prudent that she and Cody be split—since they could easily endure the bite of a vampire and return to tell any tale—he had either begun to trust her, or he'd still rather risk himself than Brendan Vincent.

"Where do we begin," Cole murmured at her side, looking out across the vast and lonely expanse of the grounds.

"I think we need to wait a moment. There are several families here—look, just behind that little hill. There are people at that grave."

He nodded. "It's very new. No marker as yet." She was startled when he suddenly took her arm. "Let's stroll. We'll appear to be seeking the grave of a father or brother."

She nodded, surprised to feel a sensation of quickening within her, and aware of the warmth in his form, the strength of his hold.

"So," he said. "Not long ago, I wouldn't have believed that I could ask such a thing, but…did you always know that you were a vampire?"

He asked the question lightly, as if it were casual conversation.

"To tell you the truth, I'm not sure exactly what we are, Cody and I," she replied. "I can be injured, and I do age. I heal overnight when I am injured, that's true. And

I have survived when I should have died. But I have a heart that beats, I breathe."

He paused, looking down at her, and she was surprised that he almost seemed to be smiling. "That's—wonderful. But it's not the answer to my question."

She shrugged. "Well, I don't remember my infancy. I remember that I was always extremely fond of a rare steak, and that my mother always had me drink a strange concoction. I suppose the day she actually talked to me was when I was very young and had been punished at school."

"For what?"

"Samuel Reeves."

"You were punished because…"

"Samuel was a bully. He was always teasing my friend Sally, who limped. She'd been born with one leg a bit shorter than the other. Samuel teased her horribly. And he was cruel to her. He'd walk by and make her drop her books. He'd trip her."

"Ah. Not at all a gentleman," Cole noted.

"One day he sat behind her. He didn't just dip her hair in an inkwell—he managed to jump up and dump the entire thing all over her. He pretended it was all a massive mistake and he didn't even get in trouble. So, when we were out playing and he started calling her Blue Face, I charged him. He and I started to fight and there were kids all around us, cheering for one or the other of us. He started to take a real swing at me and I ducked and then…"

"And then?"

"I bit him."

"And what happened? Children do bite when they're tussling on the school grounds."

She shook her head, looking straight before her, and then meeting his eyes again.

"I liked it. I liked the flow of his blood into my mouth, and I didn't want to let him go. Our teacher had to get help to drag me off him, and when my mother came for me…she was horrified and upset, and she sat me down that afternoon and told me about my father, but she said that he was a good man, and that…I had to use my powers for good, as well."

"You believe that your father is a good man—still?"

"You don't—do you? Nor does Cody. But I believe it with all my heart."

"Why?"

"Because my mother was a good woman, and she wouldn't have lied to me."

Cole lifted her chin, and his touch was gentle. He stood there, studying her eyes.

"You believe in Cody, don't you? I believed in him before I met him. When I read the articles in the papers about the outlaws in the West—I knew that Cody was the son my mother had told my father about."

Cole laughed. "The name Cody Fox didn't tell you that?"

"Fox is a common enough name," she said.

Cole still seemed to be wearing a dry half smile. "What happened to Samuel Reeves?" he asked.

"Nothing. He stayed home from school for a few days—sick. I was punished for the rest of the year—I wasn't allowed to play with the other children. But, Samuel never teased my friend Sally again. Ever."

"And did you bite anyone else? Ever?"

"Only when I've had to—and only in self-defense, and only vampires."

"They're leaving," Cole said, pointing ahead. Visitors who had been praying at graves were heading for the gates.

"We'll have to split up and start walking fast," Megan said. The ever-so-slightly-civil-almost-tender moment they had shared was gone. He had become all business. She could certainly do the same. "Look for disturbed earth."

"I know what I'm doing. You head easterly, and I'll go west. Try to keep visual contact with me."

"Of course. I won't let you get hurt," she promised sweetly.

"You're Cody's sister. I'll look after *you,*" he responded over his shoulder.

"As you like, cowboy," she said lightly, aware that her teasing response was patronizing but unable to help herself from making the statement. She didn't want anyone getting hurt looking after her; she was what she was.

She was alarmed to realize that the day was quickly waning. And it was disheartening to know that they had fought so hard the day before—and that at least one of the creatures had escaped.

She could see Cole at a distance, long strides taking him swiftly across the cemetery. She saw when he paused and reached into his coat for one of his slender honed stakes, then switched it backward to dig in the ground.

She waited to see if he had made a discovery.

He had.

She watched as he swiftly found the mallet in his inner coat pocket, and slammed the stake downward, honed side first. He drew out his bowie knife and she turned her head.

It seemed that he was quite competent at what he did.

He was seeing to it that for certain the creature would not come back. If diseased men had died, they were vampires, or would be soon, and they couldn't be given a chance to rise again.

There was a group of trees ahead of her and she continued walking toward them. As she neared the little copse, she felt her muscles suddenly stiffen, and it seemed that the breeze blew chill against her flesh.

She saw a shadow, something, like a wisp of movement through the trees, almost a trick of the eyes.

The sun had not yet fallen, though it was sinking low in the western sky. A sense of great unease filled her. She was suddenly certain that they hadn't taken down even the majority of the vampires in the prison; in fact, she wondered if the prison had been nothing more than a prelude to a huge infection about to overrun the entire capital city.

Then she wondered if something hadn't been acting on her to lure her into the trees....

She held her ground, dead still and waiting.

Shadows moved again.

She refused to be trapped. She wanted the creatures out in the open.

And so she stood. Dead still.

And waited.

And finally noticed the first of the shadows coming for her.

Young vampire. It approached as a shadow, slowly, but quickly turned. Her stomach became a knot. It was a young Rebel soldier. His uniform. His face. He barely had a beard. But he came at her, and she had no choice. She ducked and turned, grabbing him by the shoulders, and hitting his jugular—as he tried to do the same to her.

She had barely ripped at his throat before the next shadow fell upon her. She reached into her skirt pocket, then stabbed a stake into his heart. Before that one had even fallen, another was after her, this one in the uniform of a Union prison guard. She ripped the stake from the one body to strike into the heart of the other—

And saw more shadows and figures, bloody and gaunt, dressed well and in tatters, coming from the woods.

At least ten of them.

A chill at the back of her neck and she knew something was behind her. She spun to tend to the attack. Speed was everything; she had to be prepared to defend herself from those coming at her from the woods. She wanted to call for Cole, but with their speed and her breath seizing in rhythm with her movements, it was too much all at once.

The *thing* behind her was little but flesh and bone. He went down quickly, having used whatever fledgling strength it had to become shadow and slip behind her. She faced the trees again, with trepidation. There were so many of them. They had never imagined so many.

In a fleeting second, she saw that something more was in the copse of trees. A greater shadow, a darker shadow. Fear set a cold grip around her heart, and yet, even as she felt the terror, she realized that the shadow-thing, only noticeable because it was even darker than the rest of the blackening night sky—it was actually battling the creatures within the trees, preventing them from spilling out to assail her.

"Megan!"

She heard Cole's cry as she met the Union sergeant running toward her.

Cole ran past her and into the fray precisely prepared.

He held a stake in one hand, and a bottle of holy water in the other. When two of the beings fell upon her at once, she'd have to admit that only because one of them was stunned by the holy water did she survive. She struck out with her stake, and then struck again. Cole was moving expertly at her side. Despite the massive ebony wing of the giant shadow-thing in the trees, at least six more of the beings escaped the copse of trees and came at them.

But she wasn't fighting alone anymore.

One by one, they went down.

She was fighting with Cole. And the black shadow had saved them from the full force of the mismatched *army* in the woods.

Suddenly, there was nothing.

She and Cole had set their backs to each other, and together, they had fended off every assault; they had actually been an awesome force.

They remained still, tense and waiting. She could hear the thunder of his heart, and the heave of his breath as they waited.

That, and nothing more.

When she looked to the trees, there was nothing.

"It's over," she whispered softly.

Around them lay a field of rotting dead. Blue uniforms, gray, butternut. They wore insignias that denoted them as militia, captains, privates, Army of the Potomac. The Southern boys were mostly in rags.

"Wait, keep an eye on the trees," Cole warned.

"No. There is nothing more there."

"How do you know that?"

She turned to look at him at last. "Because we weren't

alone, Cole. Someone was in among the creatures there, someone who helped us."

He shook his head. His words sounded harsh. "No, Megan. Why do you think that Brendan Vincent went to find your brother in the first place? A staunch Federalist seeking the help of a Rebel doctor? You and Cody are anomalies. A vampire is a predator. A disease. A mass of infection. A parasite that must thieve blood to survive."

"You're wrong. Some can be…nearly human," she said.

Cole paused, and she knew that she had struck a chord with him. She didn't know what had really gone on in Victory, Texas, but she was pretty sure that Cole had seen infected people become *decent* vampires. He had to know it could happen.

"This thing could just have been some kind of a trick, or even a trick of your eyes," he told her. "What exactly did you see?"

She wanted to explain, but when she opened her mouth, all she could think of to describe what she had seen was, "A shadow."

"A shadow?"

She nodded.

"Megan, they come as shadows, they can move like the wind. You know that. You've done it, I'm sure." She was surprised when he touched her arm, gently. "This is our battle," he said. "It would be nice to think that others were helping, but it's doubtful. And we've got to get moving here—we have a bit of a problem."

She looked around at the fallen. The corpses were far too new to have dissolved to ash.

"Good point. How do we explain all these dead?"

"And how long do we dare stay here without…without

reinforcements?" he asked. "The sun is falling. We have to make sure that we've completely dispatched all these men, and then we have to get out of here. I'll find Lisette and have her see that the burial detail that cleaned up at the prison gets here, too. We've got to get back to Cody and Brendan and find out what they discovered today. Hopefully we got a fair number of the loose vampires here."

She nodded. She didn't know why, but she felt a sting of tears in her eyes. So many dead! It was war, and men were dying every day. But this… Her heart went out to the beings she had taken down. The Rebels that lay dead had endured battle and capture, but not this unnatural thing.

They shouldn't have ended this way.

"Disease," Cole said sadly, looking down at a soldier. "Ah, yes, Cody told me once that disease and infection killed far more men than bullets. I guess he's right. The gangrene and the vampire diseases, both."

Wincing, Megan silently agreed, and together they hurriedly made sure that the "diseased" could not come back to strike again.

The sun was almost completely down. They hurried from the cemetery, hitching a ride into the city on a medical supply wagon. They sat in the back, on a flatbed filled with crates, forced to nearly sit atop each other.

But it wasn't a bad position, Megan thought. She was tired, and the afternoon had left her worried and confused. Her fears of a greater threat came to the fore again, and she considered mentioning something to Cole, weighing her combat-born fears against rational thoughts.…

And was surprised when Cole once again took her hand from where it lay on her knee and squeezed it.

She was more surprised, at herself, when she leaned against his shoulder to rest.

He didn't move away.

THEY ARRIVED AT THE BOARDINGHOUSE to find that the rest of their party had had an uneventful day. Cody and Brendan had scoured the churches with burial grounds, but had run out of daylight time to go on to the other cemeteries.

Brendan Vincent announced he would head to the small office of the Pinkerton agency, which dealt with many secret matters of state, so as to see that the cemetery was cleaned of the evidence of combat before morning.

Before letting Brendan go, Cody hunkered down by his wife and asked, "Alex, do you think that it's safe?"

Megan was surprised by Cody, Alex and the question.

Alex hesitated before answering him. "Cody, you know that—that I can't see things on command."

He nodded. "I was hoping that you might have a sense."

"I'm not feeling that it's unsafe. I *was* worried when you all left this morning, but that was quite natural, don't you think? I can't conjure a vision of the cemetery, but…I don't think we have a choice, do we?"

Cody looked at her awhile longer, smiled and nodded. "All right, Brendan. We don't have much of a choice."

"One of us should go with the crew," Cole said. "Me, I suppose. I know where…I know where the corpses lie."

"Well, that's foolish. If we did miss any of the creatures, you'll be as vulnerable as any of the men," Megan told him. "I can go."

"You were falling asleep on the way back," Cole said. "I'll go. You must have realized by now that I do know exactly what I'm up against and how to fight this enemy." He was irritated when he first started speaking, but she supposed, even if she did have a natural immunity, she ruffled his pride when she suggested that he wasn't competent—or that he didn't have the strength. He spoke more gently when he added, "You were fighting that bunch several minutes before I reached you. You have to be far more worn-out. I'll go."

Megan frowned, wanting to protest, but Cody put an end to that. "He knows what he's doing, Megan. Let him handle the situation."

Cody left with Brendan. Alex rose. "I have a plate of supper for you, Megan. I saved a plate for Cole, too, but… anyway. You need to have dinner. And sustenance."

Sustenance appeared to be a steaming cup of tomato soup; she knew that it was not. But though Megan hadn't thought that she was hungry, she was famished.

Cody went out while she was eating. Alex stood looking out the window in the boardinghouse kitchen; there was an actual kitchen building behind the house, but Martha had put in a sink with a water pump and a stove when she had begun letting out rooms. Megan knew that when she wasn't cooking breakfast for a household of guests inside the house, she prepared food for her children and herself in the kitchen building out back.

Alex seemed anxious as she peered out.

Then she turned and smiled. "Cody is taking a few precautions. He's setting up an alarm system, arranging crosses, sprinkling holy water around Martha's little carriage house, as well."

"Thank God," Megan said.

Alex smiled at her, a twinkle of amusement in her eyes. "You knew Martha before you were brought here, didn't you?"

Caught off guard, Megan nodded. "I was afraid to say so. Brendan Vincent is so staunch a Unionist, I was afraid he would think that Martha was a Confederate spy if I let on that we knew each other."

"Is she a spy?" Alex asked.

"No," Megan said, with a stone-serious expression Alex could not misinterpret.

Alex smiled and took a seat at the table across from Megan.

"But you are."

Megan shook her head. "I was a courier, and sometimes I carried information that fell into my lap. I was never actually a spy. And now...well, we're all fighting a different war." Megan looked at the woman, staring into her eyes. "*Your* turn, Alex, please. What was Cody talking about when he asked you if it was going to be safe for Brendan and Cole?"

Alex sat back. She was quiet for a minute. "I have dreams. I see things that happen, or may happen. When I can, I try to prevent them from happening. Actually, I was once brought in for being a spy, but—" she smiled "—I became friends with the U.S. government instead."

"Who?" Megan demanded, wondering if highest government and military leaders in the land really understood the reality and seriousness of the vampire situation.

"We're not totally sure we trust you yet, you know," Alex replied.

"I am Cody's sister."

Alex smiled, curling her fingers around the cup of tea she had poured for herself. "I believe that biologically, yes, you're his sister. But this country is currently full of brothers who grew up in the same house, loving the same two parents, going to war against one another. I've personally seen this travesty ripping apart the country. So, whether we all believe you're Cody's sister is rather a moot point. None of us knows you."

"Martha knows me. And you know Martha, too, don't you?"

Alex laughed. "Yes, I do. I know a lot of people in Washington."

"Then ask Martha about me," Megan suggested with both force and exasperation at this tension between them.

"I'll probably do that."

They sat in silence for some minutes, whatever had spiked up between them dissipating for the most part. Though questions still remained.

"And you do trust some vampires," Megan said.

"Some," Alex agreed, smiling. She hesitated for a moment. "Actually, I have good reason to believe in the goodness of *some* vampires—as do Cody, Cole and Brendan." She stood. "You are looking a bit worse for wear. Why, actually, you look like you've been digging in a cemetery. I had the tub filled in the back kitchen. I'll add some water and you can take a bath."

"I'm not going to take your bath," Megan protested.

"Oh, seriously, I insist. You look like you need it much

more than I do!" Alex told her. "I'll put more water on to boil."

It would be good to take a long, hot bath.

Alex provided her with a nightdress and robe and a cake of her own soap; it smelled deliciously of lavender. It seemed such a luxury that night—she hadn't seen decent soap in a long time. It was growing scarce in the South.

Cody was putting the final touches on a bell-and-wire alarm system on the carriage house where Martha slept with her children. Megan made a mental note to find time with Martha alone in the morning; she didn't know what Martha knew about Cody and Alex Fox and their friends, Brendan Vincent and Cole Granger. She thought she'd be much better prepared for whatever might come if she studied up on her new associates.

She carried the water to the tub herself, determined not to let Alex tote it for her on top of the kindness she'd shown already. Once she was in the external kitchen, she bolted the door and noted the many windows she had never much paid attention to before. They were closed, the drapes drawn. It was nice. She was beginning to feel as if she was being watched far too easily.

She had never been afraid, not since she had bitten Samuel. Then her mother had sat her down to explain that she was a being of free choice, and that she must choose for herself, but that using her strength for good would certainly prove to be the best thing to do, at least in the long run. Once the war had begun, she hadn't thought much about *what* she was; she had thought about little but the men on the field who needed help so desperately. The Minié ball and the other amazing rifle technology in the North had made it certain that many soldiers would be shot, and that most of those hit would die. She'd left Richmond with the Army of Northern Virginia, always on the lookout for the brother she knew had to be out there somewhere. She'd heard he was in New Orleans, and she'd planned to go there. But then a courier told her that he had gone out West, and that he was some kind of a hero in a town called Victory.

Impatient with herself, she dropped her lace-up boots and her muddied outfit to the floor and sank into the water. It wasn't as warm as she would have liked it, but it was delicious anyway.

And the soap! The sweet scent of lavender was a true wonder.

She leaned back and simply enjoyed the scent and the feel of cleanliness, closing her eyes and letting the water ease around her.

Then she heard a knock at the door.

She stiffened, then relaxed. "Alex? Come on in."

She had bolted the door, she remembered. "I'm coming. Hang on just a minute, please."

She hesitated, though. There had been no response from whoever had knocked at the door. Someone tried to twist the door handle. She heard the sound. She saw it move. But it was bolted.

There was another noise.

Now at the side window.

Then…

At the rear window.

Megan scrambled to her feet. She hopped out of the tub just as she heard the shattering of glass.

And saw the figure of a man crawling heedlessly through the shards of the windowpane that clung to the frame.

He was wearing butternut and gray. A Confederate Uniform worn by the Virginia Regulars. His uniform was worn and frayed on his gaunt, tall frame. Creeping menacingly from beneath his hat, a straggly beard, green eyes and dusty brown hair.

She knew him.

He laughed, staring at her, and she realized she was still dripping wet, and naked. She grabbed the bright white towel and covered herself haphazardly.

When he spoke, his voice was strange.

"You! Ah, you, Megan Fox. Imagine. I smelled the intoxicating scent of blood…and it's *you!* How delicious. Now, I know. And now, I have the strength, and the power—and the hunger!"

She blinked, unable to believe her eyes—or ears. And, yet…

Not so strange, not so ridiculous. So many of the young men her own age had answered the call to war—Virginians, fighting for the Commonwealth of Virginia.

He opened his mouth.

His fangs dripped saliva.

She knew this man-thing.

"Samuel Reeves!" she gasped.

CHAPTER FIVE

BURIAL DETAIL WAS grim, but, although Cole had expected that someone—*something*—would leap from the small copse of trees by the cemetery's edge, nothing happened at all.

He and Brendan arrived in a military conveyance with four soldiers that had been trusted to understand that no matter how bizarre the orders given to them might seem, they must be followed to the letter.

Coming to the ground where the corpses lay, Cole saw that the soldiers with him wore bleak expressions; some of the bodies had decomposed unnaturally quickly. Sergeant Terry Newcomb was in charge of the detail, a crusty old Irishman who still bore traces of his native accent. He had seen action through the first battles of the war and been sent back to D.C. for guard duty after he'd somehow survived a shot to his leg just a fraction of an inch from a major artery. The doctor on duty had not amputated, and Terry Newcomb was damned lucky on that score. He hadn't gotten gangrene. He limped, but he was still feisty and fiercely loyal to the Union. Those under him were war-wounded, as well: Michael Hodges suffered hearing loss, Gerald Banter had lived through a bout with malaria but was still considered too weak for duty and Evan Briar had lost the tip of his trigger finger.

He was learning to shoot left-handed, but it was going to take some time.

They stood with their shovels and picks, surveying the field of dead. "It's a disease that brings on madness?" Sergeant Newcomb asked, looking at Cole.

"Yes, you could say that it brings on madness. A bloodlust. The disease is quite serious—a man may look dead when he is not," Cole explained. "There is no cure, that's why—"

"You don't need to explain, laddie," Sergeant Newcomb said. "I was at the prison. I didn't think that I'd see the light of day again. All right, boys, let's get to digging."

Cole picked up a shovel. Newcomb stopped him. "Laddie, you don't need to do the grunt work with us. We know that your loyalties lie elsewhere."

"My loyalty is to stopping this infection that kills men and women regardless of their size, their sex, their color—the uniform they choose to wear," Cole said. "And I'm good with a shovel."

"As am I, sir!" Brendan Vincent said, taking up the task himself.

"You're really here just to stop this—trouble?" Evan Briar asked Cole after they had worked in silence for several long minutes. "You're a Texas sheriff. You gotta be a Reb."

"I suppose I am. But, we're so far out on the frontier, we struggle just to keep life going on a daily basis. We don't pay it much heed," Cole said.

"But, you're still a Reb. There ain't no neutral in this war," Briar told him.

"Look, sometimes, we're so far out, we're not even

sure we're in *either* country," Cole said. The last thing he wanted to do was get into a political argument.

"Reb, yep. You're a Reb. So why don't you let this disease just tear up the Yankee capital?" Briar said, persistent. "Why, I'd think that your side would be sitting back in delight."

"No man delights in the deaths of others. And we're here because we've seen this plague before. We don't want it in the North or in the South."

"Oh, Lord Almighty!" Gerald Banter said suddenly. "You drag the body, and the head comes right off!" Gerald stood back from the hole he was digging, his mouth agape.

"It's one way of making sure that the diseased are dead," Cole said.

"We take their heads off?" Banter asked, his tone thick.

"Yes, we take their heads off." He might as well make it a lesson in vampire killing, since it seemed that the "plague" wasn't going to end anytime soon.

And he might as well end it all with the North and South, too.

He leaned on his shovel. "Look, fellows, this isn't an issue of the war. Let's clear that out right now. Think of it like you might think of the plague hitting Europe in the Middle Ages. It killed everyone. Commoner and nobleman alike. Frenchman, Englishman, Spaniard. Young and old. We have to stop this plague. Northerners would carry it to Southerners, and vice versa, and once a man is diseased, he doesn't care if he gives the disease to his own mother. When you're up against them, you've got two choices—you take off their heads, or you impale them through the heart. Remember that the heart is on the upper left side of the chest. When you can, you impale them through the heart, remove the heads and burn them, but that's not often going to be too easy, so make sure you've gotten the head or the heart. I'm no man's enemy in this thing, so get that straight, too. Trust me—no man in a secret room in the U.S. government is planning to harness this plague and set it loose in the South—and no man in the South is thinking he can harness and set it loose in the North. It's a killer, bold and simple, and that's that. Can we finish?"

There was silence. They all stared at him.

Then Newcomb came over and slapped him on the shoulder. "Damn, laddie, why someone didn't just give us this information from the beginning, I don't know. Take heed to what the Reb says, my boys. We're going to stay alive in this thing, and we're going to protect our city. Let's get this done. Heads off these poor men if they're not severed already. It takes some strength to sever a man's head, so see to it that your knives are honed!"

When Cole and Brendan returned to the house, tired, weary and dirty, they headed toward the door, hoping to clean up some of the mud in the rear kitchen. As they walked around, Alex came flying toward them. She nearly collided with Cole.

"Alex!" Cole said, catching her.

"There's something wrong!" she told him.

"What?" he asked sharply.

She turned and pointed toward the outbuilding kitchen. "I brought some more hot water for Megan—thought she might want a little more, and I didn't have a fire going in the hearth back there, so I brought it from here. But I heard things flying back there—and she's got the door bolted—and there's shattered glass—the ground by the back—and there's sounds of fighting going on in there.… I was on my way to find Cody when you came around."

"Go on then, get Cody," he said.

Cole grimly set Alex aside and he and Brendan headed for the freestanding kitchen building. He didn't go around the back to crawl through a shattered window; he put all his size and muscle into kicking in the front door. It burst off the hinges, and he was met by two people who had been locked in battle suddenly freezing and staring at him.

The man was dressed in the tattered remnants of a Southern regiment, one that appeared to be from a Virginia outfit. He had his fingers tangled in Megan's hair, and it appeared that he was trying to rip out her throat. She was clad in a white towel that she was losing—he was gratified to see that she was more concerned with remaining alive than she was with modesty.

The reborn Rebel soldier looked at him and laughed and made another move for Megan's throat, but Megan let go of the towel and caught him with a right hook that seemed to knock his head out of alignment.

"No more!" the creature cried. "No more. I am alive, and I will take you with me into the depths of the realm, Megan Fox." He jerked, gnashing his fangs, trying again for her throat.

Cole strode in, reaching into his coat pocket for one of his remaining vials. He tossed the vial of holy water at the being, and a burst of steam sent the man into a whirling, burning frenzy.

"No!" Megan cried in distress.

Cole ignored her; his movement was practically automated, and the protest didn't register. He lurched on forward, drawing out his stake and mallet, and pinning the creature to the wall. The body began to jerk and spasm even as it burned from the holy water meeting the evil within.

"Oh, Lord! Oh, no! Why did you do that?" she demanded.

Brendan had been behind him, waiting at the broken doorway with a vial of holy water in one hand, a stake in the other.

"Oh, my," he said. He flushed brilliantly and backed away.

Cole let the body go. It was safe to do so. The being had gone limp after the tremors of its death throes.

For a moment, Megan stood there, sleek and damp and entirely naked, hands on her hips as she accosted him.

Then she quickly ducked for her towel, wrapping it around herself, her cheeks flaring red as she stared at him again.

"What the hell are you talking about? I just saved your life," he told her.

"I was holding my own!"

"You were about to become dinner!" he told her.

She shook her head. "That—that was an old friend."

"That was a vampire trying to rip you apart." Cole yanked the stake from the creature and let it fall to the floor. He'd become adept at decapitation with a bowie knife, despite the impossible strength it seemed to take when he first began doing it. But he'd known Cody long enough to become excellent at the task.

There was no blood; the creature had not dined in a long time, so it seemed. He must have been ravenous.

Brendan noted that the man must have been long seasoned in battle. He had pinned a note with his name and unit on the bottom left leg of his trousers.

He stared at Megan suspiciously. "Samuel Reeves?"

Holding her towel tight, she nodded.

"Did you ask him here?" Cole demanded, incredulous.

"No! No, of course not," she protested.

"Was that entire story some kind of a trumped-up and sardonic lie? That's a coincidence that's too hard to believe!" he accused her. He didn't want it to be, but he was finding it hard to believe that they had brought up the man's name earlier—and here he was.

She gasped. "I haven't seen him in years."

"You're certain?"

"Of course! Oh, how dare you. If I'd invited him here, would he have been attacking me? What's the matter with you?" Megan cried.

He was angry, but she was furious. She was wearing a towel.

It was an incredibly uncomfortable circumstance. He kept fighting himself to stare into her eyes—eyes that usually seemed as mesmerizing as the sun.

"You didn't want me to kill him," Cole said harshly. "Because, in truth, he was a friend?"

"Because he—he might have given us information. Please! Stop it! It's not a shock, really. Think about it! He would be fighting with a Virginia regiment, he would be an officer, and it's not at all surprising that he'd be held in prison in the capital. But, damn you, Cole. I can take care of myself. And I didn't want him dead."

"He was dead already," Cole reminded her.

"There are good vampires," she protested.

He held very still, not wanting her to see the nature of his thoughts. There could be *good* vampires. That was true; he had seen it. It was unusual, and, sadly, many of those who might have proved able to retain their decency in their death or life after life couldn't be given the chance to prove it. Vampirism was a plague that spread too easily.

"He didn't look like a good vampire."

"Maybe not, but we'll never know," she told him irritably.

"And he didn't manage to rip out your throat, so you might say thank you!"

She started to speak, then closed her mouth.

"If you're telling the truth, then you really are being foolish. You were more vulnerable than you want to admit."

"I'm telling you the truth!" she insisted indignantly.

They stared at one another for a long moment.

"Damn it!" she said. "You've got to start trusting me or we'll all wind up in serious danger."

"Trust has to be earned," he said.

She swore softly.

He fought to control his temper, and he knew that fighting then was no good for either of them. He shook his head. "Another body we've got to bury."

"I could have reasoned with him," Megan said.

"What? You're crazy. And why would you reason with

him? Are you feeling some ill-conceived guilt over what happened when you were child? Dear girl, that's insane," Cole said, irritated.

"No, it has nothing to do with guilt." Her voice had become raw and edgy. "He would know where all this started. What's happened is insane. These outbreaks… here and there. Someone is starting them, and—and there's someone besides us trying to fight what's happening. If you hadn't been so knife-happy, we might have gotten some information out of him. Look at his uniform! He was a lieutenant in the cavalry. He might have known where it started."

Cody appeared at the doorway then, tense, ready for action. He stared from Megan to Cole—and to the corpse on the floor.

"Thank God you were here in time," he said to Cole.

"Yeah, that was my thought. But apparently, Megan didn't want help. She was going to reason with the man. Before or after he ripped open her jugular, I'm not sure. But I'm done for the night. You two figure this out. Oh, and Megan, if you're such an excellent fighter that you can *reason* with a starving vampire, I'm sure you're also adept at the disposal of bodies."

He turned and strode past Cody, who stared at him with surprise but didn't say a word. Alex was just outside, standing with Brendan. He shook his head and walked past them.

As he did so, Martha Graybow opened her door so that it was just ajar, saw him and stepped out. "Cole?" she asked softly.

He inhaled on a deep breath. "Martha, everything

is all right now." He saw that Cody had set up alarms, and that he'd made her house safe by erecting wooden crosses—that might pass for structural supports—at the corner joints at the roofline. He was sure Cody had taken a few other precautions, as well.

He took her hands and looked into her eyes.

"I'm all right," she said. "I was worried about Megan."

"Megan is fine. And I'll fix the door to the kitchen tomorrow…and we'll put in a new window. Look, Martha, these are really bad times. We'll be here for a while, and you'll be paid while we are. But don't bring anyone else in. Don't ask anyone in, for the love of God. I can't really explain, but—"

"There are vampires loose in the city," she said flatly.

He hesitated. He'd always suspected that she knew more than they had realized. But his protective instincts wanted to guard her against even knowing this level of evil existed. "There's something like a plague. It—it makes people crazy and murderous."

"Right. A plague of vampires," she said.

"That's not something you say out loud, you know. People will lock you up." He looked at her very seriously.

She smiled. "I know that, Cole. I'm glad you're here."

"How do you know about the vampires?"

"I've known Megan a long time," she said. Then she added worriedly, "She's a good soul, Cole. She'll never hurt you. She'll never hurt anyone. You—you wouldn't ever hurt her, would you?"

Hurt Megan. Could he ever hurt Megan? he wondered.

"She's Cody's sister," he said. "But you must have known that."

"I knew that she was looking for a brother," Martha said. "And I knew Alexandra because she lived in D.C. and we were friends. I didn't meet Cody until you all came here. But I do know Megan. And I care about her."

"Why didn't she tell us that she knew you?"

Martha's smile deepened. "She was protecting me, I believe. She wouldn't want anyone thinking that I was a Southern spy. I told you—she would never take a chance on hurting anyone. And the vampires are just a bit of something more hideous in the midst of a hideous war. But, it means that we all have to be careful on many levels."

He nodded. "I guess I'm glad you know. It will help make you truly vigilant. Make sure everything is locked up, Martha. And get some sleep. You have little ones to attend to."

"Thank you, Cole. Thank you for being here."

"We'll do our best, ma'am," he told her, tipped his hat and bade her good-night.

As he watched Martha leave, Cole was suddenly aware of just how tired he was. He was bone weary. He thought that surely he'd go to his room, clean up the best he could for the night and fall sound asleep.

But, of course, he knew that Megan was sleeping down the hall.

He was highly irritated with her—good God, she

couldn't seem to think rationally. What kind of information had she thought she'd get from the man?

He lay down to sleep with that thought in his mind.

And with a vision that crept in, as well.

Megan, alabaster pure and perfectly sculpted from head to toe. Naked head to naked toe.

He was, after all, human.

And the day hadn't been half-bad. She could be charming. She could be sweet. And no matter what she was beneath, when he touched her, she was warm and vital.

She was dangerous. She was eager to insist that someone else was out there, and ridiculously certain that a dead man turned vampire could tell them where this disease of the East had originated.

He punched his pillow, adapted his position and fell asleep at last.

That night, he dreamed.

He and Megan were in a misty place, and he could hear water running, dancing as it rode over boulders and pebbles in a clear, clean brook. There was a hazy moon somewhere above the mist, casting an opaque light upon the world.

She came forth from the light: ever beautiful, sleek, porcelain. She walked through the mist, and he waited, thinking that he had lived his entire life just to reach out to her and hold her. Her smile held the charm she so easily offered. Her hair seemed spun gold in the moonlight. Her eyes were light, gold and red and green, a promise of fire.

She came to him. And he reached out.

And she turned, her smile broadening....

Fangs longer than those of a cobra or an Arctic wolf.

The dream ended in a burst of red—bloodred.

He sat up with a jerk. He was alone in his room at Martha Graybow's boardinghouse.

And he had dreamed, nothing more.

And yet…

He wondered.

MEGAN WOKE SLOWLY in the morning. She did so with a bizarre sense of serenity. The sun had risen, birds were chirping, and the air in her bedroom seemed light and beautiful, with dust motes dancing within it.

Then, memory of the day and night gone by returned to her, and she jumped up with a jolt. She dressed quickly and hurried downstairs, making it in time to hear the wheels of a carriage clip-clop down the street. She walked to the front door and opened it. The carriage was gone.

Frowning, she went into the kitchen. There were still biscuits and bacon on the table, but the kitchen was empty.

Had they all gone and left her?

Cole was completely mistrustful of her.

But did Cody doubt her, as well?

The sound of hammering attracted her attention and she hurried out to the backyard. Cole was near the doorway to the outer kitchen, attaching new hinges to the wood that used to be a door.

He looked at her without warmth, and with a fair amount of suspicion in his eyes.

"Good morning," she said carefully.

"Grab me a handful of those nails over there. Please," he added at the last.

She did so.

"Where is everyone?" she asked.

"Out," he said simply.

"Out where?"

"They've gone off on business."

She sighed with exasperation. "What kind of business?"

He didn't answer. His attention was reserved for the door he was repairing.

"What kind of business?" she repeated.

He looked up and stared at her, arching a brow.

"Oh, all right," she told him. "Fine. I've got it. It has something to do with the *Union* government. And I'm not trusted. But I guess you're not trusted, either. Well, you are from Texas."

He leaned back, staring at her. "Brendan Vincent came from Texas. He was with the U.S. military most of his adult life. He chose to stay with the Union. Every man has to make a decision, and every decision hasn't been dictated solely by where a man was born."

"So, you're a Unionist?"

He set his hammer down, impatient. "I don't rightly see myself as either. I think that it's all just a damned sad thing. I dream of a day when it will be over, and that's that. And the next person who asks me my opinion of the war...oh, God, never mind. I am a Texan. I love Texas. I love the frontier. I've spent endless days keeping the law with Indians, Comancheros and plain old horse thieves. I don't feel like fighting the fellows with whom I went to the academy. I'm here to fight vampires. Then I'm going home, and I'm going to hope that the human war doesn't ever reach Victory, and that my quiet little town's still there when I get back."

"I'm sorry. I'm just curious why you're not with them."

His head was down and he didn't answer her.

"Oh. I see. You were left behind to watch over me."

He finished hammering a nail and looked up. "You did tell us that you had arrived when you did because of the Southern government. You might want to explain that."

"I told you. A certain general—"

"A certain general?"

"Yes, a general."

"*Which* general?" Cole demanded.

"Does it matter which?"

"It could."

She stood stubbornly for a minute. Then she sighed. "Look, Cole, I already tried to explain. It was a long time ago—after the battle at Sharpsburg—that men in the military realized that something more was going on than simply the slaughter of war," she said drily. "After the last battle, at the Wilderness, when so many Southern troops were taken captive, we were on the battlefield trying to sort the wounded from the dead. Some of the dead—weren't dead. Or they were dead, but when we tried to bury a few, they came back to life. I was there. And there are those who still believe that men suddenly rose from mortal wounds to fight one another."

"Um. So there you were. Conveniently. Fighting in the war, are you?" he asked casually.

"No. I was on the field helping the injured. I explained

everything to you, told you the truth at the beginning. You know who and what I am exactly!"

"Yes, you've given an explanation."

"Oh, please! What do you think I'm doing up here? You've been with me. You know that I'm Cody's sister, and you've seen that I'm very good at what I do—and that I'm no more lethal than Cody."

"I've certainly never suggested that Cody can't be lethal."

"Oh!" she said, exasperated. She turned to head back into the house.

"Hey! Where are you going?"

"Back in. Obviously, we have nothing to talk about."

"We'd have a lot to talk about—if you actually talked," he said. "But that's beside the point. You don't have to talk. Just give me a hand with the door. It's your fault that it's broken."

"What? That is ridiculous. You broke the door down."

"To save your life."

"I'm very good at saving my own life."

"I saved it anyway," he said briefly. "Get over by the doorframe. I need to align the hinges."

She was tempted to leave him to fix the door himself, but since there were a number of people—including Martha and her children—who used the outer kitchen, she gritted her teeth and walked stiffly to where he'd indicated. He hiked up the heavy wooden door and grunted as he shoved it in place, spare nails in his mouth, the hammer balanced in the crook of his arm. She stood to support the door as he grabbed the hammer, but the door was well behaved, and stayed in place easily as he secured the new hinges.

When all the nails were out of his mouth and hammered in, he stepped back, then swung it open and closed.

"Is that it?" she asked.

"Go in and try the new bolt."

She did so, sliding the new wooden bolt. It worked well, sliding easily in and out of place. It was larger than the previous one.

She opened the door and came out. "I thought we were supposed to be heading out to more of the cemeteries and burial grounds today."

"Soon."

"Soon?"

"When the horses get here. You ride, I assume."

"Of course I ride," she said. "I'm from Virginia."

He smiled. The point he had been making all morning, apparently.

"Well, you may come and knock on my door when you need me. I'll remove my untrustworthy presence until then," she told him.

"Suit yourself."

She started walking toward the house, angry and not sure why. She hadn't imagined that anyone Cody was with wouldn't just welcome her with open arms. Stupid, on her part. She hadn't known her brother. He hadn't known he had a sister. Maybe she had just known about Cody and wanted family so badly that she'd expected a miracle. But Cody did seem to care about her now. He *knew* they were related. Easy enough to see. Cole seemed to accept the fact that she was Cody's sister easily enough. And she had even thought that he was beginning to trust her.

Until last night.

Maybe guilt had inspired her determination to try and capture Samuel Reeves, rather than immediately dispatch him. And maybe he couldn't have been saved. So few could withstand the agonizing hunger that true vampirism caused.

At the rear door to the main house, she paused.

"Yes?" he said.

She spun around. He'd been watching her go.

Maybe he had even known that she was going to stop.

She strode back to him.

"Lee."

"What?"

"You asked which general. Lee. He's an amazing man. He's a brilliant general and the finest humanitarian you'll ever met—all in one. He keeps it private, though. His face is a mask of stoicism and courage when he's on the field. But I've heard him weep at night. You say you love Texas. Well, Robert Lee loved Virginia, and Virginia seceded. The death appalls him." She stopped speaking, knowing that she was passionate about the man who was leading troops to certain death on a daily basis. That's what a general did.

His head cast warily to the side. "You're telling me that Robert E. Lee sent you to Washington, D.C.—but you're not spying in any way?"

She waved a hand in the air. "It's a long explanation. My mother is loosely related to his mother, or some such thing. I volunteered my services as a nurse on the battlefield. No one wanted to allow me to follow the army at first, but I kept coming back from the field unscathed, so...I was useful."

"And sometimes you were a courier—who happened to be in the right place to overhear things at certain times?" he asked.

"Yes, I've admitted that. But I'm telling you that I'm here now because I heard that Cody had gone West—and then I heard that he was traveling to Washington, D.C. And it was right after the horrible, horrible battle at the Wilderness when something came and attacked after darkness fell, and the corpses came back to life. We'd dealt with it before, but we had thought that we'd managed to stop things—where they were. Many of the wounded and captured from the Wilderness had been taken to the prison. I swear to you, it's as simple as that. Lee never forgets the battle dead for a minute. But not even he had ever seen anything like the men with their throats ripped open, or the strength and horror of some of the undead who dismantled their prey by ripping off their limbs."

"So, he sent you North," Cole said.

She hesitated. "He allowed me to come North."

"Why did you hesitate?" he asked immediately.

"I just— I think that a number of people know... I think that they can't admit that there are really monsters out there. They are afraid to believe in monsters, because if they did, they couldn't hate their fellow men so much."

He was silent for a minute. Then he seemed to be listening. She heard what he heard; the arrival of horses out front.

"Someone is coming?" she asked. "And you know about it?"

"Transportation. Come on."

To her surprise, rather than heading out front, he went back in through the house. She noted, approaching the rear door, that there was a cross on the pane—as if it were structural for the window. Above it, as if in design, were a Star of David and a crescent moon.

She looked at Cole.

He shrugged. "Yeah... We're covering all the bases," he said and smiled. "You can come in, can't you?" It was a challenge.

She smiled sweetly. "Oh, yes, Sheriff. Watch me."

She entered the house ahead of him. He followed her, locking the door behind him, grinning.

"Why are we in the house when riders came to the front?"

"Because I want the front door kept locked at all times, as much as possible," he told her. "Can you ride like that?"

She was wearing one of Martha's dresses.

"Never mind. They probably brought a sidesaddle."

"I can ride any way you want me to," she assured him.

Cole stared at her, a brow slightly hiked, a small smile curling into his features. She flushed. "Any horse out there!" she said quickly, turning away from him.

He stopped by the hook near the door to get his coat—the coat with all the pockets and vampire-killing paraphernalia—and led the way out the front door, closing it and locking it once she was out.

A rider had come, a man in a Union uniform with sergeant's stripes, leading two handsome bay horses.

Well-fed horses, looking much better than most of those she was accustomed to seeing in Virginia.

"Where are we going? And who is that?" she whispered.

"Sergeant Newcomb. And he's brought us two of the North's finest military horses. It's time. We're on cemetery detail again. Let's go," he said.

As he spoke, a bolt of lightning flashed across the sky, followed by a deafening clap of thunder.

"Let's get moving. Quickly," Cole said. "The rain... well, God knows just how hard it will be out there once the rain starts."

He was right. The sky, so beautiful by morning, was darkening. She looked up at it, disheartened.

"If you're afraid of a little rain..." he suggested.

She lifted her chin and smiled. "I'm not afraid of the day, the night, the lightning or a little rain. However, if *you're* feeling uneasy..."

"If we were smart, we'd both be afraid," he said. "Miss Fox, after you."

CHAPTER SIX

FOR ALL THE clouds, it might as well have been night, and Cole rued the fact that, despite the fine mounts they had waited for, they hadn't started earlier.

There seemed nothing so desolate as a cemetery when the sky darkened by day and the chill wind whistled and moaned through the trees.

Apparently, Megan Fox could ride even in a dress; she moved effortlessly. Cole was curious about her background, how it had felt all the years to know she was different—to have the choice to give in to the side of death and devastation, or to take up the fight against the creatures of evil, of which her father had been one.

Sure, she spoke earnestly and passionately enough, but he could tell she was the ultimate actress when she chose to be. He'd seen her in action at the hospital. And still, there had been something in her voice when she had spoken about General Robert E. Lee that had rung agonizingly true. She admired the man, and more. She loved him.

Oak Hill was a beautiful place, with a chapel built in 1849, natural garden pathways and monuments that lent it an air of bittersweet melancholy. It was large and sweeping, and, like other cemeteries these days, many graves were dug in anticipation of occupants that might never find such a peaceful, final resting plot. There were plots for families, vaults for families and individual graves. In the mist and darkness, the Gothic chapel stood like a testament to the finality of death, both welcoming and sobering.

The ride had been long through city streets filled with troops on the move, citizens trying to carry on with their lives and, always, the dust of construction. Heading out to Georgetown lessened neither the constant flow of humanity nor the grind of wagons supplying for the massive war machine.

But the cemetery, when they reached it, was quiet. Peaceful beneath a heavy, storm-laden sky from which the gray clouds seemed to cast a fog, rather than rain, down upon the ground. Oak Hill was comparatively new, impressively designed and, therefore, lonely and barren and seeming like a monument to death that stretched forever.

"I don't see anything," Megan said quietly.

Cole was tempted to whisper himself. The very air around them seemed to demand it.

"What were you expecting? A vampire picnic, tables of the undead, fellows playing cards?"

She cast him a glance that assured him she did not appreciate his sarcasm.

"Same as yesterday?" she suggested.

"Yes, but stay in sight this time."

They left the horses by the gatehouse, an impressive edifice, and moved along the pathways and small hills and valleys of the cemetery. Cole motioned to Megan that they would move toward the far left first, then, finding nothing, moved in a westerly direction, always at the same pace as one another.

They spent an hour walking, seeing nothing out of

the ordinary. There were stunning new monuments of pristine marble rising high in memory of those now gone. At each mausoleum they stopped, waving at one another before circling the houses of the dead, each keeping watch over the other.

She was good at what she did, Cole thought.

She knew how to be a partner, how to trust him and how to watch his back, as well.

So why didn't he trust her?

She was just like Cody, an anomaly, the blood of a very different creature running through her veins, yet so very human in every other aspect. She was fascinating; she was compelling. She was an extraordinarily beautiful young woman in shape and form and presence, and yet he knew, too, that it was her eyes that kept him most fascinated. When she looked at him, when she spoke earnestly with passion, and even with anger, there was something about her eyes, an emotion so clearly visible in her face that it arrested his heart.

"Anything? No freshly dug ground—nothing?" He called across the space between them.

"Some newly dug graves, but no occupants! And no young ones hiding there, either," she called back.

"Keep going. The chapel is ahead. We'll rest for a few minutes!"

Cole feared, with the cemetery so empty, that the chapel might be locked. But it was not. They had no sooner reached the doors than the rain burst down at last, and they hurried in, just ahead of the first heavy drops.

The wind whipped up to an even faster tempo. Cole pressed hard on the door to close it.

It was dark and shadowy within, but it was dry.

"It's a bit chilly," Megan said.

"It's spring, and it's Washington. Cold one minute, hotter than hell the next." He hesitated. "You do feel the cold, huh?"

She glared at him. "We feel everything. I thought you and Cody were tighter than thieves."

"Just asking."

"You never will trust me, will you?"

"I haven't known you that long," he told her. "And trust needs to be earned."

"I actually think that I earned it, saving your life," she informed him.

"I saved *your* life, young lady," he said with an indignant sneer.

She sniffed. "You wouldn't have gotten through the first night without me."

"We managed fine in many a worse situation," Cole said. "And we've really just been introduced."

"Ah, yes, but we've quickly had to get to know one another," she said drily.

The rain pounded the chapel. The wind outside made a sound akin to crying, as if the elements themselves mourned all who lay interred in the cemetery. He smiled. She seemed exceptionally *human* as they waited in the confines of the chapel—so warm, vibrant and vital. He supposed he should actually put some distance between them.

He didn't. Instead, he took her hands and rubbed them between his own. She didn't pull away. She looked up at him with her huge golden eyes.

"Let me give you my coat," he said.

She shook her head. "No, no, I'm fine, really. Your coat is your defense."

"Yes, well, you know how to use its tools as well as I."

"I don't need them, though. My blood is my defense."

"And you can be killed, just as any vampire, just as any human."

She smiled. "It would take a lot."

"All it would take is a determined enemy with a stake or a good sharp sword," he reminded her practically.

"We're in a chapel."

"And you believe that a vampire—a full-blooded vampire—can't enter a chapel? There are many religions around the world, you know," he said.

"Religion doesn't matter. What matters is the soul, or the heart. Evil can't dwell in a house of holiness," she told him.

It was so similar to something that Cody had once said to him.

"Tell me more about your life," he suggested, indicating a seat in one of wooden benches before the small altar.

She arched a brow. After she sat down, she noted, "You know my life. When I was young, my mother told me what I was."

"A vampire."

"And a bastard," she said drily. "But she used the name Fox, and my birth is registered under the name Fox. My mother was an amazing woman. She grew up in a system where love didn't really exist much, marriages were planned and expected, and she knew that her stepfather intended her for a rich planter who would make her the main household 'slave' if you will. She knew that my father was different, but she went with him anyway.

Even knowing that he wouldn't—or couldn't—stay. She made her own life." Megan sighed and explained, "She met my father at a barbecue. She hated her life, and she didn't want *marriage* to a man when there was no love, when it just a matter of the *proper* way to live her life, with a man seen as *advantageous* for her in society. She fell in love at first sight, and ran away with my father instead, knowing that he was running away with the world. They had their time together, I was conceived, and then I believe my father thought that he had to run again. My mother lived on her own and met my stepfather, who was a wonderful man. He accepted me, another man's child. For all that I was."

"How?"

She smiled at him. "She taught. She taught young ladies, but she did much more than teach them the proper way to sit and stand and hold a teacup. She loved history and the world and old legends. She was always searching for the true roots of vampirism, and studied stories from all over the world. She did believe that it was a disease, and she was always certain that one day—maybe far in the future—medicine and science would catch up with the 'disease.'"

"Ah, a true scholar," Cole murmured.

"And I had a wonderful stepfather," she said.

"Had?"

"He was a scholar, too, a teacher. They had a good marriage, and he was kind to me. He died just before the war, of natural causes. If I had known…"

"Known that he was dying?" Cole asked her.

She nodded, smoothing a fold in her skirt. "I would have been tempted to save him. His heart gave out. Suddenly. If I had been there…I might have saved him."

"Turned him?" Cole asked. She looked so distressed, looking intently at her skirt still. She was about the fiercest creature he had ever met, and yet he wanted to touch her and console her. Hold her.

It seemed bizarrely comfortable in the chapel then, the two of them sitting close together, taking warmth from one another. He set an arm around her, rubbing her shoulders, to give her more warmth.

"And it might have been a mistake. Your 'friend' from last night was a mistake, no matter what you might wish to believe."

"Killing him?" she asked.

He shook his head. "Him being a vampire. He needed to be—put down."

"It sounds like we're talking about horses."

"We're talking about something akin to rabid dogs."

"But all vampires aren't rabid dogs. In the eyes of most men, I'm a vampire. My stepfather never suggested that I should have been put down."

"Where's your mother?" he asked.

She winced. "Dead, too. The first year of the war. She was young, she was healthy...but she caught a cold and it worsened and...and I was gone. So I have lost them both."

"I'm sorry," Cole said gently, and he meant it.

She nodded, and he could feel her squaring her shoulders; she didn't want to talk about the past.

"What about you—cowboy?" she asked teasingly. "You're a sheriff on the frontier, you have apparently dealt with Indians, outlaws—vampires—and more. And yet you loathe war."

"Well, I'm not particularly fond of outlaws, either," he told her lightly.

"How did you escape the war?" she asked him. "I mean, at the beginning, young men were fighting to get into units. And you went to a military academy, didn't you say? Wouldn't you have been in the military then, an officer of some sort?"

"I was in West Point briefly ten years ago. Many—most—of our Mexican-American war heroes became teachers at one time or another, still were leaders after the war." he told her.

She drew away from him, astonished. "Then, you are familiar with most of the leaders—on both sides!"

"Yes."

"How did you secure an appointment—and how did you leave without going into the military?" she demanded.

He laughed. "I didn't desert or any such thing. My grandfather was a Revolutionary War brigadier general, and so my appointment at the Academy. I went through school, but resigned my commission when my father died. I went home to Victory. They needed a sheriff."

"Your father had been the sheriff?"

"Exactly. And it's my point as regards the war, as well. I knew many of the fine officers leading both sides of the war effort now. They're mostly good men. They believe that they're right. They all believe that God is on their side. Most of those men fought *together* in various skirmishes, and though on the field they may be enemies, in their hearts, they're still friends."

"It was after Joseph Johnston was injured at the Battle of Seven Pines that Lee took control and called his forces the Army of Northern Virginia," Megan said. "He's simply an excellent tactician."

Cole nodded. It was impossible to know what the

horrible conflagration would come to before it ended. Mothers in the North often thought it would be good riddance if they all just said goodbye to the South. The newspapers thrived on printing the horrendous photos taken on the battlefields. Political pressure could end it all. Abe Lincoln was coming up for reelection, and though the North had started winning some of the major battles, there were many antiwar politicians who just might win election. If they did so, the tide could be turned and Congress might vote to stop the war and give the South the freedom to become an independent country. Lincoln, with his passion and determination, was the heart of the Union.

Even with its brilliant military men, the South was slowly strangling. The coastal blockades were keeping supplies from arriving from Europe. Food grew scarcer daily. The industrial North was producing guns and bullets on an unholy schedule. Lincoln's Emancipation Proclamation had turned into a war with a cause for the North, and that would influence voters, as well.

Cole wondered what would have happened if the South had taken the battle onto Northern soil immediately, while its troops were young and fresh and still in decent boots, with food to give them strength.

They'd never know. Amazing, though, how much he thought about a war he purportedly didn't give a thought about at all….

"Cole," Megan said, so softly he barely heard her.

But something in her voice alerted him.

What? he mouthed.

"There…in the back. I saw something. Something moved."

He looked. He saw nothing. He pulled away from her

though and rose, stretching as if he were just about to check on the rain.

He did so, opening the door just a bit. The rain had ceased. The day remained wet, gray and cold. He turned back toward Megan, who had risen, as well. He nodded to her. She saw his eyes, and she knew that they needed to take the same care they had outside and head to the front of the little chapel together.

And as they moved into the darkness, something burst out from the altar area. A shadow, so fleeting that Cole had to ask himself if he'd really seen it. It was there, and then it wasn't. The door to the chapel swung open, from a massive gust of wind—or an unseen hand.

Cole reached into his pocket coldly for a stake and started for the door. Megan raced after him, grabbing his arm. "Cole, no!"

"It's out there—whatever, exactly, it is—it's out there," he told her, trying to shake her off as he neared the outside.

"Cole! Wait, think! I told you—yesterday, there was something in the trees that fought alongside me. Whatever—whoever—this is, exactly, he, she, *it,* isn't out to hurt us. Cole! It was taking refuge inside a chapel!" she pleaded.

"If it's good, why doesn't it just join forces with us openly?" Cole demanded, yelling the words both at her and into the dark graveyard.

"I don't know," she admitted. "But…don't. Please! It's not trying to harm us in any way, and it might be there to help us when we need help. I'm begging you, think about it!" Megan insisted.

He felt her hand on his arm, felt the tension in

his muscles, and something he wasn't accustomed to—uncertainty.

Her hand fell away. She studied him with her mesmerizing golden eyes.

"You don't trust me, and you can't allow yourself to trust in anything that I say," she told him flatly.

He shook his head. "Megan, maybe it's watching us. Maybe it's waiting for us to be in a position of vulnerability. The old ones do that."

She shook her head. "Sometimes, you know, you have to believe in what you can't see."

He stared back at her, and slowly, the tension eased from his arms, and then the length of him. He wasn't sure he was giving in to her certainty that the shadow thing was *good,* a force of salvation.

But he was certain that they'd never catch it now. It knew that they would be looking for it.

"All right. The rain has stopped. Let's finish what we started," Cole said.

She nodded. They headed out. Cole closed the chapel door behind them.

"West angle," she said.

"All right. I'm on the east," he agreed. She started to walk away.

"Hey!" he called to her.

She stopped and looked back at him.

"Make sure I can see you at all times," he said.

She nodded slowly and then offered him a dry smile. "Is that because you're afraid for me? Or afraid of what I might do?"

"Yes. Both," he told her huskily. He knew it was a lie. He knew that he was already entranced by the woman, even as he mistrusted her.

Was that her plan? Seduction and then...what?

He didn't think so.

Or he didn't want to think so.

He gave himself a mental shake and started on his route across the slick grass, mud patches—among the fresh-washed flowers, blooming in spring despite the pervasive atmosphere of death. He walked down a vacant patch of land where future decades of dead might one day lie, and he came upon a section where many graves had been dug.

He stopped. There was an area where the dirt had recently been dug up and then hastily replaced.

Cole hunkered down over the damp earth. He began to dig at it.

Quickly, he came to a corpse.

The corpse of a Union private, Irish Brigade.

A corpse with a fine-honed stake in its heart, one much like Cody had taught him to make.

Someone, determined to hold the "infection" at bay, had been there before them.

And yet, even then, he held on to doubt. A callous killer might not care how many of his or her own were dispatched—if there were a greater game afoot.

He rose. He kept walking the cemetery, but he knew there would be nothing further for him to do, nothing to fear.

Any fresh, newly made vampire who might have taken refuge in the cemetery was dead now in truth.

For good or evil, the shadow-being from the chapel had seen to it already.

MARTHA CLUCKED around Megan like a mother hen when she and Cole returned to the boardinghouse. She had to admit that it was rather nice. She was accustomed to taking care of herself, having spent the past years doing her best in horrible conditions. It was nice to have someone worried about her state of exhaustion, determined that she have a long bath and some good hot tea with whiskey and settle down before a nice fire.

She needed more than tea at that moment, but she was pretty sure her brother traveled with a sizable stash of the *sustenance* they needed to maintain their customary lives. And she could wait. It had been a long day, the break they had taken in the chapel the only rest they had, and nothing to eat at all.

She was feeling quite loved and appreciated, but Martha was just as concerned about Cole. The minute she was out of the tub, Martha arrived to get her dressed quickly, and requiring her assistance to empty the contents of the tub so that fresh water could be heated to fill the tub for Cole.

She knew he'd see it as a bit of a luxury. During her time with the army, she and the men had gone days—weeks—without a chance to find a spring, a creek, a river, or anywhere with water available for bathing. She had been luckier than the men, since she had ridden often enough with messages from one position to another, and she'd had the luxury of sometimes being in Richmond, in an officer's home, and even in the White House of the Confederacy. On those occasions, she had felt a little bit of guilt bathing, thinking on her comrades in the camps and the dirt that seemed to cling to them all permanently.

Megan eased back into the overstuffed wing chair Martha had placed her in, closing her eyes.

She couldn't really tell anyone the truth about her suspicions.

She was pretty sure that Cody thought their father might have been the one to breed the vampire clan that had ripped apart the towns surrounding Victory, Texas. The clan of "outlaws" that Cody, Cole and friends had put down.

But she didn't believe it. Their father had left his mother; he had supposedly been dead. But he had returned to the East to meet her mother, and he had never hurt her. Her mother had always insisted he was an honorable man, even if he had to live by different rules than society would accept.

But he was out there, still. She knew it. And she didn't believe that he was evil. He had to have been a decent man to have been with her mother. And her mother wasn't stupid; she would trust her opinion.

He stayed hidden, of course. Most likely, he would reside in one place, and then another, careful to keep moving so no one would ever really know him.

But Megan believed, with her whole heart, that he spent his days searching out and destroying those who came back with the hunger to kill.

She dreamed of meeting her father.

A noise at the door alerted her that someone had come to the house. She instantly tensed, but the door opened and Alex was there with Cody and Brendan.

"Hello," Alex said. Her brow furrowed. "How was your day?"

"Fairly uneventful. We searched through Oak Hill, got caught in the rain, searched some more and came on back," Megan said. "How was your day?"

Alex hesitated a moment. "Worrisome," she said.

"I think a good supper would be in order round about now," Brendan said, walking to the fire to warm his hands. The rain had made the spring day chilling to the bone.

"Yes, of course. You look exhausted," Alex said to Megan.

"I *am* tired."

"Where is Cole?" Cody asked.

"Enjoying a bath," Megan said.

"We mustn't forget, Lisette Annalise needs to see him tomorrow," Brendan reminded Cody.

"We certainly won't forget that," Cody said.

"Well," Alex murmured. "I'll go see about a meal."

Alex went out. Megan looked at Cody, who seemed perplexed.

"What's wrong?" she asked him. She was disturbed not only that they had apparently been out on a secret mission all day, but that their mission seemed to concern Lisette Annalise.

It was ridiculous, but she didn't like the woman.

Was it jealousy? she wondered. She eschewed the idea. She and Cole made good partners, that was all. Even if the man still didn't trust her. She couldn't care in the least about his outside activities.

Cody glanced over at her. He looked at her for a moment and then said, "It's spreading. The outbreak is spreading."

"What happened? Where?"

Again, Cody hesitated. "We're—we're really not sure.... But we suspect that there are—creatures—in Harpers Ferry."

Megan stood up, aggravated and done with the way they all looked at her. "Look, I don't know what you're hiding, and I don't know why you mistrust me so much. You're all able to say that you do this—and you're not a part of the war. Well, at this point, I'm not a part of the war, either. So, as much as I have wanted all my life to meet you, to get to know you, Cody, I'm done. I'll go back to handling the situation in my way, as I see fit."

"Wait!"

Alex had come back into the room. She looked around at all of them. "Look, we're playing on a tightrope of belief and disbelief—and war—all the time. But, Cody, I think that this is getting ridiculous. What? Do you think that Megan is really trying to spread the disease, and she's just with us to find out what we know? Or do you think she's here to ask the vampires she's about to slay if they know any Federal secrets? Please. We're sleeping with her in the house—we're trusting her with our lives as it is. And she's done nothing to betray that trust. I'll tell her the truth, if you won't."

"Alex—" Brendan began to protest.

Alex cut him off with the wave of a hand. "It's my—it's actually my relationship to begin with. It's my right to tell Megan what I choose." She turned to Megan. "I think I mentioned that *I* was actually taken in once—with a canvas bag over my head, at that—on suspicion of spying. Because I have dreams, and the dreams sometimes foretell the future. Well, when I was in prison, I was visited by someone else who has dreams."

"Who?" Megan asked.

"Didn't I tell you? President Lincoln. He has seen terrible things happening in Harpers Ferry. Things that go beyond the scope of the town changing hands every other month in this war."

Megan stared at Alex, frowning. In 1859, John Brown

had attempted a seizure of the arsenal there, taken the armory, lost most of his men and been captured at the town's firehouse—the "fort" he had been using. Now the raid was famous—or infamous, depending on whose side one was on. She didn't feel a tremendous amount of sympathy for John Brown, though he was a hero in the Union. She didn't dislike him because of his determination that slavery be abolished, but because he had thought that any means justified the end he wanted—he had committed cold-blooded murder in his quest. It now seemed an odd piece of history: Robert E. Lee and Jeb Stuart, two of the South's most brilliant generals, had been charged by the Union government with putting down the raid and the violence. John Brown had been hanged at Charles Town, south of the border region at the junction of the Potomac and Shenandoah rivers, a town the Union only took recently.

Megan shook her head. "I thought that now the Union army was firmly entrenched at Harpers Ferry."

"It is. And there are Confederate soldiers being held there, as well. It's a political hotbed at the moment. The area, you know, is no longer part of the Confederacy—or the Commonwealth of Virginia—it was admitted to the Union as the thirty-fifth state on June twentieth, 1863. It's now part of the state of West Virginia," Brendan said, still staring at the fire. "I don't know if you're aware of this, but when the vote was taken for secession in the Virginia legislature, most of the northwestern counties voted against seceding. The Southern forces still keep attacking. You never know who might be who down there—who might be in control, who might be a prisoner."

"But right now, it's West Virginia, and the Union is in control, right? And so—we're going to Harpers Ferry?"

Megan asked. “But what about the capital? This capital—Washington, D.C.? What about here? Isn’t the president worried about what may be happening here?”

“Yes,” Cody said.

“I’m lost,” Megan admitted.

“We’ll detail the strategy tomorrow. It may mean splitting up,” Cody said. He added a hasty, “Tomorrow!” in a whisper.

Megan quickly realized why. Martha had come in. “I’ve had a ham shank basting throughout the day. I’ll bring it on in, if I may, and if I may rely upon you all for a bit of help?”

“Of course! And get the kids—we’ll all eat!” Megan said quickly. She stood up and, with the others, followed Martha.

When they were settled in, it looked like quite a feast to Megan, again having to push images of past Southern comrades, most likely hungry and tired at this hour, out of her mind. Artie and Marni were charming children; Artie, determined to be a man of the house at age twelve, and Marni, a little lady at seven. They had helped bring in the food, Artie peppering Cole with questions about being sheriff in the frontier.

“I would like to grow up to be a sheriff—and see the West!” Artie said as he excitedly ate.

“It’s a vast place,” Cole told him.

“Yes, but I would like to live there. I would like to ride horses every day, and I would very much like to bring bad men to jail and justice,” Artie said.

“You should stay right here and perhaps study medicine, like Cody,” Martha said.

Artie had solemn eyes. “I don’t want to be in a world

where we're all fighting all the time. I want to go West, where I'd be looking for men who committed crimes, and not soldiers who do what they're told."

The table went silent at the child's grave wisdom.

"Well, then, Master Artie, some time you must bring your mother and your sister and come out and visit us in Victory," Cole said.

"Yes, that would be most pleasant!" Brendan Vincent said energetically.

Megan lowered her head, hiding a smile. She hadn't realized the older Brendan was quite smitten by their hostess.

Supper was cleared away and when it was done, nobody made the usual suggestion that the gentlemen retire to one room for brandy and cigars, the ladies to another for a sip of sherry. They had all grown quiet while clearing after the meal, and Megan excused herself to go to bed.

She was exhausted, and worried. She wasn't at all sure that she wanted to leave Washington—not since she had seen the shadow again. Something about it made her think it might have something to do with her father. Maybe she was just being the hopeful daughter...but she longed to meet him.

And she was afraid for him.

She tossed and turned, but exhaustion overwhelmed her.

She slept, and she woke, and slept again. Visions tormented, and she wasn't sure if they were patches of nightmares or thoughts that came unbidden to her mind.

Alex had dreams that sometimes foretold the future.

The President of the Union, Abraham Lincoln, had dreams—visions—of what might come to pass.

She saw something in her own mind's eye, so vivid it was that she didn't know if she was awake or asleep. She saw Cole, and he was lying on a poor cot, someone moving toward him. Megan tried to see who it was, but all she saw was a shadow.

She needed to warn him, but she was afraid that he was expecting the visitor.

The visitor was a woman.

Embarrassed, flushed, Megan wanted to move away. But something held her in place.

It was dark. It was night. The woman had come for a clandestine appointment. And still Megan couldn't move. She watched, and a sliver of moonlight cast a soft glow over the scene.

It was in that glow of moonlight that she saw…

Something shining, something glittering.

It was saliva, dripping off fangs….

Megan jerked upright. She was trembling.

She groaned softly. The vision had been terrifyingly real. It was a dream.

But, still…if the man was idiot enough to fall for a rabid fanatic like Lisette Annalise, that was *his* mistake.

Lisette Annalise was not a vampire. She was an actress turned Pinkerton agent.

And still…

Megan realized that she was never going to go to sleep unless she checked on Cole. She silently crawled out of bed and to her door. She listened for a moment, then opened it and went out into the hallway.

She tiptoed down to the door to Cole's room.

She listened again.

Nothing.

And then…

CHAPTER SEVEN

HE WASN'T DREAMING—it was real, right?

He had just lain down. Therefore, he wasn't dreaming.

Some hint of sound at his window had disturbed him earlier, and he had found himself up again, securing the house, looking out to be certain that the carriage house sat in peace in the night darkness.

But his vision came to him that night.

Then again, it wasn't *precisely* his dream.

She wasn't naked.

Cole saw his door open and, in the dim sliver of light afforded by the one gaslight they kept burning in the hallway through the night, he saw her.

The pale light filtered through the light cotton of the nightdress she was wearing, making a perfect silhouette of her figure. She might not have appeared half so tempting if she had just slipped it off altogether.

Actually, maybe naked would have been just as arousing.

And she stood there, staring at him from the doorway. He didn't move. He watched her.

Had he been right to mistrust her all this time? Was she standing there, assuring herself that he was asleep, so that she could easily, silently, slip in and sever his jugular?

He waited, hoping that the darkness was deep enough that she wouldn't realize he was watching her as he lay there. She wouldn't. His eyes were barely open.

She tiptoed in.

And stood over him.

She had said that he smelled good once. *Good enough to eat.*

He could have returned the—compliment? He breathed in her scent, and it was lavender soap, clean sweet flesh and that hint of an individual that made them different, that called to him on every basic level. With his eyelids low and his vision down to tiny slits, he still saw her face and her eyes, and to his amazement, he saw something tormented within them.

She just stood there.

Was she debating a meal?

He knew he couldn't maintain his dead-still secret vigil forever. And he didn't intend to give her the first chance to move—that might be dangerous.

His eyes flew open and his arms stretched out in the blink of an eye. He bore her down beside him, leaning over to pin her on the mattress.

She didn't scream; a gasp of surprise and dismay escaped her, but nothing more.

She didn't fight him; she just stared up at him.

If she had fought, could he have won? Yes.

Or at least, he wanted to think so!

If she had screamed…

He could just see the explanation.

Yes, your newly discovered sister is in my bed, yes, beneath me—but honestly, it was all her fault.

"What in God's name are you doing? Or, should *God's*

name be invoked?" he asked her, his whisper tense as he leaned over her.

She stared back at him with no alarm, and almost as if she didn't comprehend his words.

"I was afraid for you," she told him quietly.

"You were afraid for *me?*" he repeated her words as a doubtful question.

She nodded gravely at him.

"I—I had a dream that you were under attack."

Her eyes fascinated him. He wanted to forget that he had anything to say to her. He couldn't begin to understand what in life and death, and all the miracles in between, managed to make her half human and half vampire. He knew that she was flesh and blood and bone beneath him, and that all of it was put together in a package as feminine and enticing as the libido could bear, and that she looked at him with eyes of gold in a beautifully formed face that was angelic and yet seemed to promise every wicked pleasure to be had by man.

Looking at her, he forgot his questions.

Forgot mistrust…

All he wanted to do was cradle her cheek, stare into those eyes…

And touch her.

He forced himself to think. "I was under attack—it wasn't by *you* by any chance, was it?"

She shook her head. He frowned, torn between the tension in his torso and limbs that informed him that he was an able-bodied, hungry male next to the vital heat and pulse of an able-perfect-bodied female—torn between that and the words that were coming out of his mouth. Lie, or truth? Those eyes…

"I saw you…and I saw…a creature. And you weren't

aware. You were vulnerable," she told him. Her words remained quiet. Softly spoken, for they were in the shadows and the stillness of the night.

He did touch her face. His hand brushed past her breast, and the simple touch seemed to radiate streaks of fire and heat throughout him. Her cheek was soft beneath the exquisitely designed bone structure of her face.

"Sure it wasn't you?" he queried.

"Am I hurting you?" she replied.

Was she hurting him? God, yes, he ached in every fiber of his being—thin cotton and long johns separated them—and he was very afraid that it wasn't much of a separation, and she would notice very shortly.

Define that word! he longed to cry.

He forced a certain harshness into his voice. "I was awake. You weren't expecting that."

"I heard—noise. Noise, from this room."

That was true; he had just looked out the window, closed and bolted it, and come to bed.

"I don't know what to do to convince you that I'm—*good!*" she said.

He knew exactly what she could do that might convince him she was very, very good, at least in one aspect....

He stood quickly, drawing the covers with him to wrap around his lower body. He was in a boardinghouse and this young woman, mystery though she still might be, was his best friend's half sister; the same best friend who was right down the hallway.

"I'm going to suggest that you refrain from sneaking up on a man when he's gone to bed for the night," he said. "Go. I'm fine. Please, get out of here."

She was up like a flash of lightning, speeding across the room and to the door.

"And don't come back unless you mean it!" he muttered sharply beneath his breath.

He had forgotten just how acute her hearing was. She stopped, frowning, looking back at him.

"What? I'm sorry, what does that mean?" she asked. But then, looking at him, somehow, she figured it out. "Oh…oh!" Her cheeks flamed a glorious shade of pink. Then she was gone, with the door falling slowly closed behind her.

To his astonishment, she was back, pushing it open but not coming in.

"I will remember that," she said softly.

Then, she was really gone, with the door clicking behind her as she closed it securely.

He stared after her, wondering then what *she* had meant by the last.

And thinking that he'd never sleep—her visit had assured him a long time awake and in torment before he could get any rest from the trying day that had passed, and the longer days that lay ahead.

MORNING CAME, a beautiful morning. Yesterday's rain had caused a dampness and chill, but the sun had risen and dispersed the dampness. The air was fresh, the breeze light and it was difficult to imagine that it was a day when men would fight and die somewhere in all the glory of spring.

Megan found everyone downstairs at the kitchen table. Apparently, Martha had already come and gone, the perfect hostess for a boardinghouse: preparing a feast for her guests with apparent effortlessness and then moving on to other tasks.

She was surprised when Cole was the first to notice her, and when he rose to pull back a chair for her. Brendan and Cody had risen, as well. No matter what the situation, the men were unfailingly polite.

She murmured, "Good morning," and took her seat.

A chorus of "good morning" came to her in reply as the three men took their seats again.

"Bacon?" Alex offered, passing her the serving dish.

"Thank you," she said, helping herself.

"Blood?" Cole offered her, passing her a pitcher that had been set in front of Cody. She hesitated, irritated by his bluntness.

But then she smiled with feigned courtesy, accepting the pitcher and pouring some of the contents into the stoneware mug in front of her. "Thank you so much."

Cody cleared his throat. He was staring at her, Megan realized.

"There's a carriage coming soon," he said.

"Oh?"

"About thirty minutes from now. The president has asked to meet you," Alex said.

She could have fallen off her chair.

"President—the *United States* president?" she asked.

Alex nodded. "I received a note early this morning. I'm to accompany you. The carriage will be here in a few minutes."

Megan frowned, tempted to grab her mug and down the contents in one swallow. She felt a strange unease. An uncertainty about her new comrades all of a sudden.

She folded her hands in her lap. "Does he— I don't understand. Does he know—what Cody and I *are?*"

"He knows that the world isn't always what it seems," Alex explained. "I told you—he has dreams."

"Does he want to see me as if I were some kind of… exotic beast?"

"Oh, no, dear child!" Brendan Vincent protested, which was a surprise. She had been certain that he hadn't trusted her much, either. Not because of *what* she was, but because of *who* she was. A child not of a vampire, but of Virginia. "You don't understand the man at all. He has a heart filled with goodness. He would never treat you like some curiosity!"

She smiled, not sure whether to thank him or not. She was still confused.

"Did something more happen last night?" she asked.

"No," Cole said quickly, looking around at everyone smoothly and then back to Megan. "All was quiet. But while we were considering our next move, the message came. While you and Alex are out, we'll do some planning."

She looked around at them. Well, it was obvious that her opinion wasn't important in the planning.

But she *was* going to meet Abraham Lincoln.

"Well, then, I guess all is decided. Sir," she said to Brendan, "would you be so kind as to pass the eggs and biscuits, as well?"

Breakfast was relatively silent, the carriage arriving at the front before she had finished. She was too unnerved to really eat much, anyway. She did pick up her mug, though, and down the contents. She didn't want to meet a man like Abraham Lincoln and be distracted by a pulse against a vein in his throat.

The men escorted them out to the carriage that awaited them. After Cody got Alex situated, he helped Megan up the step to the coach seating and whispered softly, "Behave now."

She stared at him, but he was grinning. She found that she had to smile in return.

Megan had assumed that it might take them to a secret place where they'd meet the President in a dark basement somewhere, or in some clandestine spot.

But she was stunned to hear a deep, slow, throaty voice welcome her even as she was seated. "So, good day, Miss Fox. A pleasure to meet you. Though I thoroughly comprehend that your loyalties might lie elsewhere, I'm grateful for all that you're doing for the sake of humanity—all humanity."

Even seated, the man appeared tall. He was gaunt, with huge sad eyes clinging to a face that was tired, lined and long. She had never seen a man who appeared to be so stoic, weary, resolved...and kind.

In the lull that should have been filled with Megan's own greeting, Alex leaned forward and said, "Megan Fox, please let me introduce you to President Lincoln," in her most genteel manner.

Megan stared at him in surprise for a moment longer, and then faltered nervously. "How do you do...sir! It's a pleasure to meet you. Seriously. Yes, I'm a Virginian. But it's a pleasure. Well, certainly, some in the South think you're a monster, but the fighting men, especially the generals and higher officers, all know that you're a man with what you truly consider to be a mission of righteousness." She winced. *He* didn't think of *her* as any kind of a beast, but she had just called him a monster.

"I'm sorry, I didn't—"

"Miss Fox, please, I'm well aware of how I'm viewed in many a place by many a person. But that is neither here nor there compared with the great assault we have faced as the tragedy of this strange *blood* disease seeks to hunt down and kill all mankind."

He tapped at the roof of the carriage and spoke to his driver. "A loop at the Mall, my good sir, if you will be so kind," he said.

Again, Megan's jaw nearly fell. Alex was seated next to her, and she had to prevent herself from clutching her sister-in-law's hand. She was aware that the White House tended to be an open area. Lincoln had never been a stupid man, and he was surely aware of the inherent dangers in being the President of the United States amid such national strife. And she had always heard that he considered himself a man of the people, and that, as such, he should be available—*to the people.*

Still, she had never imagined a carriage ride around the Mall with Abraham Lincoln.

It hadn't been that long ago that she had been hunting monsters in a D.C. prison.

He eased more comfortably back into his seat and stared at her.

"Are you a Rebel spy, Miss Fox?"

Her mouth seemed dry, filled with cotton. She shook her head. She didn't want to sit there stupidly staring at the man. "I have tried to be truthful since I met up with Cody, Alex—and their group. I was tending to the wounded on the battlefields, and, sir, I am gratified to say that I have not personally seen a doctor, nurse or medic in any form intentionally inflict more pain or suffering on a soldier on either side of this war. I have, yes, upon occasion, carried documents from one camp to another.... But did I come to Washington, D.C., to spy on anyone or to bring information of any kind to the South that would harm any man or cause of the North—is that what you're asking?"

He nodded gravely, those great sad eyes of his upon her. She felt that they were knowing eyes, the kind that saw into the soul.

"It's my understanding," he began, "that—though we have never openly mentioned such a thing in any correspondence—that many of the generals and politicians involved with the war and government in the South are aware of the serious threat we face. *We*. As one group, united. We—*humanity*."

She nodded.

"Alex said you were sent here."

"I was."

"By one of the highest commanders?"

She nodded again and frowned. "I didn't speak with General Lee myself before my departure north, but rather Lieutenant Colonel Wilkenson of the Jackson Brigade, sir. He had his orders through General Jackson, who had them from Lee. Lieutenant Colonel Wilkenson is a surgeon himself, and the...the incidents that occurred on the battlefields when both sides tried to collect their dead and wounded were horrendous and horrifying to all who witnessed them. After the Wilderness, I wasn't *ordered* to come—I was *asked* to do what could be done. Not many truly understand the...disease. But, like you, sir, they do understand the gravity of it, and that the disease is an enemy to all men. So I am here to spy? No. No I am not. I am here to help."

The president looked out the carriage window. They were passing the Smithsonian "castle," an edifice that spoke of science and industry, and man's thirst for knowledge and understanding.

"Somehow, it seems fitting," he murmured.

Next to Megan, Alex sat silent. They both waited for the president to speak again. When he did, he seemed to be speaking to himself more so than to them.

"How it breaks my heart! I think of the beauty and grace of the mansion at Arlington, and how dead men now fill the acreage. I think of Lee and I think of Mrs. Lee, who had to leave the beautiful home bequeathed to her by her father. Arlington was built by George Washington Parke Custis, the step-grandson of this nation's most elite founding father and the first president, a man who would not allow himself to be crowned king." He turned from the window to look at the two women again. "Mary Lee left notes, you know. When Robert warned her that the house would be taken because of its military position, she left notes for the Union troops who were sure to come. She didn't want the house harmed—the house, or the objects that had belonged to George Washington that were of great historical importance to all of us. What heartbreak she must have suffered! And, yet, a good wife, she stands by the loyalty her husband chose. My own dear Mary has many family members fighting against us in this war. She… I digress!" he said. "My apologies!"

"Please, you mustn't apologize," Alex said, setting a hand on his knee with the affection of a daughter. "How is Mary? I'd hoped to see her soon."

"Troubled," he said. He stared at Megan again. "The war draws upon us, all of us, to face such tragedy. I think of Jefferson—Jeff Davis—who I must admit, I pray will be the only President of the Confederate States. No malice intended, but God has willed my journey, I do so sincerely believe. I lost my dear Willie, you know, my precious son, while in the White House. I know that the Davis family lost a precious child in the White House of Confederacy, and I grieve with them, as I have grieved for my own. We serve, and we do our best to be husbands and fathers. We cannot ever really ease this pain. We received condolences from my 'enemies' in the South, just as we received them from friends here, and we send out condolences to those in the South for such tragedies, as well."

"Sir, all men rue the death of a child."

He set his mouth grimly. "Not all men. This disease… my wife cries about it at night. She believes that our Willie comes back to her at night, that he comes with his friends who have died at the hands of the deranged afflicted—and they cry out to her. She speaks to me sometimes, as if she has engaged in conversation with our dead son. It breaks my heart. And I…"

"Yes?" Megan whispered.

His gaze was directly on her. "I dream of a place that is Harpers Ferry. I see the mist, and I see soldiers—they are playing a game with a terrified little drummer boy. They like the boy, and they want to be friends, but they are soldiers, and they tease him. In their play, he falls out a window. He is crushed, and they believe him to be dead. But when he is hastily buried, there is something there, something that is hungry and watching and…it is a shadow that digs in the darkness, raising the boy and tearing into his broken body. For blood."

"Perhaps it is a nightmare, sir, and nothing more," Megan said.

He shook his head. "I dreamed of the battlefield where we first heard of the disease," he said. "I saw it, I saw the shadow, and I saw the men rise, and begin to tear at one another like rabid dogs." He looked over at a group of boys teasing one another in the friendly manner of young children. "I am afraid, not of war, not of struggle, not of hardship or privation. I fear the unholy that comes to torment us all indiscriminately."

His rich, deep, husky voice had seemed to fill the carriage air with something tangible. A sadness so deep that it took on life.

They were all still, and Megan was aware of a shout from the street, of a child's laughter, of the clip-clop of the horses' hooves.

Then he spoke briskly. "I fear that there may be danger yet in the capital, and though Mr. Vincent, Mr. Fox and especially the sheriff, Mr. Granger, have worked with some of our troops and men that they may go into battle rightly armed, I dare not leave the capital here at risk. But as your great general might suggest, my dear, I'm asking that you go to Harpers Ferry, and seek out the truth of my vision, and my wife's tears."

"So—I'm to go for you?" she asked. She knew that she wouldn't say no. She knew that whatever loyalties she might have once felt, she knew this man now. If he asked her to do something, she would do it.

But it had nothing to do with loyalties, or with the fact that Virginia was her home. It had nothing to do with the war whatsoever, the fact that the North was most probably far more than right when it proclaimed that slavery was simply wrong no matter how practiced, even if, as some of the politicians in the South argued, it had existed back in Biblical times. They had been wrong then, too, which Ramses II had learned the hard way through the seven plagues of Egypt.

It had nothing to do with men who based their lives on the economy of cotton, with Southern boys who couldn't buy a horse, much less a slave. The war itself and all the politics that went with it meant nothing to her.

She had known that. In her heart, she had always known it.

She was sad, and she wished that she could say no, *because she was convinced that the shadow that had been in the chapel, the shadow that had fought at Prospect Hill, had been her father. And she wanted to find him, so desperately.*

What if she was wrong?

Abraham Lincoln looked at her and nodded gravely. "I need someone here, you understand that I still need someone here."

She swallowed. "You want me to go to Harpers Ferry alone?" she asked.

"No. I'm aware that you arrived in Washington alone, my dear. Many of the Pinkerton agents are really very good." He waved a hand in the air. "In the private sector, is such secretive spying a detriment to our freedoms? Possibly, but we are at war. No. The Texas sheriff, Mr. Granger, will escort you. He is well aware of all the elements that are involved. Cody Fox will have his knowledgeable wife—" he smiled at Alex, for whom he seemed to have a true fatherly affection "—and you will be escorted by Mr. Granger. I will have Cody Fox remain here because he is better acquainted with this area, while I'm certain that you're familiar with Harpers Ferry."

She nodded, feeling as if her heart was sinking.

But I believe our father is here, she longed to cry out.

She did not. She uttered no protest.

"I'm sure you are aware, as well, since you've nursed men on the battlefields, that enemies may still remain friends," he said to her.

She frowned and then nodded. "Yes, they manage to trade tobacco for coffee, and to send notes back and forth by way of creeks and streams. And, of course, messengers under flags of truce bring news."

"I have papers that will take you safely to Harpers Ferry no matter whose battle lines you cross. They have already been delivered to Mr. Granger at your boardinghouse. If you'd be so kind, I'd deeply appreciate it if you would plan on leaving by morning."

"Of course, sir." The words came from her lips. She wished she hadn't uttered them. But she had. And she knew that she would go. She knew that she would never be the same again, and it was in a way that seemed to cut into her like a knife. She worshipped General Robert E. Lee. The South's President, Jefferson Davis, was a staunch, well-educated and articulate man. He didn't have quite the same…sadness in his eyes. Varina Davis, however, the first lady, was gracious and warm and truly admirable.

Now she was entranced by this man, as well.

And she thought of all the men fighting one another who were fine, good, giving men, brothers, husbands, fathers, sons and friends, and she truly understood the depth of sadness in the great man's eyes.

The carriage had stopped.

Lincoln leaned across to her, taking her hand. "I am forever in your debt, my dear," he said quietly.

The door opened. He smiled at Alex. "Alexandra, I thank you."

"Good day, sir," Alex said.

Megan managed to murmur something similar.

The coachman helped her down, and she was standing in front of the boardinghouse again. The carriage pulled out onto the street and was away, and all of it might have been some kind of a wild and distressed daydream.

"Well?" Alex asked, the one word soft.

She looked at Alex. The young woman had accepted her completely, she knew, more than the others had. More than Cody even.

"Thank you," Megan said.

"You're thanking me?"

"I believe I will always cherish the fact that I met that man."

Alex smiled. "Perhaps some men are born into destiny, truly. Or, perhaps, sometimes, fate simply finds the most honorable men. He mourns the loss of his child. And his wife… Mary is so sad. And frightening—she can be so emotional. Disturbed, really… But…I was asking about the journey you're to undertake. Are you really ready and honestly willing?"

"I'm going with Cole," Megan said, shaking her head.

"It will be all right. He is always a complete gentleman. Honestly," Alex said. "But that's not why you're really disturbed. You can hold your own with any man…."

"There's something still here," Megan said.

"Yes. That's why Cody and Brendan must remain."

Megan shook her head. "No, no, that's not it. There's something here that—that I'm convinced is good, as well."

"Your father?" Alex said, reading into her heart and mind.

She nodded. "It could be, Alex. It really could be."

"All things are possible, so I've learned," Alex told her. "But you don't need to worry. Cody is always wary, but..." Her voice trailed, and then she stopped speaking. "Cody isn't a fool, Megan. And he—and Cole and Brendan—know that sometimes the afflicted *can* be saved. Cody is a doctor, and he can work with those who might just be...*tainted.* What's happened here, though, doesn't seem to constitute a series of slow seductions, in which a vampire seeks to bring more into a clan or organized family. *This* is a feeding frenzy." She paused for a minute and then said, "Have faith in Cody, Megan. Have some faith in him."

"I have faith in him. But do you think that Cody really has faith in me?" Megan asked.

"If he didn't, do you think he would have let that carriage ride happen?"

"All right. I'll be ready to go tomorrow," Megan said. She looked back toward the house. "I don't think I'll go in though, right now. I'm not needed this afternoon, am I?"

Alex shook her head. "No one knew exactly when we would be back."

"I think I'll take a ride then," Megan said. "And, please, don't let anyone worry. I'm not planning a ride down to Richmond with Union secrets."

Alex smiled a reassuring smile. "I wasn't worried."

Megan started around to the back, where the handsome

horses they had been given by the U.S. government were tethered beneath the eaves of the house. The saddles and bridles were laid over a wooden sawhorse and she made quick work of saddling the mare that she had ridden the day before.

She detested a sidesaddle, but opted to use it anyway. She didn't want to listen to Cole complain that she'd jeopardized all their lives by making someone ride out on the sidesaddle if some mission presented itself that afternoon.

She was quickly on the road, determined on reaching her destination with as much speed as possible. The day had a tendency to disappear far too rapidly.

She had been to Washington many times when she was younger, before the war had descended.

But in a few years' time, the city had changed completely.

She stopped several times for directions, and was again surprised by the simple humanity of the courtesy she found from those who were happy to stop and help her.

War went on.

But away from those fields, life went on. Children walked the streets with their books belted and carried at their sides.

They kicked cans along the way, old bean cans with rusting, twisted tops.

Women shopped and walked along with their baskets, and businessmen checked their watches as they hurried to banks or law offices or other places of day-to-day employment.

Eventually, she left the crowds of the city behind, reached Georgetown, and the gatehouse to the cemetery.

She left the horse tethered there and nearly ran across the lawns and graves toward the chapel.

She was certain that no corpses that might return remained. The shadow in the chapel would have seen to it.

The sun was still in the sky, though the intense oranges and reds that should be of a *lowering* sun dominated. A gentle breeze moved through the cemetery, touching upon monuments, stirring the brilliant display of spring flowers that grew along the many paths.

Trees dipped their branches and gently listed in the air.

She came to the chapel, opened the door and slipped in. For a moment she stood there, trying to sense her surroundings.

She walked to a bench and sat down, staring at the altar.

"I know you're here!" she whispered aloud. "Please... I know that you're a being of decency and goodness. Please..."

There was no response.

Then...

She thought that she heard the creaking of the door.

She started to turn.

And that's when it seemed that a brick building fell on her head, and the world began to spin.

CHAPTER EIGHT

COLE WAS FAIRLY certain that Megan Fox hadn't known that he was following her, keeping his distance. She hadn't seen him at the house, but neither had he seen her. He knew how to track someone *discreetly,* essentially hunting them down.

He knew how to do it, having certainly done enough tracking in his day on the frontier. It was definitely different in the big city, but then, Megan wasn't exactly hiding, didn't expect to be followed. She was easy to follow. Even with his late start.

He'd had his own agenda while she'd been in the carriage with Mr. Lincoln.

He thought over his own meeting that morning. After Alex and Megan had left, he'd convened with Lisette Annalise at the Willard Hotel for an early lunch. He'd thought that she had some factual information to give him, information that would have helped them get their way into Harpers Ferry.

But she had met him to give him a serious warning. At least, that was all he could surmise the purpose had been by the end of their meeting.

Lisette was not happy with the circumstances. She knew that the group intended to split and that Cole would be alone with this mysterious half-vampire woman that they had known for less than a week.

Lisette had promised him that she would join them in Harpers Ferry as soon as certain matters were handled in the city. In the meanwhile, she didn't trust Megan, and had urged him to talk with Cody, convince him that Megan was dangerous—that she really should be imprisoned, with hand-selected guards to watch her until the danger was past. She was adamant that Cody himself get to know his sister better before he entrusted her with anything of importance. Moreover, Cole noticed that she carefully termed her every word, and did everything short of suggesting that Megan needed to be taken care of *on a permanent basis.*

He understood Lisette Annalise; the woman was a fanatic. She was loyal. She loved her country—almost to a fault, if there be such a thing in a time of war. It was understandable—to many people, at least. Cole was sure of that. There were many who believed that the assassination of certain generals would end the war more quickly. That agile spies, willing to give up their own lives for the greater good, should simply arrive at battle stations as messengers, draw out guns and start blazing.

Though the citizens at home longed to applaud their generals, they usually wished that meant men such as Stonewall Jackson, Robert E. Lee and Jeb Stuart. They had ruled the beginning of the war. But now, the North was adhering to more drastic tactics than before, and hard-knuckled men such as Sherman and Grant were beginning to sacrifice numbers for battles. If they could do so long enough, those tactics might win out.

But no military man would condone cold-blooded murder, even though one could reasonably argue that thousands of boys went down in cold-blooded murder on the battlefields, face-to-face, on a daily basis. Though of equal tragedy, the two things were always different to generals and commanders.

And so, because most men did have a sense of right and wrong and honor, Lisette hadn't managed to get her thoughts and passions through those in power and into action. Cole wondered though, sometimes, that she had never tried such a tactic herself. The more he saw her, the more she seemed alarming in her determination.

It had been strange to sit in the restaurant at the elegant Willard, sipping coffee from delicate cups and dining on fine china set atop snowy white cloths. The hotel was Lisette's home in the city, and she reigned there as if it were her castle alone, that her presence is what made it special, despite the fact that it had hosted many famous persons. Pinkerton had arranged for Lincoln's stay there before his inauguration; the songbird Jenny Lind had visited; and Julia Ward Howe had written the words to the *Battle Hymn of the Republic* while a guest at the hotel.

People chatted. They were dressed in elegant clothing. Politicians sat with other politicians. Constituents fiercely spoke to their representatives. There was many a man in uniform, as well as some women training to be field nurses. The war was all around them—and yet it wasn't. In this social setting, it seemed far removed.

Only the soldier missing an arm or a leg, balancing on a prosthetic here or there, gave credence to the real world hinted at beyond the fine linens and sparkling dinnerware.

While Lisette tried to emphasize the danger Megan Fox presented, basically suggesting that she be eliminated in whatever manner necessary, she still maintained the appearance of a tiny angel. She was exceptional in her ability to speak to him in a passionate whisper then turn graciously to accept an acknowledgment or compliment from a fellow diner.

Despite the elegance and the comfort, Cole couldn't wait to escape.

He was most eager to return because, he'd admitted to himself, he was afraid to be away from Megan. He knew that he wasn't afraid of her—but afraid for her. He couldn't explain that, since he knew she could protect herself.

He listened to Lisette, but when he realized the subject of her tirade, he began to daydream a bit and became simply anxious to leave. He'd been saved by the appearance of her assistant, Trudy Malcolm, the timid, mousy little woman who drifted about like a shadow, a pale shadow, albeit. Thankfully, Trudy had a note from the office, and Lisette was disturbed to discover that she had been asked back immediately, regarding information just received from the telegraph office.

He was grateful that somehow, despite the time he was gone, he managed to return to the house in time to see Alex heading for the doorway—and to learn that Megan had just left.

Thankfully, she hadn't been in a hurry. And she had far from perfect traveling instincts and had to stop for directions.

He tried to keep his distance from her, fooling himself into wondering what she was planning to do, even as he intuitively knew. Megan was convinced there was a benevolent presence in the cemetery.

He simply wasn't so trustful himself.

Of her, or of her hopes?

He wanted to believe in her completely, and to believe in this hopefulness of hers. He wanted to be with her, and know more and more about her. Frankly, he wanted just to *be* with her in every sense of the word. She was Cody's sister, and of course that meant…

He wasn't sure what that meant. She wasn't Cody's sister in the traditional form. Cody was ethical, a man with far more honor than most he had ever met. Others might speak well, but Cody lived his life by his beliefs. Still, Cody hadn't grown up as the big brother protecting her. Those feelings might be absent in him, for all Cole knew.

Of course, for that matter, Cole himself was an honorable man, or so he wanted to believe. He had come from the frontier, where life could be harsh, where people—men and women—did what was necessary to get through life, raise their children, survive. But there was still honor there, even when survival was paramount and sometimes desperate.

What he wanted, and he knew he wanted it, was…

Night and shadow. A dream that stayed a dream.

A woman with the fierce passions, the determination, courage and beauty that Megan Fox possessed. The sensuality that was so naturally hers.

He still imagined her coming to him in the night, but seeking no evil, just to be held, just to be…

She might be in serious danger, and here he was, his mind working below the belt. He gave himself a shake.

She'd tethered her horse at the gate. He did the same.

He was positive that she had gone to the chapel.

He did the same.

He wondered what it was with this cemetery. It was still early enough in the day—afternoon, but far before the night should be coming on—and yet the cemetery seemed darker than time would merit.

Maybe it was the day, and maybe it was his mood. And maybe something that had shades of pure evil was casting something malignant over a place where the hallowed dead should have rested easily.

Storms were gathering again. The storms that seemed to plague the capital as spring began its slow roll into summer.

Graves and monuments shrouded in mist.

Rain coming again.

It was the season, he told himself.

But he felt…something.

Being with Cody, learning to listen, to sense the environment around him, what he could see and what he couldn't, all had had their effect on him.

And he didn't like what he was feeling that afternoon.

And yet he wondered if the elements themselves feared a presence of evil and cast the gloom over the cemetery and the city as a warning. Was the encroaching darkness the problem, a warning about the problem…or all in his mind?

Cole gave a mental shake and reminded himself that he wasn't a fanciful man. He wasn't, but then again, life itself was proving that bizarre and ghastly fancy could be real, and thus it might have been a preternatural instinct for self-preservation that made him wary. He wasn't fanciful; he was aware.

He moved swiftly yet carefully through the abundance of graves, angels, obelisks and assorted shapes that marked the last resting places of many a good man and woman. And some not so good. War was not careful; the decent died with the liars and the rogues.

He paused briefly now and then, assuring himself that he heard or saw—*sensed*—that he was alone in the field of grass and stone.

The sky grew darker as he neared the chapel.

He was ready, however, as he moved. Alert to every sound. He could even hear the grass bend beneath his feet.

His bowie knife in his right hand, a fine honed, razor-sharp stake in his left, he came around to the chapel and neared the door.

It was ajar.

He was but twenty feet away when he saw what appeared at first to be a dark whirlwind taking form in the doorway. It was like a black shadow-wind that burst out, swirling and twisting in a growing fury. He held still for a moment, waiting, tensed and ready.

But the thing didn't come near him. It appeared like a tangle of rain clouds, battling for prominence, and swiftly it shot off as if caught by an even greater wind, or engaged in a deadly race.

Against…

He didn't know. He watched it disappear toward the north.

Against the wind.

Then a sense of dread and fear, unlike anything he had ever known.

Megan.

His muscles came to life and he sped across the remaining distance to the chapel, kicking the door fully open and shouting her name.

"Megan!"

There was no answer, and he ran down the length of the chapel.

He found her at last.

She was on the floor, fallen at an awkward angle, her face toward the floor. He raced to her and dropped his weapons, hunkering down at her side, reminding himself that she healed quickly as long as…

He turned her and saw her face, beautiful features pale, lustrous lashes closed over the golden orbs of her eyes.

He touched her cheek, lifted her chin, desperately looking for where she might have been wounded. He sat, sprawled on the ground, and pulled her onto his lap.

She was warm. She had a heartbeat. She was breathing.

"Megan!" he whispered in anguish.

Her lashes fluttered, her forehead creased in a frown, and she seemed to grimace in pain. Then her eyes opened and she was looking up at him, or somewhere just past him.

"Megan," he said again, unaware of how his voice trembled.

She blinked. "What—Cole? What happened?"

For a moment, she didn't even try to move. She just stared at him in confusion.

"I can't tell you—you have to tell me," he said.

She drew a hand to her head. "I—I don't know." She winced again. "My head hurts. It's—it's killing me, actually…."

She blinked and looked at him again, puzzled that he was there. Suspicion clouded her eyes for a moment. She tensed in his arms and he found that he held her tightly in return. "Oh, no, no!" he told her. "I came here to rescue you."

"Rescue me from what?" she asked him.

"Whoever attacked you," he said gruffly. "Megan, you had to have seen something!"

She eased in his arms, though she still studied him.

"You were following me," she accused.

"Yes," he agreed flatly.

"Why?" she asked, but then answered herself. "Why? Of course. You don't trust me. You were trying to find out who I was meeting. What other spy was going to relay all the brilliant military information I've amassed here and take it down to someone in the South," she said bitterly.

He smiled grimly. "No."

"Then?"

"I was worried about you."

She shook her head. "Why?"

He angled his head slightly, his smile deepening despite their situation. "Hmm...I was following you to see what you were up to, of course. And it was good, because I was actually..."

She flushed. She tried to sit up, but grimaced in pain.

"Easy," he said, holding her tight and pat in his arms.

Her lashes lowered and she nodded. "I'll be fine in a minute."

He tenderly touched her head. There was a good-size knot on her skull. "Someone really belted you. If you weren't who you are, it might have been a hard enough blow to kill."

"I'm all right."

"You're not all right."

"I will be," she assured him. She stared up at him with those enormous gold eyes of hers.

"I told you," he said softly, "I know you want to find your father, but you can't be certain that he's here. He could be anywhere."

She shook her head. "He's here," she whispered.

"And he conked you on the head?"

"No, of course not," she protested.

"Then you must realize that you're being far too trusting—because you so desperately want to believe. Megan, someone was here who wanted to hurt you, surely you realize that by now."

She shook her head. "No, no..."

"Megan, I didn't attack you."

"No...I know that."

"Then," he said very gently, "whatever force it is that you think is here to help us—isn't. You were lured. Something very evil wants to reach you—remove you from the equation of whatever game this is."

She struggled to sit up. He helped her. "But—if something meant to hurt me, why didn't it...finish me? I was out. I was down. It could have killed me."

"Maybe—I was behind you. It knew that it wasn't going to be alone."

Her lips curled into a slow smile. He was surprised and oddly affected when she reached up and touched his face. "I know...you came gallantly to save me. But...I don't think *it* would have been afraid of the two of us as a force."

"Wait a minute. We're a pretty good force!" he protested with a smile.

Her knuckles brushed his chin. He was startled by the

way her touch sent warmth radiating throughout him. The world came down to the two of them, alone, in a mystic pool of light that streamed through the chapel window.

"No. I agree," she said quietly, looking into his eyes. "There was something *evil* in here, too, but I think that my father was here and stopped whatever force it was that wanted to harm me. Don't laugh at me, Cole, please don't laugh at me. And don't tell me that something like that couldn't have possibly happened. Yes, of course, it's what I want to happen, but it could be the truth."

She was so earnest. And young. Though hardened by the war, by her own existence, she was still laden with hope.

He remembered what he had seen, or, what he *thought* he had seen.

A whirlwind, like twin tornadoes, meeting and melding in a storm of spinning darkness, flying away from the chapel.

He had thought that it was like a pair of thunderclouds, clashing with a tremendous violence, battling their way into the wind, together.

The light around them dimmed as the sun was setting.

"We need to get going. You're not particularly strong right now, which is going to make us both vulnerable." He eased her from his lap and stood, supporting her, helping her to her feet. "Are you…are you still in much pain?"

She shook her head and gingerly touched the back of it.

"It's already dissipating."

"Put your arm around me."

"I'm already better, really."

He asked her, "Why don't you accept help, just for a minute?"

She lowered her head with a soft sigh, then let him slip an arm around her and support her as they started from the chapel.

At the door, she paused, looking back.

"What is it?" he asked tensely. The *beings,* the clouds, whoever or whatever they had been, had gone, heading north.

But this place now made him uneasy.

"I don't really want to leave. My father has been here. I have faith in that, Cole. Please, until something is proved otherwise, please let me have that belief."

"If your father was here, and he's protecting you, he knows about you. And Cody. And if and when the time is right for him, he'll let himself be known, Megan," Cole told her.

She looked up at him. "But we're leaving tomorrow. For Harpers Ferry. He's here."

"Megan, if your father is the force for good that you want him to be, he'll fight this battle the way that he sees fit. If he's good, he's been fighting this for a long time most likely. And you have to trust that if he's not revealing himself to you now, it must not be the time for him."

"All right," she said after a moment.

"I really think we should leave."

"I'm better," she told him.

He touched the back of her head. Already the lump was disappearing.

"Still, you're susceptible at this moment."

He led her out. He was ridiculously glad that she didn't

push him away, and that she seemed content to lean on him as they walked from the cemetery.

The rain was going to come again soon. The air was damp and heavy with the portent of the coming storm.

He moved quickly, but she seemed lethargic, caught up in her own thoughts. He reminded himself not to allow his mind to wander too deeply into thoughts of her. He needed to stay alert as they left the cemetery.

As they neared the gates, he turned to look back. There was nothing behind him but gravestones, monuments and praying angels forlorn in the shrouded air. The wind blew through the beauty of the spring flowers that had bloomed. The sky looking the way it did, it was almost as if time had stopped during their escapade in the chapel.

When they reached the horses, she straightened. She looked at him gravely. "I'm fine now. I'm really fine. I'll be ready to leave first thing in the morning, whenever you wish."

"So, you're really fine with the appointment, after your meeting with the President?" he asked, ready to help her mount her horse.

She was quiet for a moment. She leaped up on her horse without assistance.

"No," she told him. "I was never here for any political reason, for any government. And now, I'm not going to Harpers Ferry for a president or a government, either. I'm ready to go for that one man, and for *people*."

He mounted his bay.

"We'll be on our own, you know. We'll really have to trust one another."

"I always trusted you. It's you who's suspicious," she

reminded him. "'Trust has to be earned'—you're the one who said that."

He glanced at her sideways. "Maybe you've earned it," he said.

"Really?" she said, and he was glad when she laughed. "How? When?"

He shrugged. "I'm not sure, just feels that way. Then, maybe I'm going on a little bit of faith, too. C'mon, let's get on out of here and back to Martha's before the rain starts, shall we?"

THEY RETURNED IN time for supper, a feast Martha Graybow had prepared in light of the pair's departure the following morning.

Cody and Cole were sequestered in the parlor, talking with one another while Martha set out their meal with Alex and Megan—and Brendan Vincent.

Brendan was being more than courteous, trying to help carry everything while Megan and Alex set the table. Alex glanced at Megan, giving her a quick grin.

It was obvious that romance was beginning to flourish. The Unionist had to be almost twenty years older than Martha, but he was a wise and gentle man, in very good shape—from the military and vampire hunting, Megan assumed—and the widow seemed not at all averse to his attention.

Megan hoped that this meant good things would happen for Martha and her young children. As far as being the perfect gentleman, someone who would truly love and care for Martha—and her children—Megan could think of no finer a man.

She was curious, however, that he wasn't with Cody

and Cole, and if she began to wonder if their conversation wasn't more personal than professional.

"I think that we're just about all set," Martha said, flushing, "thanks to Brendan giving us so much help. Will you call in Cody and Cole, and would someone mind stepping over to my house to fetch the children? They've been doing their homework, or, at least, they've supposedly been doing their homework!"

"They're good children, Martha, I'm sure it's all done," Alex said, smiling.

"I'll run out back and get them," Megan offered. As she opened the back door to go out to the carriage house, she was startled to see that there was someone just slipping out the door. His back to her, the man was essentially nothing but a large hat and long, black coat, but even with that, Megan could sense something dark and sinister about him.

"Hey! What are you doing? Who are you?"

The person froze. Then, as she ran toward him, the back of his black coat become a swirl of black movement. Shadowlike bat wings lifted up toward the sky and the figure shot up in swift flight.

Terrified, she watched it disappear, but only for a split second, before racing into the carriage house, dreading what she might find.

"Artie? Marni?" she cried, bursting through the front door, even as she heard Brendan yelling from far behind her.

The carriage house had been divided into four rooms: the entry, set up like a parlor, two bedrooms to the left and right down a hallway and Matha's larger, master bedroom at the rear.

There was no one in the parlor.

Megan hurried down the hallway, calling out to the children. "Artie? Marni? Please, answer me, where are you?"

She burst into Artie's room, a perfect room for a growing boy. It showcased a train set, books on the military heroes and a desk with a telescope and schoolbooks spread out over a blotter. The inkwell had been knocked over; a quill pen lay in the midst of the ink.

Panic began to lodge in Megan's soul. She hurried into the next room, Marni's room. It was a charming room for a little girl. Martha had sewn a ruffled canopy for the small four-post bed, and the curtains matched. Dolls lay on the bed, and Marni's young reader lay on the floor. It looked as if the little girl had been doing her reading, just as her mother had said.

Megan ran back into the hallway and looked down to Martha's room. She ran to the door, not wanting to open it.

When she did so, she had to swallow back the scream of horror that had lodged in her throat before she could breathe again.

CHAPTER NINE

"ARE YOU GETTING along any better? It appears so, at the least. But I have to admit that I don't like the situation we're in," Cody said, leaning forward. They were both sipping shots of the delicious, aged Scotch that Martha had offered them, and it was good to sit with Cody in the relative ease of the parlor and talk out some of the things that had recently happened.

Things that had happened. Not things that he was feeling!

"We're getting along fine. That's not going to be a problem," Cole said. "What I'm worried about is Megan's almost desperate insistence that your father is here, and that he's somewhere in the background, helping us fight the scourge that's upon us."

Cody leaned back, shrugging. "Odd. I was convinced that my father was a monster, and that I had to find him for *that* reason. Stop him—before he was the scourge. Or kept being the scourge, but then again, we know now that he *didn't* create all the tragedy and travesty out by Victory, Texas. We *found* that culprit."

"No, and we've seen that some people can hang on to their *souls,* I suppose you would say, their decency," Cole agreed. "We've seen it—we know it. But we also know just how damned rare it is."

"And so we're left to wonder—how many more like Megan and I might be out there?" Cody said.

"That an interesting question," Cole agreed. "And..."

"And what?"

"Well, if they all grew up to be as decent as you. And Megan," he added quickly.

Cody offered him a small, dry grin. "So, you do believe in her. In truth, and deep down. Because I was afraid you'd go to West Virginia on this hunt simply because you'd been asked—even if you didn't really trust Megan."

Cole laughed. "No. I'm not that decent a human being. If I still didn't trust her, I wouldn't be going."

Cody smiled, and then his face quickly turned grave. "You won't have much help. Well, from what I understand, the Union officers are aware that something far more dangerous than a Union spy or a sniper is about. Apparently, from the conversation I had yesterday with some officers, they've learned on their own to stay locked inside at night, to have their guards on duty in foursomes—and to wear their best Sunday, go-to-meeting crosses. But they're mainly working off superstition with that last bit. It will be you and Megan, really, who understand the heart of the matter."

"But I will have the *cooperation* of the military?"

"Yes, of course."

"And *not* to start hunting down poor locals who Northerners might think are Southern sympathizers or monsters themselves?" Cole asked.

"You'll find that the orders on this have come straight down from the top—from the supreme commander of all the forces. I doubt if you'll spend your time arguing over the finer points of States' Rights," Cody said. "Not in the midst of this. Once people face it, they realize they have a much greater enemy than the one they already know."

Cole nodded. He'd been through Harpers Ferry once, years ago. Oddly enough, he remembered it as one of the most beautiful spots he had ever seen. The mountains rose high above the rivers, the terrain was rich and filled with trees and foliage. The waters of both rivers converged with crystal beauty as they danced over rapids beneath the sun.

He knew, too, that the military firmly held the lower town with stations planted along the heights, as well. The lower town provided greater safety, being highly developed. A man named Harper had, definitively, started a ferry at the junction of rivers soon after he received his patent in 1750. The town had been a gateway for those moving into the Shenandoah Valley. Construction for the United States Armory and Arsenal had begun at the end of the last century, and the town became famous for its production of guns. In the mid-1830s, the Ohio and Chesapeake Canal had created a boon for transportation, and true industrialization had taken root. Early in the war, Southern forces had destroyed the arsenal and armory—before the Union forces could take it over.

Cole had the feeling he wasn't going to enjoy the changes in the town he remembered fondly. Once, it had been bustling, filled with life.

"We'll be fine," he said at last.

"It's been decided that you'll have a military escort," Cody said.

"Oh?"

"The same fellows you worked with before. Apparently, when asked for volunteers among the unit, the four stepped right up. They admired you, said you were a damned good man, and they even thought you were so decent, there might be more decent folk back in Texas," Cody said lightly.

Cole nodded. Good. He could work with that crew. Which reminded him that he needed to acquire the necessary weaponry still.

"Arrows," he said to Cody. "Bows and arrows. And I think we'll make sure we're carrying plenty of vials of holy water. Each man needs to be wearing a cross—or Star of David, or some sign of his affiliation. They'll need their rifles, bayonets and sidearms, as well. Knives. A good bowie knife or something similar. But I'll start with them on bows and arrows."

"Good thinking. I should get some of the men here trained with those, too." His eyes were light. "There's a lot to be learned from the West, and I should have thought about that before now," Cody said. "Out in the West, we had the Apaches and John Snow and his mixed-up family, and they were open-minded—not so disbelieving of when the unusual happened. And their expertise with arrows was certainly a boon."

Cole started to answer him but he broke off, staring as he heard the kitchen door slam open and Megan screaming for help. He and Cody jumped to their feet, racing back to where the others were.

Megan hadn't come into the parlor. Apparently she had just opened the back door to the house long enough to scream that horrible sound. By the time Cole reached the back door, Brendan, Alex and Martha were already out of the house, having followed Megan. He and Cody followed in their wake, bursting into Martha's carriage house.

He heard Martha scream as they rushed down the hall to the woman's bedroom.

And then he saw why.

Her son and daughter were laid out on the bed.

As if they had been prepared for a death viewing by an undertaker.

Martha had thrown herself upon her daughter and was trying to gather her son into her arms. Cole saw that Cody looked instantly at Megan, who was staring back at him, her eyes betraying the fact that she was praying for help—hoping against hope that he knew something that she didn't, something that would help make this better.

"Marks?" Cody asked Megan.

She nodded.

"Is there any life left?" Cody asked, walking forward to take her arm. Brendan and Alex were trying to gently wrest Martha from atop her children, lest she smother them herself.

Megan nodded. "The heartbeats are faint, but I found them, and they're both breathing. But…their throats… yes, the marks are there."

"How? Oh, they *knew* not to ask anyone in!" Martha wailed. Then she grew desperate, panicking and looking at them all with wild eyes. "No, no, no! I know what you all do—as vampire killers—and I will not let you. You will not kill my children. You will not impale them, and…oh, God! You will not decapitate my children. You will not, you cannot, I will not let you, I will fight and scream and I will…" She couldn't speak; her rash of desperate fury ended as she burst into a wail of tears again.

Brendan pulled her into his arms. "Please, please,

Martha. All is not lost if there is still a ghost of life. Please, please…Cody?" He looked back to his friend.

Cody nodded. Megan was still staring at her brother, confused. "I need my medical bag," he said.

Alex nodded and hurried past them. Megan still stood there, looking lost.

"He's going to give them a blood transfusion, Megan," Cole explained to her.

"A blood—*transfusion?*"

Cody was already rolling up his sleeves. "Actually, several doctors have been experimenting with blood transfusions in this war," he said. "In this situation, there's no other choice. It's all right. I know what I'm doing. But there are two children, so we'll both need to be donators."

She continued to stare at him blankly.

"It's all right, Megan," Cole said. "Cody has done this before."

That seemed to surprise her more than the fact that Cody was going to attempt to transfuse blood from someone into someone else.

"But—is our blood *tainted?*" she asked.

He shook his head. "No—it will actually give them the strength and power to better resist another bite. All right. Lie down next to Marni."

"Oh!" Martha gasped, sagging against Brendan. "But you had rigged the house with alarms. There were… there were crosses around the house, there was holy water around the house… Cody, how…?"

"Someone powerful did this, Martha. But, I *can* save the children. They were left yet alive to torture us, as a warning, but we won't let them die. We'll save them. You have to have faith in me."

Martha looked around at everyone. Tears continued to stream down her face. "But—Cody, I've only vaguely heard about this…this operation."

"Several physicians have worked transfusions in different way, but it's all the same thing, really. I have needles that basically attach to tubes, and the tubes will carry the plentiful blood from Megan and me into the children. It takes some time, but it's effective. Brendan, take Martha into the parlor, where she can gain some calm while she waits."

As he spoke, Alex returned.

"I can't leave the children," Martha said weakly.

"You must," Cody told her gently. He nodded to Brendan, who nodded in return, and with firm tenderness steered Martha out of the bedroom. "Alex, Cole, you'll have to listen to me, and help when I need it. Megan, lie down next to Marni. Cole, can you please tie one of the tourniquets around her arm? I'll set the tubing and the needle."

Megan looked at Cole with wide eyes. She did as Cody instructed, lying next to the little girl. "We need some leverage, so get Megan up—gravity will be at work here, too," Cody explained.

In a matter of minutes, they had her on a stack of pillows and clothing. Cole smiled at her gently and warned that the tourniquet would pinch. She looked up at him with wide eyes, enigmatic, but apparently she trusted him. He wound the tourniquet around her arm, and Cody tested her arm for a vein before setting the needle and instructing Cole on how to watch the flow in her tubing while he set the instruments up for the child. When he was finished, he lifted Artie; they were going to have to take the boy, larger than the girl, into his own room to set up a similar circumstance. Cole started to follow Cody, but he stopped him.

"You have to keep watch here. Watch Megan, and Marni, and most importantly watch the flow of blood. Shift the tubing around if it slips, and make sure it stays in her arm. Alex can help me. If the flow stops, Megan, pump your arm. You should be fine. You're my sister, which means we have the same systems."

Alex followed Cody out. Cole was left to kneel on the side of the bed, hovering over Megan and trying to keep an unblinking eye on the apparatus. He saw the blood flow from Megan and into the tube, and then onward through into the little girl. He felt numb. He knew that Cody had done this before—he had faith. But the little girl had been so pale....

So close to death.

"Are you all right?" he asked Megan.

"Of course. I would do anything to save Martha's children."

"I didn't ask that," Cole said, trying to smile. "I asked if you were all right."

She nodded to him thoughtfully. "It's strange. I can feel it. I can feel the blood flowing from me." She hesitated. "Will they really live?"

"I believe so," Cole said. "But the situation disturbs me."

"We were here—and that put the children in danger."

Cole nodded. "I'm afraid so."

"We have to get out of here," she said flatly. "All of us. We have to get away from Martha and her children."

He shook his head and she frowned. "No. The creature that did this will only come back now that he knows. You and I have to leave as planned—and Martha has to move into the house with Cody, Alex and Brendan."

"But what if whoever did this gets into the house?" she demanded.

"Cody will be there. It won't happen."

She shook her head in distress. "We can't leave anymore."

"We *have* to leave. It's imperative that we get to Harpers Ferry before it—before it doesn't exist anymore. When an outbreak that severe happens... Well, there's a ghost town near Victory now. We have to go, and we have to have faith that we're all going to be able to do what needs to be done."

He looked at the tube and watched the way that the blood was flowing, then looked back to her. Megan trained her eyes on his. She was oddly afraid, he thought. And he found himself evermore attracted to her. There were so many aspects of the woman to...like. The way that she...was put together. Built. She was a stunning creature of sensuality in her frame, in her carriage, in the way she stood, in her...physical being. But it was her eyes that seemed to entrap him every time. The hazel—the green and brown, turning gold when combined—*that* seemed to sweep his soul away, every time. The way she looked at him now...so trusting.

She stared at him. "Do you think that they'll really be all right?" she whispered.

He gripped her hand and answered in honesty. "Yes. I do. Cody—*your brother*—would give his life a thousand times over to save that of an innocent child."

She kept staring at him. The blood drained from her into Marni Graybow.

"You're doing all right?" he asked her.

"I feel…light-headed. I believe that would be natural, the life force leaving me," she whispered.

He had her hand in his. He squeezed it. "I believe so myself," he assured her.

"Martha is my friend. And a wonderful person. Honestly, I swear, she was never a spy for anyone," Megan said.

"I believe you."

"Her children must be saved," she told him.

"I believe they will be," he said softly.

She closed her eyes. He knew that what she was giving cost her. She would survive it, but he was more worried about what she was thinking than what was happening. Cody was half vampire, with half-vampire blood. He had seen Cody work magic in this fashion before.

Cole reached over and set his fingers against Marni Graybow's throat. The pulse was growing stronger. When he looked at the girl, she was beginning to show color in her cheeks.

"How are you doing?" he asked Megan.

She flashed him a smile. "I'm…I'm fine. What about Marni?"

"She's looking wonderfully healthy," Cole assured her.

For a moment, he just sat there. He studied Megan's eyes. He found himself praying not for the child, because he believed in Cody.

He prayed for Megan instead. Or himself. He prayed that Megan really was everything that she had asked them to believe she was.

Because he was mesmerized. Taken by the way she looked at him. Taken by the color of her eyes. By the way that she touched him, by the sound of her voice…

He was staring into her eyes, just staring and trying to give the utmost encouragement, when Alex came back into the room.

"We need to stop the flow of blood now. Tighten the tourniquet, please, Cole. Megan can't give anymore."

"Wait! Is it good—is it enough to save Marni yet?" Megan asked with concerned vigor.

Alex assured Megan, "Yes, absolutely. Cody has the timing down on this."

She helped Cole tighten the tourniquet around Megan's arm, preventing the further flow of blood. She withdrew the needle from both their arms, and she pressed hard on the spots where each had punctured. "Cole, please, hold tightly here until we're sure the flow of blood has stopped."

"I'm all right," Megan said.

Cole nodded, but did what Alex had said anyway. He grinned. "You'd say that if you were in the midst of a volcanic twister."

"No!"

"Yes!" he teased.

"But...Marni," she whispered.

"Marni looks so much better than when we came in, it's almost unbelievable. Her color is flushed. She's breathing easily on her own, and, her pulse is very strong."

"Really?" she whispered.

"Really." He wasn't going to lie to her. Whether she had been born half vampire or not, there was just something about Megan. He would never lie to her.

She gripped her arm, rolling from the pile of clothing and looking at the child herself.

Marni was better. She was breathing audibly, and

her color was rosy again. She opened her eyes, blinking rapidly. She looked at Megan and her lips trembled. "Mama?" she gasped.

"We'll get her right away, Marni. Right away," Megan promised, and she leaped up.

Cole saw that she and Martha nearly collided with one another—Martha had heard her daughter's voice—despite its faintness—and was hurrying in. She paused in the doorway, as if afraid that her ears had tricked her. Then she saw Marni with her open eyes, struggling to get up on her elbows. Martha burst into tears, racing for her daughter and enveloping her gently in her arms.

Cole reached out for Megan's hand. "Let's give them a few moments."

She took his hand, and then balked, pulling at it.

"Artie?" she asked.

"We'll stop and see." They paused at the boy's room, looking in. Alex was sitting by the boy's side, checking his pulse. He, too, had fresh new color and a flush of rose in his cheeks. He was breathing easily—obviously alive and in far better condition than just moments ago.

"It works, the transfusion works," she said.

"Cody is a medical doctor," Cole reminded her.

She nodded. Alex looked up at them, smiling. "We were in time. Thank God. Cole, will you bring Artie into the house? There's still an empty bedroom, across from the one Cody and I are sleeping in. We'll bring the children there, and we'll try to get Martha to rest in your room, if you don't mind—and tonight, we'll have you and Brendan keep watch over the children, sharing the time. That way you can both get some rest, and I think we should keep an eye on them through the night. Cody should sleep."

"Certainly," Cole replied. He walked over to the bed and lifted the twelve-year-old into his arms. Megan hurried ahead, opening the door to the carriage house, then moving quickly across the distance of yard to the back door of the main house. Cole walked on upstairs, taking Artie to the extra bedroom. Artie stirred in his arms as he carried him. When Cole set him down, Artie stared at him with wide blue eyes.

"You're all right," Cole assured him quickly.

Artie nodded, as if he knew and accepted Cole's words. He shook his head, though, distressed. "I…heard something at the door. But there was nothing. I went back to my room. Marni was studying her reader, just like Mama said. I heard—her cry out. I rushed in…I felt it…at my back. And then…"

"Artie, it's all right," Cole said.

"Marni!" Artie cried.

"She's here, darling, and she's going to be just fine!" Martha said, following Brendan, who was carrying the precious bundle into the room. Artie scooted up on his elbows, touching his little sister's face as she was laid beside him. He looked at his mother, and he said, "Mama, I'm so sorry. I should have been a smarter big brother, a stronger big brother…."

"Hush, son, hush!" Martha said, reaching out to pat her son's leg. "You did just fine, and I know it, Artie. And we're all going to take some lessons in the next few days on what to do when monsters slip in."

Artie nodded. His eyes closed again.

"I'll take the first watch," Brendan said. "Martha, you need to get some rest."

"Why—we have a cold supper down on the dining table," she reminded them. "And it's not going to help anyone if we don't get some food into our bodies. Cody, Megan, you two especially."

"Why, Martha, you are quite the amazing woman," Cole told her. He was somewhat surprised that the woman didn't seem to hate them all—it was unlikely that her family would have been targeted if they hadn't been there. She had almost lost her children, and she had nearly fallen apart, but she had rallied, and strongly.

"No, I'm not amazing at all. We're blessed—it might have been another time, it might have been all of us... and we might not have been found until it was too late. Now, Cole, you take Megan down to get some supper, and Cody and Alex need to go on down, too. Brendan and I will stay with the children, and after, we'll go eat, and maybe the children will even be able to have a bite or two to eat. I can fix them up some plates on trays—it'll be a bit of a lark for them to have supper in bed."

"Yes, ma'am," Cole told her. "As you say."

"Martha," Megan protested. "*You* need to take care of yourself. You know I adore the children. I'll keep watch over them while you—"

"Why, Megan, thank you, but I'm right, and that's the way it is. I have all this energy just because I know they're going to be okay. You gave my baby your blood. Now get down to that dining room. Shoo!" Martha ordered.

"She *is* right. We'll get something to eat first," Cody said from the doorway. "Come on now, Megan. The children are all right."

Megan nodded. Her eyes still seemed huge. She was pale, and Cole knew that the evening had unnerved her as little else could.

She turned and followed Alex and Cody down the stairs. Cole followed behind the three and they went to the dining room almost as a troop of sleepwalkers. They took their seats at the table, empty chairs interspaced between them. Conversation was awkwardly mundane.

"Could you pass the roast, please?" Cole asked.

"Peas?" Alex offered.

"The potatoes are delicious, even cold," Megan offered.

"Well, sadly, the gravy has congealed. But if you whirl it around enough…"

Cole stood up and walked into the kitchen and opened the icebox, drawing out a pitcher of Cody's "special drink." He brought the pitcher out to the table and poured both Cody and Megan a glass.

"This might be what you need," he said.

Both looked at each other as if they must have lost their minds—obviously, this was the nourishment they needed most at this time.

"Thank you," Megan said. She swallowed the contents quickly, set her glass down and looked around the table. "How in God's name did this happen? Now Martha and the children will be in serious danger."

"How did the creature get in?" Alex mused.

"*Who* was it?" Cody mused.

Cole said, "I don't think we're going to get anything out of the children. They just don't know what happened. Marni is so young, and she was traumatized. Artie was taken so quickly, as well…they don't know anything."

Megan stared at the table, and then drew a circle in the gravy on her plate. "I saw him," she said quietly.

"What?" Cody demanded sharply.

"I don't know who it was, though. Someone in a long coat, a railway duster something like Cole's. And a big hat that covered his head. I only saw his back, and then he was gone. So, I don't know…I don't know anything more."

"Height, weight?" Cole asked, leaning toward her, and forcing himself not to grab her.

"It was fast, so fast. All I saw was its back—and it knew I was there," Megan said.

There was silence.

Megan looked around at all of them. "It was not our father!" she said passionately, suddenly focusing on her brother.

"Megan, I don't want it to be, either," he said.

"Honestly, and you all must believe me. Someone has helped me—twice. I swear that it's the truth. And I believe that… I really believe that it could be him. I don't believe—I'll never believe—that the man my mother admired so much could be doing anything evil. I just don't. And I think that… I think that I'm afraid to leave here tomorrow because I'm worried about the children, and Martha and that…and that Cody, if you do find him, you won't bother to find out the truth!"

Cody stared back at her incredulously. "Megan—"

Oddly, he seemed to be at a loss for words.

"Megan," Cole said, "Every minute of every day, the situation is growing worse at Harpers Ferry, and that could cause a ricochet effect that no one will ever be able to stop. Frankly, your father was Cody's father first, and he's been managing this kind of situation, these *feelings* you each must have, for a very long time—and he knows how to show restraint at the right time. The children and Martha will be in the house with Cody, Brendan and Alex from now on. They'll be fine. Actually, they'll be better—because of today. Because Cody did study medicine and because he learned that under some circumstances some chances have to be taken and new techniques utilized. Megan, *you have to learn to have faith in others, and give them your trust!*"

Cody leaned forward then. "Megan, I know how to show restraint."

"My father is a vampire," Alex blurted out.

Megan sat back in stunned surprise, staring at Alex.

"A good vampire," she said softly. "He was attacked in Victory, Texas, and I received word that he was dead. But he wasn't. Well, he was, but he wasn't. He's not a half-breed of any kind. He's a vampire. But he's never killed—except in our defense, and only vampires who were monsters." And then she stared at Megan with an unmistakable resolve. "And Cody *didn't* kill my father. He'll be careful of his own, I assure you."

Megan picked up her fork. "We—we should eat."

"What? The food will get cold?" Cole asked lightly.

She turned to stare at him, as if she would burst into another tirade.

But when she looked at him, she opened her mouth, shut it and smiled.

CHAPTER TEN

EARLY THE FOLLOWING morning, Cole met with Sergeant Terry Newcomb at the railway station. It was a bustling place; Lincoln had learned to use the railroads to his advantage quickly. He was fighting a war on "foreign" soil, and he had used the strategy of railroad troop and supply movement from the beginning, realizing its importance for getting manpower and ammunition where it was needed. It seemed the Confederate commanders had not comprehended just how important the rail lines might be. At the beginning, the Union did their best to tear down what the Confederates couldn't hope to replace. But as time went on, they had begun doing more repairs, as they had to move more in Southern lands.

Although many inventors had worked with model railroads and locomotives, it hadn't been until 1830 that the Baltimore and Ohio Railroad had officially opened. This explained the fact that not many of the generals in the field had actually received any kind of tactical training at West Point regarding such things. The locomotives and cars could also be vulnerable to attack. An exploding boiler could scald a crew, and coming fast on a downed bridge could kill as efficiently as a barrage of bullets.

Against such a barrage, Cole had been assured, the train was clad in the latest in metal and wooden armor They'd be riding in a small steam-powered fortress, a fortress with small oval windows to keep the heat at bay.

He'd considered that riding the fine horses the government men had given them might have been easier and shorter than the effort it was going to take to arrive not quite seventy miles away by train. But he wanted to be well armed when he got where he was going.

"Bow and arrows, without metal heads, as you asked. Fashioned of the finest cedar available and razor sharp," the sergeant said, pointing at supply boxes as he read off articles from his list. He had been staring at the paper, but he looked at Cole as he detailed the next item. "One hundred wooden stakes—razor sharp. Fifty-five carved from lignum vitae, and another fifty carved from red oak. And…let's see…one hundred and fifty vials of holy water."

"It's really holy water, and you know it?" Cole asked, staring at the man, unblinking.

"Yes, sir, it is. I went to the church myself to collect it. I spoke with Father Vartran, who didn't seem surprised that it was something you required."

"Thank you."

The sergeant stared at him a moment longer, and then looked back at his list. "Ten cavalry sabers, freshly sharpened, ten Colt army model 1860 handguns—rifled, six shot. Then ten Smith &Wesson repeaters, rifled for accuracy, as well. Ten bowie knives, and one…ladies' small arm purse pistol."

"That should do it," Cole replied.

"And the four of us," Newcomb added, at which point Cole frowned noticeably. "Sir, you're taking the railroad, and the railroad might be disrupted. There are troops moving aboard her as well, but it will be good to have us with you. As far as we know, the Rebels are in the Shenandoah Valley now, but there are scouting troops, snipers, guerilla bands… They are not going to stop and ask you if you happen to be on a mission for humanity. They will attack you—you're on a railroad under the jurisdiction of the United States government."

"I know, although I don't believe that our route will bring us into a difficult situation. We're but seventy miles from Harpers Ferry," Cole replied calmly.

Sergeant Newcomb nodded, listening. "No, sir. But we've learned about dispatch from you. We'll be good companions. And we are all good soldiers, sir—even with our afflictions."

Good soldiers, Cole thought. Terry Newcomb limped, and he came with Gerald Banter, still weakened after a bout with malaria. Evan Briar—missing his trigger finger. And Michael Hodges, who was half-deaf.

But Sergeant Terry Newcomb was staring at him with wise, steady eyes, and Cole smiled. He'd worked with these men already, on burial detail. He had been testing the man to determine his team's resolve, to make sure they weren't just following orders. For men can abandon orders far more easily than their own passions when a mission becomes hardened. But they seemed determined to follow his lead with leaden assuredness. They *knew* they were dealing with what wasn't ordinary—even if they didn't want to put a name on it. They were fiercely loyal to Newcomb, and Newcomb was determined to help him. It wouldn't hurt to have some company on the journey to Harpers Ferry—company that knew what they were up against.

Cole set a hand on the man's arm. "Sergeant, I'm willing to bet that you're one of the best soldiers to be had. I hadn't realized we had an escort," he lied.

Newcomb nodded. "You will need us in Harpers Ferry—even if it's for picking up the dead and seeing that they receive the proper burial…for that kind of dead."

"Yes. And thank you. Now, how long before the train pulls out?"

"An hour and a half, sir. You and Miss Fox will ride your horses back to the station, and the horses will be transported in one of the supply cars, so they'll be fresh upon arrival."

"Very good," Cole said. "We'll be back, ready to go. How long will it take?"

"These days? Most of the afternoon. It will be dark when we arrive," Newcomb said.

"Have your men wear crosses—crucifixes if they're Catholic."

"Yes, sir. And Star of David if they're Jewish. I'm thanking the Good Lord that I don't have any of those atheist folks in my group, so we can do as you say."

Cole started to walk away and came back. "Sergeant Newcomb, just call me Cole. I'm starting to feel like an officer. I don't want to be an officer."

"You are an officer of the law, sir—Cole," Newcomb said.

"In Texas. We're a long way from Texas," Cole said, clapping a hand on the man's back.

"You have someone waiting, Cole," Newcomb pointed out.

Cole turned toward the street where he saw the black carriage he had seen often enough in front of the house.

It wasn't the conveyance Lincoln customarily used

for his rides around the Mall. This was the carriage that meant the president was secreted in the back and did not wish to greet his constituents on a casual basis.

Cole nodded to Newcomb and strode over to the carriage. The driver hopped down and opened the door, bringing down the step. A trolley car, heavy laden with both civilians and troops, drove on ahead as he stepped into the carriage, but the door quickly muffled the sound of the draft horses' hooves.

He slid into the seat that faced the rear. The president, his hands on a walking stick, sat back, facing forward. He looked like a tired old bulldog with a worn, gaunt face.

"Sir," Cole said.

"Sheriff Granger," Lincoln returned. "I see that you've received the supplies. It might have been a great deal easier to acquire many of them with a bit more warning."

"I'm sorry. Circumstances arose last night that put the journey into secondary consideration."

"And those were?"

Cole hesitated; he knew that Lincoln had recently lost a beloved child.

But there was nothing to say other than the truth.

"Our landlady's children fell into jeopardy."

He was sorry that he'd been forced to speak. The man with an iron determination to hold a country together, no matter the cost, looked away, deeper grooves setting into his lined face.

"I spend a great deal of my day at the telegraph office," he said.

"Yes, sir."

Lincoln looked at him gravely. "My heart grows heavier with each individual death, and yet as the notices come, that toll mounts hourly. I will not argue politics with you—I will first state my appreciation that you understand we are meeting as equals. Human beings with souls and a firm belief that there is a God and all men stand equal before him."

"This different war that we fight is one that must be won," Cole assured him.

"Such a strange disease," the president murmured, looking away again. "They lost another seven men last night. I had ordered that the guard duty be doubled. I had taken many precautions advised to me by Alex and Cody Fox. And still, the men don't understand what they face. Frankly, neither do I. Seven men, Sheriff Granger. In one night. And they did not fall to enemy troops—they did not fall for God and country in the line of battle. Once they are infected with the disease, they will attack anywhere."

"That, sir, is true."

"I needed you to know about the last seven deaths," Lincoln said. "They were heinous, from what I read between the lines of the telegraphs I receive. General Bickford described that one of the dead had his throat torn out, another looked as if he'd been mauled by a grizzly. I know we have bears in the woods, Sheriff Granger, but in the town…the afflicted seem to have the power to rip up men as if they were nothing but paper."

Cole nodded.

Lincoln sat forward, leaning on the walking stick. "Right now, there is no military action in the area. The major armies in this northeastern sector are engaged in a terrible battle at Cold Harbor once again. I have found a general who will stand his ground in a man named Ulysses Grant. Heaven help us and God forgive me—our losses are already unimaginable. But Grant will not back down. I think of the thousands of men lost with horror—and yet I know that if the terrible disease raging at Harpers Ferry is not stopped, all of humanity is at risk. There will no longer be a North, and no South. There will be no Union, and certainly no Confederacy. We may not even make it to the elections, just months away."

"I understand," Cole said. "I understand that clearly. It's why I came when notified that containing the situation in that prison was imperative."

"Of course," the president agreed softly. He nodded. "And now...I did not mean to take your time this morning. I wanted you to be forewarned regarding developments in the last twelve hours."

"Thank you."

Lincoln hesitated and looked out the window yet again.

"And then...then there is Mary."

Cole held silent, waiting.

A deep, trembling sigh shook the man. His hands, giant, long, as gaunt as his face, shook lightly where they lay atop the walking stick.

"Mary, my wife...she woke me up this morning, determined that I speak with you. Willie comes to her. She sees him in her dreams. He is deeply concerned. A young boy was killed and he has come back. Willie sees him. Willie has told Mary that you must make sure you find the boy, and that you see that he—he is *not* the *walking dead,* diseased and killing others. He doesn't want to kill, but...there is no hope for him. He wants to be set free, so that he might make amends, and join his mother in heaven."

Cole felt the man's dark, sad eyes fall on him again.

He had heard that Lincoln was often at a loss, trying to care for his wife and trying to understand her deep devotion to the dreams and spiritualism that informed her beliefs. This great man seemed to suffer his own demons, and probably understood his wife's torment. And yet, as the president of a nation at war, he had to keep a strong hand on reality and the bloody, gruesome truth of battle, politics and the decisions that must be made daily.

He leaned forward. "You may assure your wife, sir, that I will find the boy, and that I will set him free, if it is the last thing that I do."

He was rewarded by a slow smile, and another small bout of trembling.

"I pray for nothing but peace," Lincoln said. "You must understand—I believe that this great nation *is* one under God. I believe that, God willing, I will win the election and that, in time, there will be peace. And I swear to you, while I breathe, it will be an honorable peace. Every man out there is an American. We are brothers, and we will be so again."

"I pray peace will come," Cole replied. And with that, he realized that they were through talking. He also realized that the carriage hadn't really gone anywhere.

He started to rise.

"There is a telegraph office in Harpers Ferry. I want to be apprised of developments, if you will be so good as to see that all news is sent. General Bickford will see to it that you are housed and given whatever assistance you request."

"Thank you," Cole said.

"God go with you."

Cole nodded and stepped down from the carriage. The

driver gave a flick of the reins the moment he was out, and the carriage lumbered onto the street.

Cole looked after him and shivered suddenly. He gave himself a mental shake. He was a Texan at heart, and he shouldn't have agreed with the ruler of a "foreign" power. But then again, he shouldn't have been in the capital of the Union.

Fighting vampires could certainly give a man very strange bedfellows.

CHILDREN WERE certainly the most resilient little beings in the world, Megan decided.

Although Artie remained afraid that he had failed his mother and sister, he was awake, aware, alert and energetic in the morning. He sat with Cody, Megan and Alex for a long time, listening intensely as Cody taught him about the things he must watch out for, and what he could do to protect himself and his family. Artie was a very sharp young man. Perhaps, somewhere in the back of his mind, he had vague memories that he could dredge up to the surface regarding the attack the night before. But for now he was focusing on defending his mother and sister.

The household was now adorned in crucifixes, blessed by the Catholic Church. Cody had spent the morning arming each room in the house with carved wooden crosses that could double as stakes if the need arose. Vials of holy water had replaced perfumes and cosmetics on the dressing table tops. Even little Marni understood that if someone should come near her, she was to toss the contents of one of the vials at an intruder, or at anyone who seemed intent on coming too close to her.

The children had to go to school. Alex or Cody could

see that they got there and back safely, but they needed to know how to protect themselves, as well.

Megan had awakened to discover that Cole was gone, and for a moment, she was torn. She hoped in a way that he had left without her—no matter what the mission, in her heart, she didn't want to leave.

And yet…

She didn't want Cole to be gone. She didn't want to believe it, but she didn't want him to be away from her, either. Which was quite ridiculous, because he still barely tolerated her, even if she had discovered that he could be kind, even tender. But she had strange vampire blood running in her veins, and she was quite sure that was something rooted deeply in his mind, whether he was already friends with Cody or not. He could completely infuriate her, and yet…

Maybe Lisette Annalise was now going with him.

She disliked the woman. Great actress, songstress—she was still a one-minded, possessed harpy, as far as Megan could tell.

But it did seem that she'd had some kind of a relationship with Cole.

And that might be why Megan disliked her as much as she did….

Then, again, she could be right. Lisette Annalise was rabid in her determination to win the war—more so than she was to kill vampires, it seemed.

But she hadn't had to wonder about Cole and the journey to Harpers Ferry long—Alex greeted her with the cheerful information that Cole was arranging for their supplies and that he would be back soon.

She was packed and ready to go, and showing Artie how to fashion crosses out of reeds for the room he would share with his mother and sister—the family didn't intend to be parted anymore—when Cole returned.

He was striking in his dark breeches and vest, white shirt and ever-present weapon-laden coat. He strode into the house and found her on the parlor floor with Artie. She looked up at him, and he smiled.

"Master Arthur! You're doing remarkably well. Sir, I look forward to returning to see you and your family again soon," he said. He offered Megan a hand to pull her to her feet, and she accepted, feeling a rush of warmth just to take his hand and feel his strength as he drew her to her feet.

"We're really going?" she asked.

Artie, who had risen as well, asked Cole, "Must you? Really?"

"We really must. But we'll be back soon enough, I warrant. And I know that you'll be here to assist your mother, Alex, Cody and Brendan with all that they might need."

"Yes, sir. I've been learning this morning. I'll be very careful from now on. I'll keep my eyes open at all times. And I can help my mother and the others."

"Good man," Cole said, ruffling his hair. "Now, Megan, where are your things? There's a wagon outside. We're taking the horses, but the wagon will take your bags."

"I travel lightly," she told him. "One bag."

"I'll get it, sir!" Artie told him.

"Thank you," Megan said, and watched the boy head for the stairs.

"Where are the others?" Cole asked.

"In the kitchen."

She followed Cole through the house. In the kitchen,

Alex was packing a bag with bottles for Megan. "You'll be supplied for several days," Alex said flatly. "After that…well, it doesn't keep forever."

"I'm good at fending for myself," she said, her cheeks reddening. She was certain that Cole had to be thinking it was quite inconvenient to travel with a woman who needed a supply of drinkable blood.

"If that basket is set, I'll take it to the wagon," Cole said flatly. He pulled out his pocket watch. "We've got to be there in a matter of minutes."

Alex came and gave him a kiss on the cheek. He and Cody started out with a handshake, but embraced briefly. Brendan gave Cole a tremendous pat on the back, and Martha held back a little sniffle.

"Do you have to go, Cole?" Marni asked.

He lifted her into his arms. "Yes, Miss Marni, that we do. But we'll be back in a jiffy. This is the nicest place to be," he assured her.

He set Marni down and she ran to Megan, burying her face in her skirts. "It's all right, little one. You know I'll come back—I always do!"

"You'd really better hurry," Cody said.

Cole nodded. He looked at Megan. "We've got to go."

They walked through the house and out the front where a wagon was waiting to collect the belongings. The horses were waiting as well, for which Megan was glad. She had grown fond of the bay mare, rather ridiculously named Brunhilda. The animal was beautiful, however—well fed, sleek and well trained. She started to mount, but turned when she realized that Cody was standing there, ready to give her a boost up.

He smiled solemnly at her. "Take care, and come home safely. It's good to have a sister."

She felt bizarrely like bursting into tears and nodded instead.

Cody stepped back, perhaps aware that he might be overly sentimental. "And watch out for Cole, huh?"

Cole shook his head and rolled his eyes.

"Cole, you take good care of Megan," Alex said.

"I'll see to it that you receive the news from the telegraphs," Cole told Cody.

Cody nodded. With a last wave, they turned the horses down the street and followed the wagon to the railroad station.

Four men in uniform were waiting for them. Cole introduced them as Sergeant Terry Newcomb, Gerald Banter, Michael Hodges and Evan Briar. The men were unerringly polite. They pointed out that they were in the fourth car. She took note of the armor on the train as she walked along the side of it to the door and as the men helped her up the two steps to the car.

Inside, the train was dark and shadowed; the windows were small ovals that opened up to the world beyond.

Cole took the seat beside her, and the four military men sat in the two closest rows on the opposite side of the train. She noted, as they waited, that a number of men in uniform were boarding the train, and their car filled up quickly. There were a few other civilians, all with their travel papers ready should they be needed.

She heard the sound of the train's whistle, and then felt the massive wheels beneath her as they began to churn. They moved slowly from the railway station.

Cole took her hand, surprising her. He drew a line over the top of it, his fingers moving down hers. It was an affectionate gesture, and she hoped that he couldn't feel the sudden heat that it sent rushing through her.

"You're unusually quiet," he said, a half smile curled into his features.

"So are you," she told him.

"Ah, well, I like to play the silent type."

"Really? I must say, I hadn't noted."

"I'd love to know what you're thinking right now," he told her.

She would not love to tell him.

She was sitting next to him, not exactly tightly, but tightly enough. She was coming to be so aware of him when he was near that it hurt. She loved the sound of his voice, and she particularly loved his face when he had that sardonic smile that seemed to be a wry look aimed at himself, rather than anyone around him. She loved the darkness of him—the deep, penetrating blue of his eyes, and still...the scent of him. And the feel of him. His fingers, a featherlight touch upon her own...

She didn't draw away from him. She tried to answer. "Actually, I'm thinking that just weeks ago, I would have been stunned to think that I could be here—wishing that I was not leaving the Union capital."

He nodded, staring out as the train continued its slow pace out of the station and through the heart of the city. The day was clear and the sky was light—now that they were leaving. There was no hint of rain. People moved to and fro; a horse-drawn trolley was clopping along while riders passed it and pedestrians seemed to crawl behind it. Shop fronts displayed their wares, and men and women went into and out of a large bank.

He looked at her again. His hand squeezed hers. "They'll be fine. Really. Cody is the most adept person

I have ever met, and Alex is excellent at his side. And Brendan! Brendan is an extremely wise man. He knew about Cody and hunted him down when the trouble began out West."

She nodded, afraid to speak for a moment.

He leaned closer to her, talking softly. "I do know the feeling, however."

"You don't want to be leaving?" she asked him, surprised.

"It isn't that. We're not going far, and still, we're going to a different world. The war effort is so visible here—and yet, there are so many civilians here, too. Life goes on. From what I've heard…Harpers Ferry, early on, became something of a ghost town. There has been so much battle and trauma that everyday life is nonexistent. And…"

"And?"

"Believe it or not, I made a promise to the president of the United States today."

She smiled herself. She'd been so distrusted herself, she'd not really realized that Cole was out of his element here, too…

"Oh?" she asked.

He nodded. "Today…ah, well, it's so strange. There are those who would make a true monster out of Lincoln. The papers in the South skewer him, as do his political enemies in the North. There are sketches of him as a buffoon in some of them—I recently saw one in which he was depicted as man dangling a group of Africans from his fingers, as if he weren't really concerned for the welfare of man, but just in having his own way. I never believed that he was a monster. In all honesty, I tried not to think about the East or any place where I knew that people were dying daily, torn apart in so many ways. But today, I saw what makes him a man who people do follow with a passion. He cares deeply. And he is torn and embattled with his own inner demons and those of his wife."

"Go on," Megan said when he paused for a moment, as if lost in thought.

"I promised I would find a drummer boy, and see that his soul was saved," Cole told her softly.

"We'll find him," she said, filling in the words but not quite knowing what he meant.

He nodded. "There were seven more deaths last night."

"Seven—what have they done with the bodies?"

"I'm hoping that we get there in time to see that—that they have been dealt with in the proper manner," he told her.

"I'm hoping we don't get there just to run into a battle," Megan said. "I know what happens when the wounded lay strewn on the fields of war."

He squeezed her hand. "I think it's quiet at the moment. The Union forces have been in control since the end of July, last year. God knows, that can change at a moment's notice. But the area has faced the same problems since the beginning of the war, when the Southern forces knew they needed to keep the town—but then realized that, logistically, it was almost impossible. I think Union forces, in leaving initially, destroyed most of the armory. The Southerners salvaged what they could, but knew they didn't have the manpower to hold tight—the heights there leave an awful lot of opportunity for snipers, for guerilla forces, to pin down the town. It's one of God's most beautiful creations—now devastated so much that it's barely recognizable."

"And now it's been carved off from its homeland. Now it's the state of *West* Virginia...." Megan commented.

Cole didn't reply to that. He seemed lost in his own thoughts.

Their route was to take them north-northwest to Frederick, then west to Harpers Ferry. They fell silent as the train picked up speed.

Cole continued to look out the window, watching.

"We're traveling through Union territory," she reminded him.

"Yes, I know. And the major armies on this front are engaged elsewhere."

She arched a brow. "How do you know that?"

"Battle is engaged at Cold Harbor," he said.

"But there are smaller pockets of guerilla bands in motion?" she asked. "And, certainly, Lee has been known to split the Army of Northern Virginia. The war isn't over, Cole. You must know that Jeff Davis and Robert E. Lee are always thinking of ways that they might invade Washington, D.C."

"Yes. But I believe that we're looking at nothing but bloodshed—until the 'rebellion,' as it's called here, is put down. Lincoln knows how many men he is losing, and the generals know how many men they are losing. While the South eyes D.C., the North is eyeing Richmond. And the North has more men. And arms."

"George Washington and the Rebels should have, logistically, lost the Revolution," Megan pointed out.

"The English were across an ocean. They didn't have a passion like President Lincoln's, and they were distracted by their other holdings."

She smiled slightly. "Have you been swayed to a cause?" she asked him.

"My only cause is a prayer that all this ends," he told her. "My cause is to save *people,* which I believe is your cause."

She looked away for a moment. "I think we'll be all right on the train."

He looked at her. "I'm not just watching for Southern troops."

"You think that a band of vampires might attack an armored train?"

"I think that anything can happen."

She discovered that she was particularly disturbed, and looked out the window again.

Anything could happen.

But nothing did happen as they moved through the countryside. Though it had picked up speed out of D.C., the train did not seem to be moving fast.

The land gently rolled as they headed west toward the mountains. They passed farms and fields, some heavy with the abundance of the crops planted this past spring.

And they passed barren areas of desolation. Farmers worked out in their fields.

And nothing happened.

She began to doze, leaning her head on Cole's shoulder.

In her dreams, she saw him. He was standing as if in one of the fields they had just passed. And there was something behind him. Something dark, like a malevolent cloud, and yet it had a substance to it, a shape....

Evil personified.

She kept shouting to Cole, telling him that it was

coming, that he had to turn around, that he had to quit watching *her* and see the truth. She wasn't the evil—the thing coming for him was the true monster, and he wouldn't see it....

The cloud descended closer and closer....

"Megan, Megan!"

She awoke with a start, ready to scream, leap from her seat and look for the danger.

She was ready to die for him, she realized.

"Megan! It's all right," he warned her quickly, his hands on her shoulders, guiding her back into her seat. His eyes were troubled; he looked past her, making sure that no one else had noted her panic. "It's all right," he said again. "We've just stopped. We're in Frederick, Maryland. We're stopping, that's all."

"Oh," she murmured, and still she looked around, trying to tell herself that it had only been a dream.

He smiled and stroked her cheek gently, a strange light in the deep blue of his eyes. "But, thank you," he said.

"For what?"

"Being ready to leap in front of fire—for me."

She feared being so vulnerable, and for feeling such a deep fascination and attraction to Cole. There could be nothing good about it, and yet...

"It's—it's just what I do."

And he laughed. "Really?" he queried in a husky whisper. "Well, may I say, I am ready to leap in front of fire for you."

"It's what you do, too," she said gravely. And he smiled, about to say more, but the train suddenly jerked and she fell forward, almost into his arms.

"We'll see, won't we?" he said and sat back. Because the soldiers across the aisle were rising, and Sergeant Newcomb was coming toward them.

CHAPTER ELEVEN

SERGEANT NEWCOMB WAS a man who struck Megan as the type of father she would have dearly loved to have had. She reminded herself that she'd been raised by a wonderful stepfather, and she should just be grateful for that fact. But Newcomb was endearing to her nonetheless.

He limped down the aisle to them. "I believe we'll be here for about an hour or so. They're adding more supplies and taking on a few more passengers."

"Thank you," Cole said. "We'll detrain for the time? Maybe find a restaurant where we can get something to eat."

"There is a place in the St. James Hotel, just up the street," Newcomb told them.

"Will you join us, Sergeant?" Megan asked him.

Newcomb shook his head. "We'll remain here, miss, to watch the provisions. You go and have a nice meal, some proper sustenance."

Cole grinned. He whispered in her ear, "Maybe we can find a very rare steak."

She forced a smile. "I certainly hope so. You always do smell good enough to eat," she replied covertly.

To her surprise, he laughed. "All right, I deserved that one! Come on, then, let's hurry. An hour isn't that long."

"I hope not. I think we might have gotten there much more quickly on our own," she said, chaffing.

"In the best of conditions, it's a day on horseback. And given the terrain—and what might be found on such a journey—the train is our best bet," Cole assured her. "Besides, with what we might be facing, we have to be supplied, and rested."

"All right. Let's find a rare steak, then," she said.

They walked through the station to the street, where they were directed to the hotel. There were many men in uniform about, and there were many men who must have been in uniform at one time or another, their shirt-sleeves clipped at the elbow, where their arms ended, or moving awkwardly on crutches, lower limbs missing. Women moved along raised sidewalks, and here, too, though some sights showed clearly that a war was in progress, people went about their daily lives. At the hotel restaurant they were ushered to a table, and an elderly waiter took their order. There was no beef to be had, so they settled on chicken.

"I'm sorry," Cole told Megan.

"I'll be fine. I have my…basket that Cody and Alex prepared."

Their plates had just arrived when she saw Cole suddenly stiffen, looking toward the doorway.

"What is it?" Megan asked.

"Trudy," he said, frowning. "Alone."

Megan tried to discern who this Trudy was that had seized his attention. She felt a fluttering of jealousy, no matter how she warned herself that she was certainly *not* the object of any real affection from Cole.

She was startled to realize that he was looking at a small, mousy little woman. She was tiny, extremely thin, and seemed to be slightly bent over. She wore gold-wired glasses, and wore her hair in an unflattering bun.

"Trudy?" she persisted.

"She's Lisette's assistant," Cole explained, rising. "Excuse me."

He walked across to the entry, startling the woman as he greeted her. She offered him a shy, meek smile, and then followed him across the room.

"Trudy Malcolm, this is Megan Fox. Megan, Miss Trudy Malcolm," Cole said, politely introducing the two.

"How do you do," Megan said politely.

Even at that, the young woman blushed. "I'm fine, thank you. I didn't mean to disturb your lunch."

"You're not disturbing us. Please. Sit down," Cole urged her.

"Oh, no, really, I..."

"Please, Miss Malcolm, we would very much enjoy for you to join us. Were you about to have a late lunch?" Megan asked.

"Yes, but—"

"I'll have our waiter bring another chair," Cole said firmly, and insisted that Trudy take his seat while he arranged another for himself.

The woman sat, looking so miserable that Megan wondered if they shouldn't have just let her be.

"So, where is Miss Annalise?" Megan asked, not wishing to let the young woman sit there in painfully awkward silence.

"Oh, well, Lisette went on into Harpers Ferry on the late-afternoon train that left last evening. I'm to board the train in about an hour."

"The train we're on?" Megan said. She forced a smile,

but her mind was working. So, Lisette Annalise was already at Harpers Ferry.

And men had been savagely killed overnight.

But the attack on the children had been last night, too. Of course, they knew that there were a number of the creatures at work in D.C. still and at Harpers Ferry.

But she had dreamed that Lisette *was a vicious bloodsucker. After Cole!*

"Well, you'll be on our train, then," Megan said cheerfully.

Cole had garnered another chair and he pulled it up to the side of the table. Their elderly waiter was a bit slow in adding another setting to the table, but they all waited patiently. Eventually, Cole told him, "We have to be back at the train, my good sir, if you'd be good enough to bring us a plate as quickly as possible for this young lady?"

The waiter nodded.

"Thank you," Trudy murmured.

"I must admit, I'm surprised to see you alone," Cole said. "I thought it was your job to follow along with Lisette."

"Oh, it is!" she said quickly. "But we came here quite late, and Lisette ordered me to just rest for the night. I believe she thought that I was a bit of a hindrance, that I wasn't moving quickly enough for her. She can be very impatient." She seemed disturbed. "It's my job, of course, to see to such mundane things as accommodations, and I should have gone ahead of Lisette, but...well, events move quickly. I do my best to be of service."

"I'm sure you do," Cole told her.

Megan noted that he was kind to the shy, unattractive woman, and she liked him all the more for his careful courtesy. Still, she couldn't help but wonder what his relationship with Lisette Annalise had been. The woman was certainly a powerhouse. She went after what she wanted, and she had evidently wanted Cole.

And? Had she had him? She'd implied that they'd been close. Intimately close.

Megan told herself that she seriously needed to remember the business at hand—and to stop indulging in this growing fascination over Cole and his life. He was a Texan, for God's sake. A sheriff. A human who knew all about vampires. A man who considered her to be...*a monster, still, no matter what his words or his apparent trust.*

Trust...she had earned.

Fine, so she was jealous. That didn't entirely preclude rational thought. And Lisette had been in Harpers Ferry, and more people had been killed. Lisette had been in Washington, D.C., when other horrible things had happened there, though, apparently, not when the children had been attacked. And, if she was to be honest with herself, the figure last night had been in a long coat and a broad hat. The figure had appeared to be that of a man, before it became a whirling shadow shooting into the sky.

"Lisette is, of course, brilliant," Trudy said, defending the woman.

"She is an excellent actress," Cole agreed.

Megan found herself clinging to those words. He hadn't said that Lisette was beautiful, or that she was a wonderful person. He had just stated that she was quite the actress.

"And she is energetic, and dedicated," Trudy said loyally.

"Very dedicated," Cole agreed.

The waiter brought Trudy's chicken. As he did so, a woman let out a cry from a table near them. Cole and Megan were both instantly on their feet, seeking out the problem.

"Joshua, my boy, my poor child…!"

She was just two tables down from them, and she was on her knees next to a boy of about eight or nine who had collapsed at the table.

Cole was at her side in two steps, inspecting the boy's eyes and face closely. "Is there somewhere I can take the child?" he asked.

The elderly waiter could move when necessary. "There are downstairs guest rooms—right this way, sir!" he told Cole.

Cole gently cradled the collapsed child in his arms and followed the man. The woman was right behind him, Megan behind her.

They came to a nicely appointed guest room and Cole laid the boy out on the bed. He turned to the hovering older woman. "Has he been ill?"

"Just…just this morning. He said that he was feeling weak, and I thought that I should I take him for a good meal and that would make him feel better. His father is far away fighting, and his mother died a few months ago, and…he's all that gives us hope!" She was hysterical, her hands grasping at each other desperately.

"I'll ask after a doctor," the waiter said.

"There's no time," Cole said briskly. "I need medical tubing and two surgical needles. The soldiers will have the supplies on the train."

He stared at Megan.

You're not a doctor! Cody is, she mouthed to him.

"I need the supplies!" was his only reply.

As she turned to head out and run for the train, she nearly tripped over Trudy Malcolm, who had silently followed her. Megan couldn't waste time being gentle. She moved the young woman out of the way, tore out of the hotel and ran back down the street to the train. Sergeant Newcomb saw her coming and raced toward her, moving very quickly for a man with a limp.

"Cole needs a medical supply bag. I didn't know that we—"

"I'll get it."

She nodded as he turned and ran. She waited—for too long, it felt!—but the bag wasn't packed anywhere at the rear of the train, and upon his return Newcomb yelled that he had to look among their things in the passenger car. Megan thanked him, and she hurried back up to the hotel.

"You could kill the boy!" Trudy was saying as Megan burst back into the room, her meek voice filled with horror.

"Mrs. Osterly, is it? Ma'am, I honestly believe this is the only chance the boy has to survive," Cole said, looking intently at the nervous woman.

Megan glanced at the boy. He was almost parchment-white. "He's right," she said.

"Oh, I don't know. Joshua…" The older woman spoke in a whisper, still wringing her hands.

Megan went up to the boy and touching his cheek. Upon his throat she saw the telltale marks.

Sometimes, vampires struck in a wild frenzy, hungry, and in a swift killing mode.

Sometimes, they were subtle, taking enough to slowly drain the life from a victim.

This boy was near death from total blood loss.

"This gentleman is right," she said, her voice strong with conviction. "The child will die without a transfusion. They've been done by several doctors on both sides of the conflict, and I've been involved, as has Mr. Granger. I will stake my life that we can save the boy."

Mrs. Osterly smoothed back a stray strand of graying hair and looked at Megan.

She nodded. "Yes. Give him a chance!" she managed.

"Height," Cole said. "Megan?"

She nodded, and quickly added cushions and pillows to one side of the bed. She lay down and bared her arm. Cole went through the medical bag and found the needles and tubes that were necessary. He tied a tourniquet around her arm.

"Have you done this before?" she asked him in a whisper.

"Not alone," he whispered back. "Do you trust me?"

She met his steady gaze. She nodded.

She closed her eyes and felt the pinch of the needle. She'd given blood so recently she thought she might black out. It seemed she could feel it flowing from her veins. She closed her eyes and tried to think of daylight, of beautiful days in rich green meadows with the sun shining overhead. She tried to think of the sound of a brook rushing over rocks....

She saw the beautiful meadow, the dazzling water.... And then shadow. The dark shadow that came to ruin the brilliance of the day.

She opened her eyes.

She was still in the guest room at the St. James Hotel,

and Cole was still leaning over her. She had blacked out. She had frightened herself back to consciousness.

Cole was looking at her with concern creating dark storms in his eyes. Tension knitted his brow and tightened his features. "Are you all right?" he asked anxiously.

She nodded. "Joshua?" she asked weakly.

Cole nodded gravely.

She tried to offer him a weak smile. "I guess you're not a bad doctor."

He shook his head. "I shouldn't have used you. I shouldn't have used your blood."

She started to rise, feeling just a little dizzy. "I do have the best blood."

"Easy," he said.

She looked around. They were alone in the room.

"Where is everyone?" she asked.

"I'm here!" Trudy said, waving a hand from the doorway, then, apparently, feeling that she had intruded, she stepped back.

"Well, thank you," Megan said, trying to make her feel welcome, yet hoping that she and Cole hadn't said anything that they wouldn't have wanted the young woman overhearing.

Trudy got up the courage to step into the room again. "I—I took the liberty of having the waiter prepare bundles of food for you, too."

"That was very thoughtful," Megan told her.

"Yes, and, if you can, we need to move. They've delayed the train, but can't do so for long," Cole said.

"No, no, I'm fine. Just so long as the boy…" Her voice trailed as she tried to rise and nearly fell back. Cole caught her, steadying her.

"You're not all right," he said.

"I will be…if we can just get to the train."

"Lean on me," he said.

"I seem to be doing that a lot lately," she murmured.

"Ah, but that's because we keep using you," he teased in a whisper, for her ears only.

She likely would have flushed, had she enough blood left to rush anywhere.

"Come on, now," Cole said.

His arm was around her and she leaned heavily against him, allowing him to lead her through the door and out to the hallway. A crowd had gathered, their waiter among them, a number of the diners from the restaurant, as well. Guests had come into the hallway, and she saw several men in suits and hats with notebooks, writing and drawing furiously as she walked into the hallway. She and Cole were met with applause.

Mrs. Osterly came hurrying toward them from a nearby doorway, her smile brilliant and lighting up her face, though tears still dampened her cheeks.

"He's so much better already! Joshua has color and opened his eyes and spoke to me—and he's telling me that he's hungry!"

"We're grateful to hear that," Cole said.

"Very," Megan agreed.

"There must be a way to repay you.… I have some money," she offered.

"Stay well and survive," Cole told her. "Keep the lad in at night, and keep him wearing that cross I gave him. That's payment enough."

"Pray!" said a man from the crowd.

"Prayer and belief are always good," Megan said.

Mrs. Osterly walked up and kissed her cheek. Her

voice was tremulous as she said, "You gave my grandson your blood! May God protect and bless you!"

A bright light suddenly burned her eyes and a puff of smoke filled the room. One of the newspapers had sent a photographer to the hotel. Megan blinked furiously, and Cole said, "Excuse us, please, we must be on the train."

"This way, this way, come along!" The speaker was Sergeant Newcomb, who was waiting at the hotel's main door alongside Gerald Banter. The two had come to bring them back with an escort so that they wouldn't be waylaid further by the crowd.

Cole led her through the mass of people to the doorway. She realized that meek little Trudy Malcolm was hurrying along behind them, the medical bag now in her hands. They walked down the street to the station with applause and well wishes following them. Michael Hodges was waiting at the top of the steps to their car and reached down to help her in. Cody followed, then Trudy and then Sergeant Newcomb and Gerald Banter.

"Let's get her to her seat," Cold said.

"I'm all right," she protested.

"You're going to need one of the drinks Cody sent," Cole told her firmly.

He ushered her into a seat by one of the small oval windows and sat down next to her. "She's fine!" he told the others. "She just needs some rest now, gents. And Miss Malcolm, if we can give her a little peace...!"

"Oh! I'm back here, if you need me," Trudy said.

As she sat, and waited for Cole to find the blood in the travel bag beneath her seat, she noted that Sergeant Newcomb had the medical bag, and apparently intended to keep guard over it. Cole produced a canteen, and she drained its contents quickly. Almost immediately, she felt revived.

"I'm better!" she assured him.

"Rest anyway. It's not far now. Close your eyes, and rest. It may be that you'll need your strength. Soon."

He reached for her, pulling her head down to his shoulder.

She liked it. She wanted to reimagine her rich meadow with Cole there at her side. With the sound of bubbling water near, and the sun overhead. She wanted to dream....

A dream in which there would be no black-winged shadows.

THE ROCKING of the train's motion, and even the click-clacking of the wheels, had a lulling effect. Megan seemed to be sleeping peacefully enough against him, and Cole was careful not to move, lest he disturb her.

They'd traveled slowly, the engineer ever vigilant for track sections that guerilla troops had managed to rip out or damage. They passed through the rolling country and headed toward the mountains, and giant, beautiful bluffs, purple and orange in the waning of the day, began to appear before them. Cole wasn't tired. He'd actually had several hours of sleep the night before. But the motion was so lulling that he'd begun to doze himself when he heard the first faint thud on the top of the train car.

He was instantly alert, and he sat rigid for several seconds, waiting.

No one else seemed to have noticed anything.

And there was nothing else...

Then he heard sound again. There was something moving stealthily atop the car.

He eased himself up, trying to slide Megan to lean against the side of the car, but she was instantly awake. She didn't cry out in alarm; she looked at him tensely, waiting.

"On top of the car," he said quietly, pointing up.

She nodded. He rose, moving back to Sergeant Newcomb, who had been dozing, rocking along with the motion of the train. He touched Newcomb and the sergeant was quickly awake and aware, as well.

"I'm going out back," he whispered. "Guard the front of the car. Take one of the knives, and if anyone tries to enter, go straight for the throat."

Newcomb nodded. "And decapitation," he said flatly. "Soldiers! To your posts," he said in a low voice as he tapped each one awake. The soldiers on board got up, deftly negotiating the tight aisle space. Newcomb and one of the men headed directly for the front of the car as the other two men began to follow Cole to the rear.

"Oh, dear Lord! What's happening?" Trudy cried out.

"Sit tight and stay quiet," Cole told her, pausing by her side to bring his fingers to his lips in a warning motion. He realized that Megan was by his side.

"*Sit.* You can't be strong enough," he told her.

"But I am," she assured him flatly.

"Megan, please?"

"Cole, I'll settle for giving you the lead," she said and looked at him. "We don't know how many there are," she reminded him.

No, he didn't know their numbers. Nor did he know their power....

"Why, Miss Fox," Sergeant Newcomb said. "You sit down. I've been on trains under attack before."

"Not like this, Sergeant Newcomb," Cole said firmly. "She knows what she's doing, and we can use all hands, honestly."

Megan looked at him for a moment with eyes full of appreciation. Then, suddenly, she was all business and supplied herself from the box they had quickly split open in the aisle. She followed Cole to the back.

Hodges was waiting by the rear door, ready to let them out. When he opened the door, Cole grasped the edging to gain his balance before straining with his all his might to pull himself up to the top of the moving car. He ducked low, aware that he might have been heard.

It seemed that Megan came up beside him with far less effort.

He saw a being ahead, clinging to the roof of the train car and bending low to push at the windows. Crouching low, Cole balanced for a minute, then moved quickly down the length of the car, learning to move with the sway of the train as he did so.

He moved quickly to reach the figure and didn't dare take the time to ask questions. With all his speed and force he pounced upon the creature's back, catching its hair and drawing his bowie knife across its throat.

There was no blood. The effort was minimal. The head came off in his hand without being severed.

He quickly tossed the head and the body over the roof.

"Cole!" Megan cried.

He turned just in time to keep himself from being swept off the roof of the car. The creature that flew at him came in a dark fury, not even a fully solid form at first, only becoming so as they both crashed down flat and hard on the roof.

The creature stood up quickly though. It stood over him, this thing that had once been a Southern cavalry soldier now missing half of its face, the other half offering a one-eyed stare as malignant and evil as anything Cole had ever seen. The mouth opened, and fangs seemed to sparkle as they dripped saliva. With all his force, Cole kept the creature at bay, straining to get his knee and leg up to kick the thing away from him. At last he accomplished the task and sprang to a crouch, ready for the next attack.

But the creature didn't come at him again. It let out an unholy scream and began to smoke, twist, wriggle and writhe. He saw Megan behind him, an empty bottle of holy water in hand. He reached into his belt satchel for a stake and dove at the being, slamming the stake down hard into the heart. In a flash, the smoking creature became deadweight and fell at his feet. It rolled and fell from the moving train.

As Cole stared at Megan, gasping for breath, he saw something else emerging from the darkening sky, heading her way.

"Megan, duck!" he ordered and pulled out another stake. Bracing himself, he waited for the flying object so intent on bringing down Megan. Lunging forward, he managed to catch the shadow on the stake, and, using the momentum of the weight that came flapping heavily against him to press hard, prayed that he had struck somewhere near its shapeless heart.

He'd struck, but he hadn't managed a dead aim. The thing became fully solid, in the form of a man, this one in a Union artillery uniform. It was injured but still fighting, still desperately hungry and still clinging to what had become its existence. Cole slashed at the thing. He cut its flesh, and, though catching the throat, realized he wasn't getting his cuts in deeply enough.

To avoid the chomping fangs, he grabbed the thing and rolled off the roof.

He desperately grabbed at the upper railing, losing his bowie knife but catching hold. To his horror, the thing didn't roll and go flying from the moving train.

The thing clung stubbornly to his back.

It was desperate, too.

Their position was perilous. Cole's legs were swinging wildly and the effort to hold on was like fire ripping down his arms. He tried to shake the thing off, but its fingers were gripped into his back like talons. He knew that he couldn't hold long, even if its fangs didn't strike into his nape or his shoulder.

But the thing clinging to him made a hideous shrieking sound, desperate. He wasn't going to be able to shake it. He had to get back on top of the train and free his hands to draw another weapon.

With all his might he strained. But then he saw that Megan was above him, casting vial after vial of holy water onto the creature—it began to shake and ease its hold. He twisted to look over his shoulder and see it turning darker and darker, see the flesh turn to ash and blow in the wind.

Briefly a skull appeared beneath the dark and smoking ash, and then the bones disarticulated and fell, some clattering away from the tracks, some crunching loudly beneath the iron wheels. Megan gave Cole an arm, drawing him back to the roof. They fell there for a moment together, gasping. Then he pushed from her, rising in a leap, balancing carefully and turning around and around.

One more shadow came out of the air that had turned

into mist as they came closer and closer into the foothills of the mountains.

Cole reached into his pocket, drawing out a vial, hitting the shape before it could take full form and substance. It shrieked, crashing down just inches before them, flapping its parts, banging wildly with arms and legs as it burned and sizzled in horrible throes. Megan, behind him, tossed another vial, and the thing began to burn in earnest. He drew a stake from his coat, pinned the creature straight through the heart and then kicked the whole of the burning, decaying, disjointed creature from the roof of the train car.

Again, the two of them adopted a defensive stance. And waited, ready for whatever might come.

Cole could hear it. The things made a sound when they came sweeping down. And he knew that the one coming was older, wiser. It didn't rush.

It landed feet away from them on the swaying surface of the roof. Megan was ready; from a crouched stance, she rushed forward, hurling holy water with a speed and accuracy that surprised even Cole. It surprised the creature, which just stood there, screeching, burning.

She turned to look at Cole.

"Cole!" Megan cried. "Duck!"

"From where—?"

"No—the railway tunnel!"

He collapsed face-first in the nick of time. The quivering, shrieking *thing* was dashed against the granite archway of the bridge. Its cry was cut off, and it was as if a *silence* now issued from the thing. Bursting into a thousand pieces, it blew away, one with the darkness.

Cole inched closer to Megan as the blackness of the tunnel and the coming night overwhelmed them. He reached for her, drawing her tightly against him until they had cleared the tunnel.

And yet, the sky barely lightened. They were nearing Harpers Ferry, and the heights around it, and the mountains were now rising like massive shadows, deep violet against the gray of the sky. Night was nearly fully upon them.

"They're gone, I believe," Cole said after a minute.

"They—they seemed to be starving. I don't think they were part of any band.… I don't see any more of them.… And I don't—hear them."

"The other cars—" Cole began, straining to see in the darkness. But he could detect nothing more either before them or behind them.

"It's over," Megan told him. "It's really over."

It was over, but he knew their real ordeal was just beginning.

They were coming into Harpers Ferry where the Shenandoah and Potomac met, where great peaks looked over deep valleys. Where John Brown had determined to free the slaves, and instead, a freed black man had been among the first to die.

Where the abolitionists had been given their cause, and bloodshed had come early.

By night, it was oddly beautiful to roll closer and closer to the depot. To see the majesty of nature in the massive cliffs, feel the soft, cool air as it rushed around them.

And still…

The cliffs and valleys held secret places where evil could dwell, where the unwary might be taken, where evil could abide.

And watch.

And wait.

The mist grew denser. The train began to chug over the bridge and then slow. Cole could see the station ahead.

They had arrived.

CHAPTER TWELVE

COLE AND MEGAN returned to the train car just before they pulled into the station. God knows, the soldiers here were probably unnerved enough as it was without watching such a strange arrival as the two of them balancing on the roof.

When the great locomotive chugged to a stop, Sergeant Newcomb stepped down first, looking around, but they were greeted by none other than Brigadier General Thomas Bickford himself and his aides. There had been other troops aboard the train, but, apparently, they had been unaware that another car on the train had been attacked. They were met by Lieutenant Dowling, who, quickly and with military precision, gave them instructions for lodging, nodding with courtesy to Megan and shy little Trudy Malcolm.

Thomas Bickford was a man of about fifty, solid, courteous and as weary as the rest of the world.

"You'll be in a house in the lower town, just up the street from the engine house," he told them. "We'll see that your horses are stabled for the evening, and you'll join me for dinner two doors down. The town has been so deserted that there aren't really many facilities to offer. You'll have one of my aides-de-camp, Corporal Dickens, to assist with your needs. Dickens is from this area, so he knows the terrain, as well. You'll find that most of my officers are housed along the road, as well. If you take Church Street, you get to the church, should you desire. Had another church up there, but it got blown to bits." He looked over at Dowling briefly. "But you can see more of the town tomorrow and get the lay of the land then. Darkness comes real quick and harsh here, so you might want to be seeing to your lodgings, first thing."

"What I'd like to see first thing," Cole told him, "is the corpses."

"Suit yourself then, Granger. I'll see to it that Dickens settles the ladies in."

"I will stay with Mr. Granger, if I may," Megan told him.

The general shook his head. "I hear that you know a great deal about men possessed by this horrible disease, Miss Fox. But I'm not sure you want to see *these* bodies."

"Sir, I must, if I'm to be of assistance."

He looked at her solemnly. She doubted that the man knew anything about her or her past. He certainly didn't know what she was. But, there was a telegraph office here, and here was a man in direct contact with the *supreme commander* of the Union forces, so there really wasn't any need for her to argue her presence.

"As you wish. I am far too eager to put a stop to this to demand delicacy in any situation these days, my dear. You may go with Mr. Granger and we'll rendezvous in two hours' time in my dining room. Dickens will show you the way."

Trudy managed to speak up at last. "General Bickford, I'm here as secretary and assistant to Miss Lisette Annalise."

"Yes, of course. Miss Annalise is lodging in the lower

level of the house. Private Anderson will take you then, and the men who will be sharing the Mickleberry house with Mr. Granger's party. And now, Mr. Granger, since you are eager… Dickens—where are you, son?"

Dickens quickly came forward. He was a young fellow, maybe twenty-one or twenty-two, with freckles and bright red hair. He quickly nodded, smiled at the ladies and tipped his cap and then said to Cole, "This way, sir."

As she followed Cole and Dickens, Megan looked around the town and felt a chill. On the main street they walked uphill. She looked at the houses, and it seemed that none of them had borne the true wicked brunt of the war. The houses lining the street remained beautiful as they went up the hill.

But it wasn't the same town at all. There was no one there. Men and women did not stroll the streets. Nobody leisurely enjoyed the misty cool air of evening.

They passed by the engine house where John Brown had reportedly holed up during his infamous raid on Harpers Ferry. It was now in use by the military, and all that remained of the fiery abolitionist was the ghost of the past. Right or wrong? Shades of gray. The man had believed desperately in freedom for all men, but he'd murdered innocents to prove his point. He had died himself, promising that the land would be washed in blood.

And so it was. In a different way, now.

"This is our temporary morgue," Dickens said. He opened a door on the street level, but when they had entered the building, he opened another door at the end of a hallway where there were stairs leading down to the coolness of a basement. "Summer's coming. The heat, even here nearly in the mountains, can play havoc with the dead."

"Of course," Cole said.

"There's gas lamps on the walls. I'll just get them on for you," Dickens told them.

They went down the darkened stairway, Dickens in the lead. When he stopped, Cole stopped, and Megan nearly plowed into his back.

Suddenly, Dickens let out a horrendous cry. He had turned the wick on one of the lights, and in the pale red glow that came to surround them, Megan saw that a man stood in front of Dickens. His head was at an angle, his throat badly slashed, and he was reaching for Dickens with a savage smile upon his mottled face. The man had risen, and recently.

Cole quickly pushed Dickens out of the way, ready with a stake for the heart of the "diseased" man. The body fell, but Megan knew as well as Cole that if one had resurrected, the others would soon follow suit.

She reached into her skirt pockets, hoping that, after their adventure on the train, she still had a decent supply of holy water. She had four vials; seven men had been killed the night before; one was down.

"Back out of the way!" she ordered Dickens, stepping around him. Cole was already dispatching the second beast to rise, one that wore a sergeant's stripes. She hurried to one of the wooden benches where the corpses had been laid out, and hurriedly emptied the contents of one vial over a corpse's heart. The water became like acid, eating through uniform wool and the man's flesh. His mouth started to form into a snarl and his eyes opened in shock. But then the man's eyes softened. He looked straight at Megan for a minute. And then he closed his eyes, and he was dead and gone, a hole where his heart

had been and the ragged remnants of his insides still visible.

"Oh, holy Jesus! Mary, mother of God!" Dickens slumped against the rough brick of the basement wall.

Megan glanced at him, and he cried out, pointing. She swung around swiftly enough to duck the attack of a private first class. Avoiding his lumbering embrace, she slashed down hard on his neck with her balled fist as he fell, then straddled him swiftly to roll him over and plunge a stake Cole tossed her deep into his heart. Another came at her, while Cole engaged another himself. They both staked their opponents cleanly.

Poor Dickens was mouthing words incoherently.

"One more!" Cole cried to her—he had already dispatched four of the undead dead, and was pointing to the last bench.

The corpse upon it was now rising. She kicked out hard, catching the head with her booted heel, and causing the thing to roll off the bench. Cole tossed her another stake from the arsenal in his coat, and she slammed the finely honed wood hard into his chest.

The dead were now—dead. Dickens had slumped all the way to the floor and was just staring at the two of them.

"Mr. Dickens," Cole said gently, hunkering down in front of him. "This is a really bad disease, and the problem is that it's contagious. Once you're ripped apart, you can end up coming back. This is the way the dead must be dispatched. Now, to finish this off, they all need to be decapitated. Can you handle this?"

Dickens stared at him, blinking.

"We've got to get this situation under control, now,"

Cole said gently. "Or...well, you've seen what can happen."

Dickens nodded. Cole stretched out a hand. Dickens took it and pulled himself up. He shivered and seemed to give himself a huge mental shake. He saluted, though Cole wasn't military. "Yes, sir!"

"I'm going to need a wagon and some shrouds. Can you get them for me? We'll get these men buried before it gets any later. This is one occasion when they just can't be sent home for proper burial."

"Yes, sir!" Dickens started for the stairs. He came back. "I have a bowie knife on me, sir. The orders came through over the wire that we were all to be armed with bowie knives. I can do my part here, sir."

Cole hesitated, wanting to keep the man's mind sound.

Megan stepped forward, touching his arm and speaking quietly. "He should learn while he's with us."

Cole nodded.

Dickens, now that he was gaining control over his shock, was going to prove to be a stronger individual than Megan had previously thought. She went quietly to work on her own kills while Cole showed Dickens how to best sever through the neck. It took some strength.

Finally, Dickens left to acquire the wagon and shrouds. Then he returned, Newcomb was with him, and between the four of them, they brought the corpses up, the heads in a separate bag, and then began the long haul to the Harpers Ferry cemetery. It was at the top of the hill, and trees surrounded it, shrouded in fog. Megan kept a staunch lookout while the men dug graves and buried the remains of the deceased.

Dickens was quiet a moment while Cole tamped down the earth that covered the heads.

"That one fellow," he said. "The one who came after me. I knew him well in life. We served together since the beginning of the war. That was Petey Marlburg. A good friend. A staunch Catholic."

"We can have words said over him tomorrow," Megan said, her tone consoling.

"That's right, son. But when you come back with the—uh, disease, well, then you need to be put down and put to rest properly, then have the words said over you, do you understand?" Sergeant Newcomb asked.

Dickens nodded. "Yes, sir. I—uh—I sure do understand. After tonight. Was it—was it other *diseased* men who did this?"

"Yes, precisely," Cole said. "And that's why we have to find the men who are out there—those with the disease."

Dickens nodded. They all walked back to the wagon and crawled aboard. Dickens took the reins for the slow and careful journey back down the hill in the dark. Megan was certain that they would be attacked any minute. She sat with her hands in her pockets, ready for whatever came.

But though the night sky was dark, and though they were surrounded by mist, no one, and no creature, assaulted them. It had grown late—they should have been at the general's quarters an hour before to share supper, but there had been nothing they could do. If they were to be of any help here, they had to see that the dead were *dead,* and not buried before then.

It turned out that they had very decent quarters, with Cole and Megan in separate bedrooms on the second floor, their four-man military escort in bedrooms on the ground level. There was a woman, a middle-aged, still-round spinster named Mary-Anne Weatherly who tended to their rooms and to their needs. They washed up quickly. While bringing in warm water so that Megan could clean herself, she informed her that no matter what people said, she just wasn't afraid of Rebs, Yankees, guns, bombs or diseases. For the good Lord had taken her first love in the war with Mexico, and her second love last year at Gettysburg. She was ready to join all her loved ones when He chose, and that was that.

She winked at Megan, though, and told her, "But I don't mind paying heed to superstition, I'll have you know. I sleep next to my own little altar with a beautiful, carved wood crucifix made by my nephew and blessed by a priest. And I go up to church every day of my life and make crosses all over my body with holy water. When the good Lord wants me, he gets me. But no other!"

With that, she left Megan smiling and a little lighter. Megan finished scrubbing up the best she could. Right as she finished, Cole knocked at her door and asked in his deep voice if she was ready.

She joined him quickly.

The general had taken up residency in an abandoned home, as well. There were still pictures of somebody's family on the mantel, and on a few of the side tables. They'd probably been taken just before the start of the war, when photography had grown so popular. Older silhouette drawings sat side by side with the images.

The family had consisted of a mother and father, two sons and a daughter. The mother had a beautiful smile. The girl seemed to adore the brothers she sat between. The grandparents had...pleasing profiles.

Megan wondered if these people were all alive. She hoped so, and that one day, they would come back and laughter might fill the house again.

Their meal had been kept warm, and it had dried out. The general had already dined with his other guests—Lisette Annalise and Trudy Malcolm.

"Well, how very lovely and charming, Miss Fox—you've accompanied Cole," Lisette said, greeting Megan.

She practically gushed the words. Her eyes were brilliant, and anyone might have thought that she was honestly open, warm and giving.

"Yes, I think I can be of service," Megan said.

"Dickens reported on your service, Miss Fox," General Bickford said gravely. "How did you come to know how to deal with this disease so well?"

"I saw it on the battlefield."

"And you were on the battlefield, supporting Southern troops?" Bickford asked.

"Yes, sir. I am from Virginia."

"Many a man from Virginia chose to stay with the Union," Bickford pointed out.

One of the general's aides handed Megan a sherry. She accepted it, weighing her answer. "And many a man did not. But I'm not here to wage a war against anything other than disease, sir. And I pray that you will take advantage of that."

"I am grateful that you have chosen to lend us your expertise," he said, jovial and expansive from drinking.

"And your strength!" Lisette said. "Trudy has told me you were amazing—better than any male soldier—when your train was beset this afternoon."

"I have had some dealings with the situation," Megan

said evenly. "Although, in fairness to the others, Trudy likely didn't see everything."

"Yes, well, your brother is quite the expert. Cody Fox," Lisette said.

"Yes, he is. He has worked with Brendan Vincent, and now Cole, for some time dealing with this plague. He is a medical man, you know," she said sweetly.

"Now, Lisette, you must give my guests the chance to enjoy their dinner," General Bickford said. He meant that it should be so. Though he had dined already with Lisette and Trudy, they all sat at the dinner table, covered in the original owner's lace cloth.

General Bickford talked about Harpers Ferry, keeping the war from his conversation. "It's sad that Harpers Ferry should have come to be such a strategic location. It is a magical spot on earth, I believe. Two rivers come together here, and the jagged edges of cliffs and mounts look down on the verdant richness of the valley! Commerce was wonderful, with the canal and then the railroad. The great father of our country, George Washington, saw the wonder here. Before him, the native peoples knew the beauty and the magic. It's said that Shenandoah and Potomac were lovers from different tribes—they were forbidden to love and marry, and thus they saw each other across a great chasm, and their tears formed the rivers when they could not reach one another. They tried, of course, and died there, in the flood of their tears, for their love was true and strong. Alas, now, the night comes quickly, fog and mist swirl around in a deep darkness, and a different sort of tears there are, with my men taken by something that seems not quite of this earth."

"Oh, it's of this earth, sir. But it's a new type of disease, and it spreads quickly. But there's no mystery as to how," Cole began. "The only way to stop it is to find all of the diseased, injured, dead and even some appearing to be all right, and see to it that the infection doesn't overtake and revive them. There are methods of dispatching the dead, and your fellow, Dickens, proved himself to be a fine asset this evening. In fact, he shows just how easily one can learn these methods. I think that the men must become aware, and they must not laugh at tactics, or think that they're silly—or assume that a dead man can no longer move and harm them. They must take severe precautions at night. I believe that some instructions have been wired to you, and that Lisette has been able to give you other suggestions."

When they had finished their meal, the remains were quickly whisked away by the general's staff. Coffee and brandy were served to all of them in the parlor, and the general pulled out a cigar. Cole thanked him, though he refused one of his own.

They were dealing with a harsh situation, but the weathered general still asked the ladies permission to light up with them in his company. Megan appreciated the courtesy, and thought it strange but nice—considering that she had spent part of the early evening severing men's heads from their bodies.

Bickford puffed on his cigar and watched the smoke. "I have been advised, even before now, that survival, faith and the hereafter may often rely upon a man's belief. Take the Catholic church up on the height. Father Costello stayed behind when many fled. He had not cared if Union or Confederate troops were holding the city. When there's fighting, he raises the Union Jack of Britain, and all of us—Southerners, Northerners, strangers!—look for different targets. That church remains, despite its location, and despite the cannon balls that have riddled other houses of worship.

"He had told me that bricks and stones don't hold God, that a man finds God without any physical doing. And yet, he tells me that I must remain blessed by his holy water, and he watches over many who were his flock, those hardy individuals who have not fled this place of constant struggle! He had told me to see that my men pray at night, that they wear their crosses and crucifixes, and even that they should sprinkle their door frames and window frames with holy water." The general looked around at them."What do you say to that—can faith fight disease?"

"I've seen faith work miracles," Cole said drily.

"Many of the men whisper that this is the work of vampires," Lisette said, looking straight at Megan.

"Is vampirism the name of this disease?" Megan asked. "I suppose that it's lore in many places," she said sweetly. "But, the point is, as Shakespeare pointed out, names mean little. But, I will say this—I've seen injured who hadn't a chance survive because of the love they bore for their family. I've seen men pray before a battle that should have been lost, and yet, they prevailed. At a time like this, I think that the good Father's suggestions should definitely be taken to heart. If nothing else, it gives people some feeling of control, some ability to calm themselves while they endure whatever this is. Besides, we do know that the disease will return if the heart is not staked, or if the head of the stricken isn't removed. Call it what you will, Miss Annalise—what must be done to stop it must be done."

"Of course," Lisette said. "But we all know, too, that sometimes the disease is stealthy and works its terrors slowly. Why, that we might be dining with one of the diseased at almost any time."

"The disease is only truly a disease when the malignance in it comes to a head," Cole said, stepping in. "And, there are times when those who are barely inflicted can be saved."

"Oh, yes!" Trudy said, speaking up ardently. She looked flushed when she realized she had actually spoken.

Lisette offered her a serious frown, but General Bickford said kindly, "Oh, do you know something about this, Miss Malcolm?"

"Well, I know that a boy collapsed early this afternoon, and that Mr. Granger and Miss Fox were magnificent. They *transfused* blood from Miss Fox to the boy, and the boy, who appeared to be at death's door, was then cured. It was—awe inspiring!" she declared.

"Do we know that the boy will survive the night? That he won't be further afflicted, or infect others?" Lisette asked pointedly. She looked at Cole. "My goodness—I hadn't known that you'd received a medical degree, Cole."

"No medical degree, Lisette. I've just worked in the field with Cody many times to help the injured—and the diseased. Like is done in the army every day," Cole said easily.

"Well, in this matter, it seems, I will follow your lead, Mr. Granger," General Bickford said. "My men have found that while bullets might slow the diseased animals, it will not kill them. They have been ordered to use knives, and stakes, as you would have them." He hesitated. "But so far, we've had mostly sneak attacks at night, so little chance to employ these methods. Attacks so stealthy that we don't even know until the morning that our guards have been killed. What I fear is that the hills are not harboring rebels, but monsters who might be gathering for an attack."

"We've come prepared for such a possibility," Cole said. "Tomorrow, if I may, I would like to work with some of your troops."

"Absolutely. And is there a specific art in which you will train them?" Bickford asked.

"Archery," Cole said, and Megan smiled inside as the solemn general's eyebrows raised just a little in response.

THE QUICK WALK HOME from General Bickford's house was uneventful. Cole and Megan walked alone, Lisette and Trudy being quartered with the general and his aides.

It struck Cole as they walked the few feet from house to house that the town was unusually silent for an army camp, and that, in the shroud of mist it wore, this was a sad and melancholy place, one of such great beauty that it mourned with pain for all that the war had cost it.

When they reached the house where they were staying, he noted that although no one was outside the house, their escorts were on duty inside.

The door opened as they approached the house, and Sergeant Newcomb was there to greet them. "I'll be locking up when you two are in," he said cheerfully. Megan was glad to see that he seemed to know his business; once they were inside, he didn't just lock the door. He set a large, plain, heavy wooden cross against it. "Windows are all set, sir. The housekeeper, that nice Mrs. Weatherly, she told me that she knew how to keep a Christian household safe, and we decided that we'd just do everything she said. Though, I must admit, she'd been at it herself already. She said that we were lucky—she already had holy water all around the place, and it wasn't likely that anything would be getting through on *her* watch."

Cole smiled. "I believe her, Sergeant. I believe her. I guess we'll go on up and get some sleep then."

"Good night, sir. One of us will be awake through the night, and not one of the boys will strive to be a brave soul and venture out on his own. If anything happens, you'll hear us a-caterwauling as if the devil himself stepped foot inside."

"Thank you, Sergeant. Good night," Megan told him.

She preceded Cole up the stairs. This, like General Bickford's quarters, had been someone's home, one set up long ago to accept visitors. It had probably been maintained primarily as a lodging house. A large hallway had become a makeshift parlor, and there was table and chairs arranged for dining. At one time, meals had more likely been brought up to tenants individually instead.

"Good night," Megan told Cole, pausing in the parlor area.

"Good night. And—"

"Scream, loudly, if anything," she finished for him.

Cole nodded and walked on into his room, closing the door behind him.

Megan walked into her own room, wondering if she would dream that Lisette Annalise was a monster again. She'd already seen tonight that the woman was a monster indeed, though perhaps only a horned toad.

In the dressing room she discovered that Mrs. Weatherly had left her fresh water, and, with the liberty of time, she scrubbed well and managed to wash away most of the dirt and dust and death of the day. It felt nice. She took her time brushing out her hair, and wished that she didn't have to turn out the gas lamps; it was darker here than she had ever imagined darkness could be. Of course, she would be best off in the dark, leaving what slim light came from the moon to illuminate any intruder, should one come. But she didn't want to be in the darkness, and that might be why she tarried so long.

Eventually, she had brushed her hair, brushed her teeth, scrubbed and brushed her teeth and hair again, and had no further reason to stay up. She'd given blood twice in two days; she needed to rest. But, still, she didn't want to sleep in the dark.

She left the dressing room for the bedroom and lit the lamp there before walking to the window and looking out. She could see the Catholic church up on the hill, a silhouette in the moonlight, and she could see the darkness, a shadowy drape as it fell over foliage and houses alike. She was at the low end of the valley. The house was barely a block up the hill, but when she listened closely, she could hear the rush of the river so near, and then the soft call of night birds. The sounds were enchanting, and, tonight, the darkness seemed to be filled with peace.

So she was startled when a tap came at her door. And again when the door opened slowly. She was framed by the window, and she knew that she could be seen clearly, just as Cole was caught in the soft glow that emanated from the lamp near the doorway.

"Is something wrong?" she asked him anxiously.

He was shirtless, in his long johns, and the gaslight cast a pattern of gold over the muscular structure of his shoulders and chest.

"No, nothing has happened," he told her. "I couldn't sleep. I heard you in here, moving. I wanted to make sure that you were all right."

"I'm all right."

"I see that," he replied. He didn't leave the doorway. She didn't leave the window.

They seemed frozen in time, and, oddly, Megan wanted the moment to remain. He was beautiful there—he was what she might have wanted her whole life, someone who knew her for exactly who—and what—she was. He was ever ready to protect her, but he knew her strengths as well, and wasn't loath to the fact that she could help him. Somehow his initial resistance to her compelled this feeling further: she had impressed him with who she was.

She wanted to touch him, and yet she was afraid to move, because she didn't want to break the spell that kept him as close as he was, even though it was too far away.

At last, he moved. "Well, good night," he said.

And she thought that he would turn, close the door and return to his own room. She wanted to cry out that she didn't want him to go, but the words froze in her throat.

But instead, he paused halfway out, and she thought that he swore just beneath his breath. And then he turned, and he walked across the room to her, pulling her into his arms. For a moment she saw the depths of blue intensity in his eyes, and then he lifted her chin, and he kissed her, and it seemed as if the entire world melted away.

She should protest, of course. She should show some semblance of dignity or pride. She should remember that she had come from society in which decent young women did not do such things....

But they were so wrong. That *she knew. All young women dreamed of being held by a man such as Cole, by someone who could be so strong and tender at once, by someone with a voice as rich and husky and sensual as finely polished mahogany.*

And his mouth, his touch, his kiss...his lips formed over hers, his tongue prodding an entrance, playing so evocatively in her mouth....

And then he broke away from her, his thumb and forefinger still upon her chin and cheek, and his eyes searched hers, for what she wasn't sure. But again she feared that he would go away—she had to say something or he would do so.

But words wouldn't come, so she stood on her toes and pressed her lips to his, and luxuriated in the way that his mouth parted, how his lips pressed tightly and hungrily over hers once again. His arms came around her then, pulling her close to him, so wonderfully close. The fabric of her cotton gown was thin, and she could feel the heat of his body through the gauzelike fabric. She felt his heart and its pulse running through his veins, and she wondered at the vitality and the passion in him, and she prayed that the rest of the world could be this, just being held by him, feeling his body tight against her own.

And then...

She wanted more. There was wonderful energy running through him. There were things happening with his size and shape, the tension in his muscles, and the feel of his sex tight against her, constrained within the long johns and yet so...insinuative.

His hand ran down the length of her back, and they were closer still. And then his lips parted from hers once again and he was looking at her, and husky, whispered words escaped him. "You're my best friend's sister," he said, with a hint of anger in his voice. But the anger was for himself, not for her.

She found her voice at last: she knew that she had to do so.

"Life is fleeting and short, and even bitter, and *I* chose this. We don't need his permission for anything. I adore my brother, but he's a man who didn't know he even had a sister until recently. I can tell about him—if he knew that we were here, together, if I've come to know him at all, he'd be glad that we were together. He'd never deny you or me something that felt so right."

She had managed, somehow, in her confusion and longing, to say the right thing. Because she knew, as his eyes still touched hers, that he wasn't leaving.

His mouth found hers again, and his kiss was deliciously fevered and wet—searing hot—and it awoke every sense in her body as if she had never felt awakened before. His lips ran down the side of her throat, pressing against the pulse there, and down to her shoulder, and he slipped his fingers beneath the shoulders of the gown, and it slipped down her body, baring her breasts in the moonlight. His hands were callused, the hands of a man who handled guns, bows and arrows, saddles and reins, but the light and caressing way they circled and cradled her breasts made the touch more than she thought she could bear. She trembled beneath his touch, returning the sensation, feathering her fingertips over his shoulders and down the length of his back. He cradled her closer but she drew away from him, stepping from the gown, and she didn't feel in the least ashamed that she should be with him so. She just wanted more.

She caught his hand and drew him toward the bed. He ripped the covers from it to bring her down upon the clean, fresh sheets, his mouth finding hers again. And then he rose over her, catching her eyes again, and he didn't smile. He seemed to be almost bleak for a moment, but then he closed his eyes and opened them, and said softly, "I don't know how I stayed away from you so long."

She smiled and reached out to touch his hair, thick and rich and so dark. His head bent, and she threaded her fingers through the richness of it as his kiss found her throat again, the pulse there, and then lowered to encompass her breasts, tender and light and passionate, then her midsection. His tongue teased and laved her navel and traveled below, and she stopped breathing, just feeling and marveling, ever so slightly in shock, at the things the intimate touch of his tongue seemed to do to her, inside and out. She began to feel a rising of something almost like insanity, a need for more of his touch that was more desperate than any hunger she had ever known. It rose within like a spiraling fire. She'd heard whispers about this kind of desire, this kind of magnificence, but she'd never imagined that anything so spectacular and physical could really be… A magic that she had never thought that she might attain…

She arched against him, writhed with an ache that kept rising explosively, and then felt as if the world itself did ignite. A burst of a thousand stars…it was a feeling almost like ebony silk, shattered with a million crystals of light. It was like basking on clouds. And she felt the thunder of her heart and realized that the gasping she heard was her own breath, and then his, for he moved over her, scrambling with one hand to rid himself of the ridiculously intrusive long johns, and then it started all over again, only more magical, for he was within her, their bodies were like one, moving, slowly…faster…

She clung to him. She was sure she whispered incoherent words.

She didn't care.

She knew that she was mindless, soaked with perspiration, striving again, hungry, wanting and yet aware now that a peak could be reached, more magnificent than any mountain crest, sweeter than any bubbling stream or flower-strewn lea. She was achingly aware of his every twitch of muscle, his pure physical being, and yet…

The world exploded again. Stars. Everywhere. Something so good and sweet it was almost agony. Incredible. Miraculous. A feeling of intimacy and fantasy that was so elusive…and yet, even as she drifted and eased to a sensible platform of knowledge and being, he was there with her, holding her at his side, and his breathing was erratic and his heartbeat was still thunder, and to know that it had been shared made it all the more wondrous. His hand, long fingered and strong, pulled her close to him. She felt the whisper of his breath against her neck, and the chill as their body heat cooled and the touch of the night air swirled around them.

Of course, a certain sense of logic returned to her then. Cole was a man who had known what he was doing.

It might not have been the magic of discovery for him.

He'd known other lovers.…

She closed her eyes, and she lay against him, her heart pounding as she charged herself not to ruin the beauty with flippancy and insecurity. And when he drew a finger down her back, she knew that she would not, for he whispered, "You're more beautiful than even I might have imagined."

She turned into his arms. She looked searchingly into his eyes. "You were never afraid," she said softly.

He gave her a curious smile, frowning slightly. "Afraid?"

"That I might have gone mad, taken a chunk out of your jugular?"

His smiled deepened. "It would have been worth it."

She started to turn away, perplexed, disturbed.

He wouldn't allow it. He pulled her back to him, rising above her on an elbow. "I was never afraid," he said softly. "I trust you completely."

Tears threatened to sting her eyes. She couldn't allow such a show of emotion.

"Thank you," she said, and her voice sounded ridiculously prim.

He looked at her searchingly. "Is that why...you never took a lover before?"

She laughed softly, the sound hollow. "Ah, well, not that I was much of a believer in the behavior of a woman in fine society..." she began. But she wanted to cry inside, for he'd discovered the truth.

She thought that now he might draw back.

But he didn't.

He kissed her tenderly on the lips, and then kissed her forehead.

"My poor, dear girl," he said softly. "My poor, dear Megan."

"Not poor at all," she said. "Just a choice I made."

He eased back down beside her, pulling her close

again. "I will always trust you," he said, "and admire you and care for you, for all that you are."

They were beautiful words, of course. She found herself imagining that he had said, *I will always love you.*

But, of course, he had not. Trust was earned. Love…

How did love come to one? Was it something like this feeling of wanting to be with someone, and then knowing that you wanted to be with them always…?

Wake with them in the morning? Every morning?

She swallowed, knowing it would be far too easy to feel that way about Cole. And she wasn't stupid or naive. Wanting someone sexually did not mean that you wanted to wake up with them every morning.

And still…

She had spoken the truth. They had both seen just how bitterly short and brutal life could be. She was happy beside him, glad to be where she was, and she would cherish the moment.

Moments…

His fingers were running down her spine to the small of her back.

And it was amazing that the sweet and agonizing feeling could begin to sweep through her again so easily.…

She turned into his arms. She didn't want to question or wonder.

She just wanted to cherish the night.

CHAPTER THIRTEEN

"MARYLAND HEIGHTS, ACROSS the Potomac River, Loudoun Heights, across the Shenandoah," General Bickford pointed out on the map he now had spread out across the dining room table.

It was bright and early in the morning, but they'd been summoned bright and early because the general hadn't had much sleep that night, so he had explained. Besides, he was a man with a great deal of energy.

The general had just informed them that the area was only temporarily under his command; he'd been brought in not long ago himself, being a Marylander who knew the area well and might have an understanding on how the strange attacks were happening, or just what kind of beast might be ripping men to shreds. When the situation was under control, he'd be back in the main action with Grant, a commander who knew how to hold his guns and move forward, without becoming cautious and failing to pursue the enemy after a victory, as so many of the other Union commanders had done.

Bickford himself was a man who intended to make things happen. He would get to the heart and truth of a situation.

They had been summoned to a "strategic meeting," but it included breakfast—and the women. Lisette Analise had made it clear that she'd come as an agent of the Pinkertons, and that her office was under direct command of the president. She *would* be there. If she was there, Trudy was there. And Megan Fox had been sent specifically with Cole; he knew there was no way she was going to be absent from this meeting.

And so, with their meal cleared away, maps were strewn out on the dining-room table.

"Here we sit in Harpers Ferry, on this little triangular spit of peninsula. You might say at the confluence of the two rivers. Here's the armory—what's left of it. The railroad. Back over here, one of tunnels through the mountains, and here, the bridge—destroyed to smithereens after the siege, put back up by the corps of engineers. And right here, the engine house. Heading up the hill you've got Washington Street. You keep going and you're on some of the old battlefields, and then on out of the town. John Brown came in from the Kennedy Farm over here, in Maryland, and took the railroad bridge on over, utilizing a lot of the track you were on yesterday.

"Stonewall Jackson had a major victory here after the 1862 siege—but he and his troops came in from the west and from Maryland, creating a circle in that battle arena and putting a choke hold on the place. Then he moved on with the campaign and joined up with Lee at Antietam. The destruction you see now mostly comes from that siege—like I said, the bridge was blown to bits—and it's a miracle so many of the houses still stood at the end of it. Thing is, holding the place is a nightmare. The manpower needed is horrendous—probably one of the reasons President Lincoln, with all he has to deal with, took note when I said men were disappearing.

"We've held it now for nearly a year, but the place has changed hands six times, I think. Not as bad as

Winchester, though. I saw action there, and it changed hands a few times in one day. But, that, my friends, was a situation we could contend with. Here, we thought at first that we'd awakened some beast, like an unknown, particularly cunning bear or a wolf pack, when the men started dying, when scouting missions failed to return. And that's what it was at first—men just disappearing. Then, we had the situation where they were being ripped up practically before our noses, with the worst being the night before you arrived—seven men dead. And now, last night, a quiet night, a peaceful night."

Cole looked at the maps with a sinking feeling. The Union had repaired so much of the damage that the little spit of land that wound down to river was easy to approach from just about every direction. Throw in things that can move with the wind, and it was especially vulnerable.

Still, it seemed that the attacks had been started with a *strategy* requiring but a few "troops" to create pure havoc. Chew up—infect—a few men, and they'd arise to do the next round of death and terror, and then it would all spread like wildfire. But before the deaths two nights ago, according to Bickford, the attacks had been confined to the small scouting groups out looking for guerilla bands and supplies.

Bickford was staring at Cole. "I'm not a man to sit around and wait for this kind of an attack, sir. I'm suggesting that you take the battle out there, to whatever it is that comes in here and tears into all these good people without mercy."

Cole studied the map again. He'd spent his time in the East, and he'd spent his time at the finest military school in the country. He knew something about the terrain, but not extensively. He thought about the ragtag troop he had with him; the sergeant who limped, the nearly deaf private, another minus a trigger finger, another weakened by malaria.

He looked up; he could feel Megan watching him. Her eyes met his, and he could see that she thought the general was right. As it was, they were all just sitting and waiting to be attacked. And, by doing so, they might just create the perfect environment for a different kind of siege.

Cole had to force himself to draw his eyes from Megan, to remember that they were fighting an extremely fierce battle here, possibly with the fate of the country more in their hands than either side in the official war.

He'd always known that she was beautiful and filled with fire, but he hadn't known just what kind of a heart might beat within the perfect body of such a creature, or what depths could exist within her soul. Or, for that matter, and in all honesty, what sensuality could come alive within her, and how she could steal his senses and his mind and make him long for the world to go away, just so that they could be alone together.

The world wasn't going to go away. Every moment of every day had to be treated with the utmost importance during these troubles. He had to give his mind over to the task at hand.

"Dickens knows this area like the back of his hand," Bickford relayed. "He'll go with you. He'll be your guide."

"I've seen enough to work with the men here," Lisette said gravely.

Cole nodded. "First thing, though, is to gather the men

and set up some targets. General, you've arranged for the archery setup I mentioned last night?"

"Down by the river, past the guardhouse. I'll give the orders for assembly and we'll rally there at ten hundred. Dickens will get some men to gather the supplies you want out on the field. Then you can instruct them how to fight these things and how to defend themselves."

"Then, sir, I'm happy to follow your orders and let Dickens guide us on a hunt, but, today, I'd train the troops who will remain here. And we'll see that we pass another night quietly," Cole said.

"A sound plan," the general agreed.

Cole rose, ready to leave. Megan joined him. But she paused before the general. "Sir, what news have you heard this morning?"

"News? War news?" the general asked, and his voice then made a sound that seemed older than the hills that surrounded them.

"From Washington, specifically, sir."

The general seemed to soften. "A quiet night in the capital, my dear. A quiet night."

She nodded. "Thank you."

Out on the sidewalk, they saw that the town, with its few civilians and heavy troop population, was awake and moving. Troops drilled on the spit of land near the engine house. A baker delivered boxes to the house where they lodged. A woman in a white apron was moving up Church Street, possibly headed to the Catholic church.

Dickens met them on the street. "Sir! What are your orders, sir?" he asked Cole.

Cole decided that Dickens was going to call him *sir* no matter how he tried to protest, so he told him, "Go to Sergeant Newcomb and tell him we're going to have archery practice. He'll tell you what supply boxes need to be delivered to the field. We meet there at ten hundred."

"Aye, sir!" Dickens said, and, turning on his heel, made haste to find Newcomb.

"We could have done that ourselves," Megan pointed out.

"Yes, but I think we need to take a walk up Church Street. I want to meet Father Costello."

She nodded. "I believe they're using the church as a hospital."

"Yes, and I think we should definitely see the injured."

Cole slipped an arm around Megan as they walked uphill to the church. For a moment, they both paused, noting the beauty that not even the bombardments on the city could destroy. The rivers moved below in crystalline fantasy, and the majestic mounts surrounding them were rich with greenery. The church sat high upon a rock formation and seemed to be a beacon to the weary. They approached, and the door was open. Entering, they noted that crosses adorned both sides of the doorway.

The air inside was cool and carried the scent of incense. For a moment, they stood, adjusting to the light.

If the church was a hospital, there were no injured here now.

There was, however, a man in a priest's robes, kneeling at the altar. He remained there for a moment, and then rose, smiling as he came to meet them. He appeared to be in his late twenties, and he had a countenance of serenity unlike any Cole had witnessed in a very long time.

"Welcome. I'm Father Michael Costello, and you are a guest in St. Peter's," he said. His accent was Irish and melodic.

Megan murmured a shy greeting. She seemed awed, unusual for her. Cole shook the priest's hands, introducing the two of them in return.

"It's a remarkably beautiful church," Megan commented.

"Yes, I think so, thank you," Father Costello said. "God's hand drew the palette upon which we sit, and he created a place of majesty here."

"And we understand that you have maintained the building by raising the Union Jack," Cole said.

Father Costello smiled and shrugged. "The Confederacy hopes to be recognized and perhaps assisted by the British. The Union officers don't want to create any problems with the British while they fight the war—and when an election is at stake. The bombardment here in '62 was so severe that many thought not a tree or bush would remain, but this church did stand while some of the others were badly shelled. Some believe that God was watching out for us, which is true, but I also believe that God leads us to do things that might be clever when necessary," he said, his humor evident.

"Father, you're aware of the disease striking the area," Cole said.

"Indeed," Father Costello said gravely. "There have been times when I have gathered what remains of my flock here so that they might seek sanctuary from the night."

"But you have also utilized the church as a hospital."

"After the battles. And sometimes, when we have injured men, they are brought here."

"Have you ever had injured men here who—who left in the night?" Megan asked him.

Costello looked at Megan and seemed to study her eyes. He smiled. "I have a deep belief in God giving us the gifts and the strengths we need to get through times of heavy travail. You must understand that, to me, death is not the end, and there are many fates worse than death. I have had injured who have passed into God's hands here, but this is His sanctuary, and none pass these doors who are not in His grace, no matter how they may choose to worship. I have not had the kind of trouble you describe, nor do I expect that it will seek to come here."

Cole nodded and hesitated for a minute. "Father, we may be needing a great deal of holy water in the days to come."

Father Costello's handsome smile deepened. "Mr. Granger, I must say that I'm delighted that you have come to see me. Men of great faith may be fighting in this war. They may even be leaders in it. They may all pray to God that their cause wins. But, I must say, you are the first to come to me, relying on what services a priest may give. I will see to it that my reserves are plentiful and strong."

"Thank you," Megan said.

"Come," Father Costello said to her. "Come to the altar, if you will, whatever your faith, and allow me to bless you both."

Cole felt a little awkward. He had attended chapel years ago as a cadet, and he hadn't been averse to attending services when preachers out in the West had what they referred to as "go-to meetings." But he wasn't Catholic and wasn't at all sure of what he was supposed to do.

But he followed Megan and Father Costello and knelt down as indicated. The priest's prayers were in Latin at first, and he didn't understand a word. But he had learned the power of holy water, even if he wasn't sure how it worked. So when the priest formed crosses on their foreheads with the water, he couldn't help but feel that it gave him a greater sense of his own abilities and determination.

He knew as well that the creatures turned away from crosses and other symbols of deep faith. And when they were leaving, Father Costello pulled the large silver cross he had been wearing over his head, and put it around Cole's neck.

"I see that Megan wears a large gold cross. This is one you may need, my friend," Costello told him.

Cole thanked him. "We have to be on the field in a matter of minutes, Father. Thank you. We deeply appreciate your help."

The man seemed to be watching them, and weighing them as individuals once again.

"Is there something more, Father, that you think you should tell us?" Megan asked quietly.

Father Costello was thoughtful. "Yes," he said, making his decision. "I do have one soldier who is convalescing here."

"Oh?"

"A Confederate lieutenant of cavalry. You will not see him in uniform—I am tending to him as if he were a civilian. He was among my flock when the war began, and he found his way back to me after some of the recent bloodshed at the Wilderness."

Megan cast Cole a quick, worried look.

"May we see him?" she asked.

"Yes, you may. I have told you the truth, and I haven't lied to others. The Union officers know that he is here, but don't know that he should be a prisoner of war," Father Costello explained.

"We're not here to fight for either side, Father Costello," Cole assured the man.

"I believe you, and that's why I've spoken freely. Come with me. He resides in the rectory."

They followed him toward rear of the church, through what had been a schoolroom in better times, and on back to the priest's dwelling. Father Costello lived modestly, with worn furniture kept neat and clean. He brought the pair out back, to an enclosed porch area, where a man sat in a chair and stared out at the mountains and rivers.

The man turned when he heard them coming. He was pale, nearly white, but beside that fact, he seemed to be whole. His hair was long and blond and his beard was roughly cut. His eyes were a dull brown, conveying a world of confusion and loss.

"Father?" he said quietly, surprised that visitors had been brought to him.

"These people are here to help, Daniel," Father Costello said. "Cole Granger, Megan Fox, please meet Daniel Whitehall."

"Hello," Daniel said, trying to rise.

"No, please!" Megan said, dropping down beside him. "Please, don't stand up. I'd just like to ask you some questions."

Daniel looked doubtful, and stared at Father Costello again.

"It's all right," Cole said quickly. "We're not with the army."

"Really," Megan said gently. Whitehall seemed to be taken with her. He stared at Megan and waited. "You were hurt during the Wilderness campaign?" she asked.

He didn't look away. He nodded.

"I was there," she said softly.

He didn't reply. His bony fingers tightened on the arms of his chair.

"What happened then, can you tell me?"

The man winced, closing his eyes. "I remember the fires, and the stinking smell of burning flesh, and the men screaming when they were caught in the woods and knew they were going to burn to death. I was disoriented, I couldn't see. I couldn't breathe.... You can't imagine the smoke. I think I fell, passed out, and then..."

"And then?" Megan prodded gently.

"And then there was something, someone on me. And I came to in the darkness, and felt something at my neck...." He touched his throat. "I looked up and it seemed there was a beast on me. Some strength came to me and I screamed, and I hurled it from me...and then I heard it scream because I had thrown it into the fire...."

"And then?"

"I passed out again. When I came to, I was alone, with the remnants of the burned and smoking forest around me. And I was..."

Megan didn't speak. They all waited.

"Hungry," he whispered.

His eyes focused on Megan again, and tears stung his eyes. "I was hungry—for blood."

She nodded, watching him with caring eyes.

"I am not a monster!" he said. "There were injured, and I wanted to tear into them, and I couldn't and...I ran." He paused for a minute. "I couldn't try to find my regiment. I couldn't surrender. I...oh, God. I found a pathetic old horse and I—I bit its neck. And it screamed—and I

stopped—and the horse died anyway, there on the spot—blood streaming from its neck and I…God, help me! I lapped it up, and then I ran and I ran and I…I didn't let myself kill the next horse I found. I traveled by day and night and it seemed to take forever, and I…came back to Father Costello."

"How did you survive, back here?" Megan asked him.

"Rats are always plentiful," Daniel Whitehall said. "Squirrels, possums and one time a cow that was loose near Front Royal."

"We manage to keep the rat population down around here now," Father Costello said drily. "And I take what raw meat supplies I can get from the soldiers' mess."

"I can help you," Megan told him.

The sickly man looked at her with disbelieving eyes.

Cole clamped a hand on her shoulder. "Megan can help you, but it will have to be tomorrow."

"He needs help now, Cole," Megan insisted.

"You can't," he said firmly. "You have helped two people in the last two days. You'll weaken yourself, and that could be very dangerous."

"You know how quickly I heal."

"Give it a day."

"How are you going to help him?" Father Costello asked.

"A blood transfusion," Megan said.

Father Costello wasn't surprised, but he was somber. "I've heard of doctors performing such operations. I've also heard that men often die after the treatment. There is one learned doctor up in Massachusetts who suggests that some men have blood that is compatible with others, and some do not."

"He won't die from my blood," Megan said.

Father Costello was silent for a minute.

Daniel Whitehall spoke up. "Father, I can't bear this existence. I'd have died long ago—if I weren't willing myself to stay alive, despite the terror of what I might become. Please, I am more than willing to try anything!"

"Then we'll do it. Early *tomorrow* morning," Cole said firmly.

She looked at him, ready to argue.

"I have to be on that field for archery practice," Cole reminded her. "And you must give yourself some time. There are bigger issues at hand than just one individual, if you may accept my apologies, Mr. Whitehall."

"Tomorrow morning," Father Costello said. "I will be ready to assist."

Megan started to rise. Daniel Whitehall grabbed her arm. "I am so afraid. Can you save me from the nightmares?"

"Yes." She looked at Cole.

"Tomorrow. Early," she said. "We're due to head out now, and I wouldn't want the general to think that we're not doing all in our power to find the beasts now lurking around Harpers Ferry."

She stood, resigned, it seemed, to his logic.

"At daybreak, we'll come back up," Cole said.

"Thank you," Daniel said.

Father Costello led them back through the church and then out. It appeared he didn't want anyone knowing that they'd been through the church, should someone be near. The ill man was the priest's secret.

When they came down the church aisle to the door, they bade the priest goodbye.

Father Costello nodded. "I am glad to meet you, and glad that you have come here."

"We'll be back, Father," Cole said.

"I admit, I still fear for Daniel's life," Costello said. "But not as much as I fear for his soul. He is a good man."

"And he will be again," Megan assured him.

They started out. Father Costello stopped them. "One more thing. A young man did come to see me this morning. A Private Dickens. Please tell him that he has done his duty as a friend. I read burial services over the graves you dug last night just an hour ago."

"We'll tell him, Father," Megan said.

When they were far enough from the church and could just spy the drill field, Megan turned to Cole. "He knows what I am, Cole. He knows!"

He set his arm around her and pulled her close to him. "He knows, and he gave you a blessing, Megan. He's a priest. He has an amazing faith—and an amazing mind. He knows what we're up against. He's a wonderful ally." He paused. "Megan, you must remember how valuable you are, yourself, and you can't risk that many transfusions."

"That man must be saved."

"That's fine, and I understand. But you do understand that you're not invulnerable yourself," he said.

"Of course," she said.

"All will be well."

She laughed. "I don't know about all, but…as for Daniel, we have a chance!"

They walked on down the hill, and all the while, Cole thought it was sadly wrong that while others did not, Megan saw herself as a monster. And he wondered if she was so desperate to find her father and prove that he was not evil because that might clear her own name, too. And maybe she could forgive herself…for merely *existing*.

He didn't know how to voice his words, to assure her that he'd seen many an outlaw who had killed ruthlessly yet left behind children that grew and became nothing but an asset to humanity.

He just pulled her closer.

As they neared the street, Megan pulled away from him. "There's your friend, Lisette. All ready for archery practice."

Lisette was on the street with the general. She had changed into a man's shirt and breeches and seemed focused and ready to work. Her hair was tied into a knot at her back, and she wore a wide-brimmed hat to protect herself from the heat of the sun.

As he watched, shy little Trudy stepped out from behind her. She, too, was dressed in a man's clothing, though she appeared to be horribly uncomfortable and not sure how to stand.

"Maybe you could help Trudy," Cole said.

"And you'll help Lisette?" Megan asked, smiling though her voice was sharp.

Cole laughed. "You really dislike Lisette."

"I'm sorry. I know the two of you are—*friends*."

He turned her around to face him, smiling. She was jealous. He rather liked that. Not if it seriously harmed their relationship, but it was nice to know that she had been noting the woman, and was wary of her—in many ways.

"I met her as a starstruck young man, watching a play. There were half a dozen of us, admiring her, enjoying a little after-the-show party. Back then, she was just an actress, charming and intent on storming the world—becoming more famous than Jenny Lind. When it came to war, she focused all that energy on the Union. I don't know when she actually went to work for Pinkerton, or how she knew exactly what had happened in Victory, Texas. But she was involved in bringing Cody, Brendan and I to Washington. But that's really about it. She's an actress, Megan. And when she's not spouting fire, she's the kind of woman who needs to believe that every man fantasizes that she's in love with him. There was never anything between us."

Megan flushed and winced, meeting his eyes openly. "You wouldn't lie to me, would you?"

He shook his head. "When I met you, Megan, I thought you were dangerous, conniving and that we should have put you down or thrown out on the street."

"Well, *that's* honest."

"I'm sorry. You asked."

"It's all right. I thought you were an arrogant, pig-headed bastard. So I guess we're even."

"I don't know," he said softly. "Because now I think you're the most beautiful creature to ever draw breath, and that you've got a soul that glitters more sweetly than the sun on a bubbling brook."

She inhaled sharply, studying his eyes.

"Well?" he asked.

"Well? I think that was amazingly romantic and poetic for a longhorn cowboy!"

"And?"

"You're still pigheaded," she told him.

He laughed. "At times. But only when I know that I'm right."

"And I guess I've waited my life to meet someone like you," she said softly.

He wanted the world to drop away. He wanted to drag her into his arms again, ravage her with kisses and feel the remarkable sexual thrill when she did the things to him she had learned to do throughout last night.

But the earth was not going to slip from beneath their feet. A general was waiting for them, and he could hear the shouts of men as they set up the targets and gathered armaments.

"So, are *you* going to teach Lisette what to do?" he asked.

"Not on your life. You're far better with a bow and arrow, I'm certain. But, believe me, I do know the art of archery. No, this is your class, cowboy. Go to it."

"Wait," he said, eyeing her suspiciously. "What are you going to do—you're not training Trudy?"

"I'm going to rest. Trudy's a particularly smart girl—she'll learn faster than Lisette, no matter how much attention you give *her*. Besides, I had a particularly invigorating night, and I wouldn't mind a bit of sleep," she said, smiling. "One of us should have some energy left for tonight," she told him, the golden color in her eyes sparkling mischievously.

"My reserves can be endless, you know, when properly motivated," he told her.

She grinned and walked away in the direction of their lodgings. He frowned, wondering what she might really be planning, but it was nearly ten hundred and he knew that the military moved like clockwork when it came to drilling.

"Mr. Granger!" General Bickford bellowed. "The men

are assembling. If you would be so kind as to accompany me?"

He strode to General Bickford, who was briskly heading down the street toward their hastily prepared archery field.

Cole looked back, though.

He wanted to make sure that Megan went into the house where they were lodging.

She did.

Still uneasy, he went on to take command of the men.

CHAPTER FOURTEEN

MEGAN DECIDED THAT she would let at least half an hour go by before heading back up the hill. She wanted to make sure that Cole was heavily involved in his activities first.

She needed to get back to the church where Father Costello could assist her. Cole just might try to stop her.... As far as Daniel Whitehall went...

She also figured she should go on over to the cemetery afterward, though that could wait. It wasn't often that the dead came back to life in the morning, but the way the priest had spoken, she was certain that he believed that certain "undead" had been abiding in the cemetery for some time. It would be interesting to see what was going on there, though they had not come across anything during the burial detail of the night before.

As far as Daniel Whitehall went, she didn't believe that she could wait. Yes, the young man had been holding his own for a long time. But he was so gaunt and pale, and so tormented. The way he spoke, she knew that he would have rather died in the agony of the flames that had taken so many lives at the Wilderness than face the demons tormenting him now. Perhaps he could wait. But she couldn't, now that she had seen him.

She hurried first to find the bag with the reserves of blood that Cody and Alex had packed up for her; now was the time to make sure that she was at her best, strong. She sat at the table in the parlor area and sipped the contents of one of the canteens. Noting that there were old newspapers lying shoved into a stand by the door, she drew one out. It featured a caricature of Abe Lincoln holding a ship and firing on New York. The headline read, Draft Riots Tear Apart New York City.

The paper was from July, 1863. On one page, it extolled the virtues of the Union army at Gettysburg, but the headline had been written by a Northerner who was against the war. The article went on to read that New York City had given the most men to the Union at the beginning of the war, but with recruitment and fighting numbers down, the increasingly frequent practice of conscription made some question whether laws that permitted such were unconstitutional and should be argued in court.

New York seemed so far away.

The author of the article tried, however, to write without bias. He noted that the riots had not just been caused by the conscription laws, but that overcrowding, decades of corrupt city politics, a lack of sewage and the astounding death toll of civilians living in tenement houses were all part of the problem.

She leaned back, finishing the contents of the canteen. She wondered what the horror would be if the *disease* were not stopped, and if it began to infect a city as huge, crowded and congested as New York. What would newspapermen write about then?

That thought brought her to swift movement. Daniel Whitehall, at least, could be saved, and she was determined that he be saved immediately. The priest had been keeping him alive, but if he were to pass away in the night, there was no way of knowing what would happen. He'd not killed a human being—she believed him on that—but he *had* felt the vampiric hunger that ripped into one with such viciousness that they became mad and assaulted the first available human being.

Cole didn't really understand that. He knew that there was salvation, and knew that it was rare, because it was. And she knew that under the circumstances in which they had found themselves, *being* a good vampire was incredibly difficult. Cole acted like it was a matter of choice, or even chance, possibly. Megan knew it was a matter of struggle. A pressure under which not just everyone could hold out indefinitely. Daniel could start out okay, but the hunger might overtake him, especially in the early weeks following infection.

She glanced at the clock above the mantel. Cole had been with the troops at least thirty minutes. She went into his room and found the medical bag and slipped outside.

The street was uncannily quiet.

She hurried back toward Church Street and headed uphill. When she reached the church, she took a minute to adjust to the dimmer light.

"Father Costello?" she called softly.

He didn't answer her, but she knew the path through the church and schoolroom and outside to the rectory out back. Approaching the small building, she heard a low murmur of voices. She hurried toward the sound.

In a ground-floor bedroom, Daniel was in bed, the priest murmuring prayers at his side.

Hearing Megan's arrival, Father Costello looked up. He crossed himself and rose and spoke softly. "He weakened when you left, so I brought him in here. I didn't want to leave him alone, and he said that he'd never risk your life for his." He paused a moment, seeing the medical bag. "You're not supposed to be here, Miss Fox. It could be dangerous."

She shook her head. "Please, Father, though I respect the opinions of others, I do know myself best. But I'm afraid you're going to have to help me."

Father Costello hesitated, and she knew that he hated going against Cole's warnings, but that as a man and a priest, he had to make a decision.

"I know myself better than anyone, Father. I will be fine."

He made his decision quickly, and once he did, he was all business, demanding that she describe the entire procedure first, and then take him step by step again as they went through it. Megan arranged the supplies and explained the tourniquets and that the process used gravity to keep the blood flow moving in the proper direction. They moved Daniel down to the floor for expediency's sake—he was already unconscious and his face was deadly pale. Megan situated herself against a wall, using pillows as a prop for her arm.

Father Costello was concerned about the needles, but he had apparently dealt with enough war injured not to be squeamish at the sight of blood. He was an intelligent and adept man, and once they began, there was little instruction Megan needed to give him. He was concerned that he set the tubes properly—concerned not to stab her or Daniel needlessly—but, once he concentrated, the entire thing went smoothly.

Megan leaned back, feeling the flow of blood. She wondered if it was something that she really felt, or just something that she knew, and it was a feeling by way of imagination only. It didn't matter, she assured herself, as long as the blood flowed from her into Daniel.

As she watched Daniel's face, to her vast relief, she began to see color slowly return to it.

"It's been some time now," Father Costello stated.

"A little longer," she murmured.

He looked at her and then shook his head. "No. Now, tell me, what do I do to stop it?"

He was firm, so she gave him the directions he requested, and he pressed the small towel he had given her against the puncture wound in her arm, then tended to Daniel.

She closed her eyes and waited for several long minutes, aware that she was weaker than she had expected. Looking at Daniel, though, she saw that his eyes were open and he was looking at her.

His lips formed two words. "Thank you."

She smiled.

But she wasn't able to reply.

Father Costello stood, frowning. "Did you hear that?" he asked quietly.

She hadn't been listening, but at his soft warning she focused her attention to any outside sounds.

Something was prowling around the rectory.

The father looked down at Megan. "We've got to get into the church itself. The church is consecrated, it's truly God's house, and we'll be safe from those creatures there."

She nodded, and nearly passed out trying to get to her feet. She had to find strength. They had to get Daniel up and into the church. Whatever was out there, she couldn't fight it now.

Father Costello steadied her. "Daniel, drag Daniel in!" she told him in response.

It was broad daylight; the night had been quiet. She shouldn't have to be afraid now. Only a vampire of some experience could easily be about and on the prowl in the strong sunlight of the morning. This was no new being.

Father Costello did as she directed him, setting an arm around Daniel. Daniel tried to help, but he didn't have much strength. They made it through the rectory to the schoolroom. Something was prying at one of the windows.

"Take Daniel in, please, go!" Megan begged. "Bring back holy water, Father, in your hands…any way that you can!"

There wasn't time for the priest to reply. He rushed through as best he could, dragging Daniel along.

The first of the creatures burst through the window.

It was a man dressed in the suit of a businessman or banker, though the suit was ragged. He was covered in dirt, mud from the cemetery, she presumed. He may have been an accountant once; he was a being thirstily bent on survival now.

She rifled through her pockets, but she hadn't come armed. She watched him come at her until, finally, she drew back her lips and displayed her fangs, hissing in warning.

That gave him pause, but another muddy creature—a woman with ferocious features—crawled through the window behind him. She had been middle-aged in life, and her graying hair was in tangled skeins around her pinched face. Her calico dress seemed at once too festive and sufficiently morbid for her actions. Behind her came a soldier in the remnants of a Confederate uniform—Louisiana militia—though with pants replaced at some time with those probably stolen off a clothesline.

There were so many of them. She tried to hiss out another warning that would give them all pause, but they knew they outnumbered her and that she was the one in danger.

She had managed to buy herself a little time, though. Father Costello came rushing back in, his hands cradled with a scoop of water. He raised his voice in prayer, and again the creatures gave momentary pause. But then they came forward.

Father Costello aimed the water in his hands the best he could, catching the first man in the face, which elicited howls of agony. The others fell back, but then, as Father Costello stared at them—empty-handed—they started forward again.

Megan found the strength to reach for a child's wooden chair and slam it against the wall at her back, breaking off one of the legs to use as a bat and praying she might manage to make it work as a stake.

The woman came at her. Megan picked up her weapon and prayed. She was aware of a whoosh of the air…and the creature didn't reach her. It fell, just inches before her. She stared in disbelief, then looked up to see Cole at the window. He was armed with a bow and notched another arrow from his quiver.

Another swift movement, another and another. Not thirty seconds had passed, and Cole had killed the entire horde, so quick with the weapon was he, and so accurate with his aim in the close quarters.

Finally he crawled through the window…staring at her with his features hardened in anger.

Father Costello sank to the floor, his prayers of thanksgiving mere whispers.

Megan stared back at him. "Thank God," she said simply herself.

The words didn't appease Cole.

He walked from corpse to corpse, rolling each over, impaling it with a stake from the supply inside his coat. "We'll need to finish up here quickly," he said curtly.

"Of course," she said, and moving forward, wavered. He came to her and grabbed her roughly, with little tenderness in his touch.

"You just won't listen to me, will you?" he demanded. She didn't remember the blue in his eyes as being so much like cold steel as when he looked at her then.

"Daniel was dying," she said. "Ask the father."

"You couldn't have known that, and you ignored me anyway."

"But he would have died or been taken. Cole, it's a *good* thing that I didn't listen to you this time!" she pleaded.

Whatever her logic, he wasn't interested.

"Father, get her into the church for now, please," Cole said. "Dickens will be here in a minute and can help me manage in here." He ruffled through the pocketed lining of his coat again, producing another of the canteens. "Make her drink this," he said to the man, ignoring her completely. "Please, get her into the church now. Who knows? There might be a grand old tea party rising from the graveyard."

Father Costello didn't argue. He set a supporting arm around Megan and led her into the consecrated area of the church. He sat her down on a bench and handed her the canteen.

Megan held the canteen and looked at the altar. She was tempted to weep. Something felt so wrong.

"Drink it, please!" the father urged her.

"It feels...wrong."

"Ah, well, the Great Almighty supplies what we need, and there is nothing wrong in your efforts to save your fellow man. Drink, child, and with His blessing, I am sure!" the Father told her.

She did so. She felt strength seep back into her body and limbs. The world still seemed to be so—vague. Spinning before her.

Father Costello eased her down to lie on the pew.

She was vaguely aware of Daniel Whitehall's face before her.

Against it all, she was gratified to hear his words.

"Thank you. You have saved my soul," he whispered.

She allowed blackness to engulf her.

COLE TRIED HIS HARDEST to tamp down the fury he felt. He knew that it had to do with fear. It had been terrifying to see Megan and the father facing down the ravenous vampires that had boldly broken in by daylight.

He was shaking.

"Heads off, sir?" Dickens asked quietly.

Cole managed to nod. "Drag them out to the cemetery first, Dickens."

The church and the cemetery were close enough that it wasn't a major project. Even though they had been staked, Cole wasn't comfortable with leaving the dead unattended. He and Dickens took turns dragging the bodies back to the cemetery where their graves—looking as if the sod had burst open—were easy enough to find.

Dickens was a fast learner; as soon as they were both at the graveyard together, he got busy sawing away at the necks of the creatures and decapitating them. Within thirty minutes, they had completed the task of assuring that the dead stayed dead and weren't going to return to the realm of the living.

Hot, dusty and worn, Cole returned to the church where Father Costello informed him that both Daniel and Megan were resting peacefully in the church itself.

"I've wondered," the holy man said. "I've seen the graves disturbed, and I thought at first that it was some sick joke by Confederate soldiers or Union soldiers or even the few adolescents who remain in the area. Once Daniel came to me, I stayed in at night. But I have seen things that..." He shuddered, stiffened and asked briskly, "What do we do now?"

"None of this was happening at Harpers Ferry until the war began, is that right?" Cole asked him.

"No. In fact, not until rather recently." He looked at Cole and shook his head. "And don't think that Daniel caused any of this—because he *did not,*" he said firmly.

"Daniel was actually with you several days—weeks?—before it began, is that right?" Cole asked him.

"I'm telling you. It wasn't Daniel."

"Father, I'm not trying to blame Daniel. I need a time frame because it's important that we save time. We're going to dig up every grave from the last several weeks—the period of infection that we can determine, at least—and I want to be thorough, but I don't want to waste time," Cole explained.

Father Costello nodded. "I believe that Harpers Ferry

was free of this scourge until recently, but I can't give an exact date."

"We'll go to May seventh, to be safe. That was the last day of the Battle of the Wilderness," Cole said. He charged Costello to find all the burial records from that date forward, and left with Dickens to return to the makeshift archery range. He would have to let Megan rest where she was. He was too angry to deal with her anyway.

Upon returning to the field, he was pleasantly surprised to discover that the troops were enthused with the new challenge of the bows and arrows, and that many of the soldiers, though not adept at first, were able to grasp the trajectory of the arrows and learn to string a bow and shoot with damned decent aim.

When they finished up, the light was waning, and he knew that he had to get back to the graveyard quickly. He brought Dickens and his four-man crew from Washington.

At the church he was annoyed to discover that Megan had returned to the house, but he couldn't afford the time to engage in a renewed battle with her. Daniel Whitehall was standing on his own. He looked like an altogether different man. He had bathed and groomed his beard and mustache, and even trimmed his hair. He intended to help them that night, even if it all he had the strength for was carrying the picks and the shovels.

In the cemetery, Father Costello, armed with an incense burner and receptacles of holy water, led them to every recent grave. The dead were disinterred. Some were in coffins. Some had been lowered into the ground with only shrouds around them.

It didn't matter how they had been buried, nor their

dress, sex or age. Coffins were burst open with the pick. And though it pained every man there, even the heads of children were separated from their bodies. Each body taken from the grave, beheaded and returned, received a prayer from Father Costello for their souls. The sun sank as they neared the end of their task, and it wasn't until they came to the last of the graves that its occupant burst out of the earth, lunging for the closest man.

That was Dickens. But he had learned well and stepped back, letting Cole slide by him with mallet and stake. The vampiric dead had been a Rebel soldier, returned here perhaps from a faraway battlefield. He went down with an expulsion of dust and earth, and, like the others, the men decapitated him and he was laid back to rest.

"There's just one more," Father Costello said, reading from his book of records. "Twenty feet or so to your left. You should see that the grass hasn't grown over it. Betsy Jennings. She died a few weeks ago of tuberculosis. Poor thing—she was only eight years old. How young to have acquired such a devastating illness!"

Cole followed the priest's directions but when he came to the plot indicated, he discovered that the earth was greatly disturbed.

The grave's occupant was long gone.

He took his shovel and dug furiously around the area, to no avail. There was no corpse in the grave.

And all he could think was that Megan was alone at the house.

MEGAN FELT FINE. She had indulged in another of the canteens, which worried her some, but then, they wouldn't keep forever anyway. She had allowed herself the luxury of a long and relaxing hot bath with the help of Mary-Anne Weatherly—easy enough! They had a lovely supply of fresh water, thanks to the rivers, and she had even sipped at a sherry. But none of it made her feel any better about the way that Cole had looked at her that afternoon.

She had been right: Daniel might have died if she hadn't come. And beyond that, the infected dead had risen to attack the church. If she hadn't been there—if Cole hadn't guessed that she might be there and arrived—truly horrible things might have happened. The good father would have died trying to protect Daniel.

She had been right to do what she had done.

And she continued to have a hollow feeling at her core.

She was still sipping the sherry, waiting for darkness and the men to return, when she heard sobbing outside the window.

Looking down, she saw a child sitting on the sidewalk. A little girl with long dark hair, a doll clutched in her arms. The sobbing was heart-breaking, and she wanted to run right out to the child.

Something however, stopped her, when she leaped up to do just that. There was something incredibly sad and poignant about the scene, and very disturbing. She hadn't seen any children in the streets of Harpers Ferry before. She had hardly seen any civilians for a town this size.

But then the sobbing seemed to strike something in her heart, and she moved about preparing to get the girl with an unnatural haste. There was danger inherent here, no matter what, and so she quickly filled her pockets with vials of holy water before heading down to the sidewalk.

Trudy Malcolm, notepad in hand, had apparently heard

the sobbing as well and was already heading toward the child. "You poor little thing!" Megan heard Trudy crooning in a gentle voice. She reached for the girl.

Suddenly, the situation seemed wrong to Megan. *This was the first child she had seen. And even a child, a sobbing child, might have been a victim...*

Might have been turned!

"Trudy, wait!" Megan cried, and ran toward her, but Trudy had already picked the little girl up and held her in her arms, staring at Megan as if she had lost her mind.

"Megan, she's just a little thing, so skinny and lost!"

The girl was dirty. With her keen vision, Megan could see that even though the light on the street was poor. Megan did slow as she came forward, wanting a good look at the child, not wishing to startle Trudy further. The little girl had her head leaned against Trudy's. She stared at Megan with giant blue eyes. No signs of fangs, no movements to take a bite out of Trudy's neck.

"Honey, what's your name?" Megan asked. The child continued to stare at her.

"I'm going to take her up to the general's quarters," Trudy said with a joyfully matronly sense of purpose. "Maybe one of the men will have an idea of who she is. I believe some of the officers do have their wives and family staying here."

"No," Megan said. "Let's take her up to my apartments, and see if we can get her to talk to us." She reached for the child.

"Miss Fox—I have her! Oh, I know I look like the wind could blow me away, but I'm stronger than I look."

"Trudy, I don't doubt your strength, but you know that people can be very sick. She might be infected.... Trudy, you've seen what can happen."

"But she's just a little slip of a thing!" Trudy said.

"Still..."

Trudy set her jaw at a stubborn angle. Megan slipped an arm around Trudy, leading the way as they headed back to the house and then up the stairs to the parlor area she shared with Cole.

"All right, set her on the sofa, please, Trudy?" Megan begged.

Trudy did so, kneeling down before the child and smiling. "Honey, we really need to know your name."

The little girl wiped at her face. She shuddered, staring at Trudy.

"She's filthy," Trudy said. "Oh, the poor little thing! She must have been wandering around lost forever. Megan, do you have a washcloth? Maybe we could clean up her face?"

"I'll stay here with her. You can find a washcloth in my room," Megan said.

The little girl sniffled. "Betsy," she said. "I want my mommy."

"Oh, poor child. We just have to find out who your mommy is, Betsy, and then we can get you to her," Trudy said. She glanced up at Megan. "Oh, Megan, I can't just leave her. Please, you can see that she's all right. The—the—*things* turn into rabid beasts and attack. She's just a lost little girl."

Megan headed toward the bedroom backward, wanting to keep her eyes on Trudy and the child. She understood that poor Trudy seemed to be living a lonely life. She had work to keep her living well enough, but that work was at the beck and call of Lisette Annalise, who treated her with absolute disdain.

"Trudy, move away from her for a minute," Megan said firmly.

Trudy looked at her and frowned, but sighed and stood and took a step away. The child burst into tears and Trudy moved back to her, cradling her into her arms. "It's all right, little one. It's all right. Um, Aunt Trudy is here!"

Megan decided to make a quick run for the washcloth and water. She turned her back for one second.

And in that time, she knew.

She turned back around, to see that the child was behind her. The blue eyes had been filled with a glitter of evil laughter and cunning, and she stared at Megan, ready to fly at her. Trudy was lying at a skewed angle.

Megan vaguely heard the downstairs door burst open and Cole shouting her name while the child lifted from the floor as a black-winged shadow to come flying at her. She was prepared. She had the holy water out of her pocket in seconds, and flung it while the creature was still two feet away.

The scream that resulted was wild and shrill as the thing died in a thrashing pile of agony before her. She stared at it, detesting her own failure to read the truth—to insist on her instinct no matter what Trudy implored.

Cole saw the writhing mass and rushed to her, taking her into his arms. She allowed herself a split second of trembling gratitude that he still cared enough to hold her, but then she pushed away in fear.

"Trudy!" she said, pushing past him to where Trudy was being held up by Dickens.

"She's passing out!" Dickens cried, the sound of his voice helpless.

"Get her to the sofa," Megan ordered. "Quickly, I have to see her throat!"

She fell to her knees next to the woman as Dickens laid her out. Cole hovered behind her and his Union troop came bursting through the door to their parlor.

She searched Trudy's neck for any sign of violence, but none had been done to her. "Cole, there must be smelling salts in the medical bag." She looked back at him. He arched his brows at her, and she flushed. "I brought it *back* from the church. It's where you keep it—at the foot of your bed."

He returned quickly and she found what she needed, wafting the little pellet beneath Trudy's nose. The woman began to cough and sputter, waving a hand in the air. Her eyelids fluttered and then she opened her eyes fully and stared at the group blankly.

"What happened?" she asked weakly.

"Sweet little Betsy *was* a monster," Megan said. "You tell me what happened. You were holding her, and then she was attacking me."

Trudy shook her head, giant tears forming in her eyes. "I don't know! She just burst out of my arms and I—I don't remember anything else!"

"She didn't touch you, didn't scratch you, didn't hurt you in any way?" Cole demanded, his tone harsh.

Trudy cringed, bringing her hand to her throat. "No… no. She just burst out of my arms with such strength that I fell back, stunned. I was on the sofa…getting up, and then I felt as if the world was rushing all around me and I was…oh, goodness. I fainted. Please! Don't tell Miss Annalise! She'll think me a worse fool than she already does. Please! Please!"

Trudy clutched Megan's arm, her eyes filled with such misery that Megan couldn't help but be touched, despite her anger. In truth, she was angrier with herself than she was with Trudy. She should have tossed some holy water on the girl immediately. Had she been but a mortal, it wouldn't have hurt her; otherwise it would have clearly notified them that she was a monster.

"We'll see to the remains," Sergeant Newcomb said, his tone that of the practical soldier. He paused, though, to put a gentle hand on Trudy's head. "None of us will tell Miss Annalise a thing, you can be sure."

The men headed into the bedroom to collect whatever remained of the child. Cole walked over to the liquor stand and poured out a portion of straight whiskey. He paused, drank the first one down himself, and then poured a second for Trudy.

As she eased herself up to a sitting position, Cole handed her the whiskey. "Here," he said, "drink this."

"Oh, sir! Good heavens, I don't drink whiskey!" she protested.

"You do now," Cole said.

Trudy looked at Cole with pure adoration. "Oh, thank you, thank you, thank you all so much." She clutched Megan's arm again, her expression one of horror then. "My dear God, I am so sorry, Megan, you tried to tell me. But she was a child. A *child!* How could I possibly believe that such a pathetic little thing could be such a monster?"

"It's all right, Trudy. She didn't get to you," Megan said. "I'm fine. It's all right."

She was afraid that Trudy was going to start crying in gratitude, so she rose quickly.

"Oh, Lord," she heard Cole murmur, and she quickly knew why.

"What in God's name is going on?" Lisette demanded angrily. "Where are you all?"

Dickens seemed to hear the voice of authority in her cry, and he quickly answered by rote—the soldier accustomed to command. "Come on up, Miss Annalise. We're all here, ma'am."

Cole glared at Dickens, who went white. But it was too late. Lisette Annalise was already stomping up the stairs.

She looked around and seemed to quickly assess the situation. "One of them got in here," she said flatly, and she stared at her assistant.

"It wasn't her fault. It was mine," Megan said. "And we've handled the situation."

"Were you near the diseased?" she demanded, staring at her assistant.

"Um, um—" Trudy stuttered.

"You were!" Lisette said.

The woman might have been working with the archers on the field all day, but now she was dressed elegantly in a silk gown, and her hair was perfectly coiffed in an upsweep. She looked as ladylike and poised as a plantation wife greeting her husband's guests, but there remained that unmistakable air of steel about her.

"Did you see everything that happened?" Lisette demanded.

Cole said, "Lisette, it's over."

"So, no, you didn't. And I believe there was a time when Trudy must have been alone with—whatever creature made its way into this house! Megan, accompany me, if you will. I'm afraid we'll have to have a complete inspection of my assistant, and don't you dare start blubbering, Trudy, that's the way it needs to be and every one of you knows that I'm right!"

"Oh!" Trudy cried out, and she swayed on the sofa, crashing down into a dead faint once again.

CHAPTER FIFTEEN

COLE PACED THE parlor area, waiting for the women to come out of the bedroom. He wished he'd had an argument with which to counter Lisette, but it was true that they needed to make sure that Trudy Malcolm had not been bitten covertly, despite Megan angrily declaring that it wasn't possible for her to have been bitten so quickly.

Lisette was not to be dissuaded, reminding them all that the things could strike with the speed of a cobra and incubate inside someone for a long time.

Dickens alone remained with him, pacing in the opposite direction. Newcomb and his men had taken the corpse back to the graveyard. Betsy would now rest in peace.

The two men had passed each other five times when Cole finally barked out, "Dickens! Grab a whiskey. Quit that walking up and down."

Dickens jumped. He stared at Cole, but was too polite to mention that Cole was doing the same thing.

"I'll have a whiskey, too," Cole said.

"That poor woman. She must be humiliated. She is such a lady."

"Trudy. Trudy Malcolm?" Cole said, pouring the whiskey himself since Dickens seemed to have it in mind that he was an officer.

"She's—she's gentle, she's kind. A true lady."

"Okay." Cole wasn't sure how to respond. He poured the portions of whiskey and handed a glass to Dickens. "Well, don't worry. We...will...all treat her like a lady, have no fear, Dickens."

"Yes, sir. Well, you would, sir. You're always courteous. Not everyone is."

"Well, probably there are those who wouldn't say I was always courteous," Cole told him. "But, we will take special care of Miss Malcolm."

Lisette came out of the bedroom. His bedroom. Since the child-vampire had exploded just inside Megan's bedroom, Lisette had lifted her nose and headed into his.

Neither would prove to be a comfortable place, conducive to a romantic evening, he thought.

"She's clean. Not a mark on her," the Pinkerton said, heading straight for the liquor. She poured herself a sherry and sipped it, then spun around to stare at Cole and Dickens. "But mark my words, gentlemen, this is a brutal war we fight. Nothing can be taken for granted." She looked at Cole, and, apparently, realized the sheriff eyed her like one might an icy dictator. She instantly managed one of her sweet smiles. "You know, Cole, that we can't be too careful. We can't trust in children, and we can't allow ourselves a the naive niceties of life, not all the time." She scanned him with a head-to-toe gaze, and then glanced at the clock. "The general has been waiting supper so that we all might join him, but..." Her voice trailed. "I will tell him another hour, Cole, dear. That should give you time to clean up."

"Yes, Lisette, I will need an hour. Digging up corpses and beheading them has been dirty work."

"Cole, you needn't be so crass," she said, as if she

hadn't just forced her assistant to strip for a puncture search.

"Dickens, you can escort Miss Malcolm back to the general's when she's finished dressing. I'll go on over and inform him that dinner will be delayed."

She swallowed down the sherry and headed for the stairs.

Megan emerged from the room, looking as if she was about to explode. She closed the door behind her, giving Trudy the privacy she surely needed.

"She's gone?" Megan asked Cole.

"Yes. We're invited to the general's for dinner again."

Megan didn't look happy. She glanced at the boyish corporal mindfully, and then decided that she was going to explode anyway. "Lisette Annalise is her own form of monster!"

Dickens gasped and then laughed, and then sobered.

But Cole was glad, because Megan managed to smile. It occurred to him then that it was odd: a vampire *could* strike with the speed of a cobra, yet it hadn't gone for Trudy. Rather, it had rushed to attack Megan when her back was turned.

The church had never been under attack.

The vampires had broken into the schoolroom section of the church while Megan had been there—at her weakest.

He kept quiet then because Dickens was with them, and Trudy Malcolm emerged from the bedroom at last, redressed, but with a face as bright red as that of a lobster. To the young spinster, an inspection must have been mortifying.

"Miss Malcolm," Dickens said politely, "I'm to see you

back to your quarters at the general's lodgings, whenever you're ready to go."

Trudy didn't say anything. She just nodded miserably.

She headed for the stairs, and then stopped. She looked back at Megan. "Thank you."

"I'm sorry, Trudy. I'm so sorry," Megan said.

Trudy smiled weakly. "I'm all right. I mean, I might have been viciously attacked by that child…and…I guess it's better to know for sure that I'm not bitten.… Oh, it's so terrible that a baby like that could be…" She let her voice trail, and then she lifted her chin. "I'm not sorry. We still have to look for the good in people, right?"

"We do have to be very careful these days," Cole said.

"But, no, tenderness and caring are not bad things, Trudy," Megan said.

Trudy nodded, and then started down the stairs. Dickens looked back at Megan and Cole and then followed her out.

They were alone, and for a minute, they stood in silence.

"I'm supposed to wash up," Cole said at last. "For dinner. I suppose I'm not in any shape to dine politely with a general and an actress."

"I'll go out back and fetch more water from the well," Megan offered.

She started for the stairs and he caught her arm. She looked at him, waiting. But he wasn't sure what he wanted to say, and to his relief, she spoke.

"I'm sorry, Cole. I'm really sorry. I just felt that I had to go back there today. And I believe that Daniel is going to prove invaluable to us. He was stricken badly, yet he managed to survive. He didn't attack human beings—he sucked the blood out of rats, for God's sake. It was important. Please, I don't intend to ignore your wishes all of the time. Honestly."

"Just when you think you're right," he said quietly.

She was silent.

"I was right—you were severely weakened today."

"But we don't know what could have happened to him," she reminded him.

He didn't know how to end the argument. He certainly didn't want it going on through the night.

"Didn't you find the last hour strange?" he asked her.

"Oh, yes. Very strange. You didn't have your actress friend making a pathetic girl strip and turn in circles so she could assure herself there were no bite marks. Oh, yes, that was strange—perhaps *acutely uncomfortable* is the better term."

"No, I mean before that. Tell me what happened."

He released her arm. She frowned, thinking, and wandered back toward the liquor table. She poured herself a whiskey neat, and swallowed it in a gulp. She set the glass down.

"I've seen children turned before," she told him.

"But you brought that child into this house."

"Trudy was convinced that she was but a lost child, and I'm sorry to admit, I wasn't as resolute as I should have been. I was a little taken in myself. Betsy was able to maintain tears, to speak, to lure us into believing in her, and I'm usually pretty good at knowing when I see—when I see one of my own kind."

He strode over to her, taking her by the arms. "There are only two people I know who are exactly your *kind*.

You two are nothing like the others." He winced. "I know a few people who have been turned and somehow managed to retain their souls."

She studied his eyes. "Alex's father?" she asked.

He nodded.

"And maybe mine?" she queried softly.

He shook his head. "Megan, a vampire doesn't get as practiced as that child without the help of some kind of a—a mentor, I suppose you could say. When they behave just as beasts, attacking wildly, at anyone, then you know that they were turned, taken for food, and then just deserted. But that child—someone had to teach her to control her hunger to get what she wanted. To lure people to a point where she could attack."

She studied his eyes, and he knew that she agreed with his train of thought.

"But, we've known that…we've known that someone has been out there. Since the Wilderness, at the very least. It seems we can track all this back to that battle. The fires and the carnage were so terrible…no one knew where bodies would be. No one knew who many of the dead were.… Some bodies were burned so badly, no one knew which side they'd been fighting for. And this has all come from then, the best that I can tell," she said.

He nodded. "You're probably right. So, if we're figuring this correctly, there's an older, practiced vampire out there who decided it was time to get into the war."

"On which side?" she asked drily.

"This vampire doesn't care which side. This vampire has started a war against humanity, and intends to take it as far as it can."

She pulled back, studying his face again. "Not my father, Cole. Not my father."

"That's what you want to believe."

"I think I learned a lot about belief, that it's a good thing. Father Costello believes, and his belief keeps him strong."

"Don't mix up faith with what you want to be truth, Megan."

"I'm not doing that!" she protested.

"Look, we don't know if your father still exists, Megan. You want to believe that there's someone really evil out there, and that your father does remain, that he's out there combating the evil. You're stretching the limits of probability."

She shook her head. "But not of possibility."

He looked into her golden eyes, and at the hope there, and he knew that he'd found another argument he wasn't going to win.

"No, not possibility," he agreed. He stepped away from her. "I'll go downstairs. My Federal boys will be back and they'll get enough water in for me to do a nice cold cleanup job. Get a little more rest, if you can. I'll collect you when I'm ready."

TRUST WAS SOMETHING that had to be earned.

Despite everything that had happened during the day, that was the one thought that kept going through Megan's mind. She'd been so gratified that he'd leaped over the remains of the child vampire to check on her that she hadn't realized that there was now a new distance between them. A distance that became evident when they had spoken.

She took another swallow of whiskey, watching the fire that burned in the hearth. It was probably going to be their last night for such simple pleasures as a fire, the comfort of a plush sofa, the solace of a liquor table. But though she enjoyed such niceties, they weren't necessary to her—she'd spent far too long on far too many battlefields, praying for alcohol just to ease some pain, not for fun, and for fire, just because the earth was so damp and the temperature freezing.

What disturbed her was Cole himself, and the fact that he had left her to freshen up, preferring the company of the Union men to a prolonged conversation with her. She tried to reason with herself that there might be a real bathtub down on the ground level. And yes, of course, the well was much closer and it was easier to haul water in on the first level than the second.

And she asked herself if there was anything she might have done differently that day, and there wasn't.

But she had just lost ground again in that effort to be really trusted.

Maybe there was *trust,* and then a different kind of trust.

She looked around the rooms that she had so enjoyed when they had somehow belonged to—or, at least, were borrowed by—just her and Cole. Now, the remnant of ash from a diseased and cunning vampire lay about her bedroom, and she didn't think she could even venture into Cole's again after the humiliation that Lisette Annalise had inflicted on Trudy.

Trudy had stood shaking like a windblown branch while she removed her clothing. It had been worse when she had shed it all and stood in there with her eyes closed in her nakedness. Then, she had been trembling like a terrier who knew that his master was going to beat him again.

It had been horrible to witness, but she didn't doubt that

Lisette would have dragged one of the men in as a second set of eyes if Megan herself hadn't been there. She'd tried to speed up the process as best she could, at least helping Trudy with the many ties on her garments.

Megan leaned back, hating what had happened. Even worse was the breach of trust for Trudy, owing from her simple, desperate determination to give love and help to a little girl.

"Well," she said aloud, lifting her glass to the fire. "At least, I'm not jealous anymore. Any man who might want Lisette Annalise could not be a friend of mine!"

"Here, here!"

She startled and swung around. Cole was back at the landing, grinning at her. She flushed, and she felt slightly warmed and renewed by the light in his eyes.

"Liar! You admired her and found her attractive," she accused him.

"Well, guilty, once. I admired her. I never said that I wanted her."

"But—surely, you did. You don't need to lie. I'm not in the least naive, you know. She does have certain assets."

"Yes, and if she'd never spoken, never looked about a room with her ever-watchful and plotting eyes, yes, possibly, she'd have been appealing. A puma can be beautiful—but far too deadly."

Megan studied her glass. "Would you say that of me?" she asked.

"Are you fishing for a compliment—or worried that I might see you as a puma?"

She looked up, flushing. "I don't fish for compliments."

He smiled and joined her on the sofa. “I'm sure you've never had to,” he said.

“That's nice,” she told him gravely. “But it doesn't answer my question.”

He took the glass from her hands and indulged in a sip himself. “Whoever owned this house certainly enjoyed fine whiskey.”

“Cole?”

He turned to look at her again, and his curious half smile was in place on his features, and she thought that he had to be the most charming and yet most masculine man she had ever met. From just being near him she felt fire ignite within her, and she suddenly wished that she hadn't come to want him, even need him, so very much.

“I think you're amazingly strong and resilient, and that you have been blessed with extra strengths—and weaknesses,” he told her. “If I had ever thought of you as a puma, my love, I'd have never been with you.”

“Cody made you come,” she reminded him.

“Cody never *made* me do anything,” Cole assured her. “Every move I've made, I've made because I chose to.”

“Yes, you chose to, but not because you actually trusted me,” Megan said quietly. “You were going to come no matter what—despite me. We want things for different reasons. You nearly lost a town over an—invasion, or infestation, however we decide to look at it. You came with Cody to D.C. because you knew that you were needed. You came here for the same reason.”

He stood up, walking to look out the window to the street. “The drummer boy,” he said slowly. “I promised that I would find the drummer boy.”

She waited.

He shrugged. "The world is an amazing place, full of hopes, dreams, ideals, indignation, wants and desires. And then people don't agree on what is right and what isn't, and suddenly, you're at war. But then you're looking at the person, the human being, who should be your enemy, and that person is just another human being, flesh and blood, and he's your enemy, but if someone told you to shoot him, stab him face-to-face without battle surrounding you, no cannons blasting and gunfire exploding, no pretty banners and slogans, you'd realize that all we're doing is murdering one another. And worse, your enemy is someone you admire maybe, and someone who even touches something in you that makes you want to achieve greater things, fight the braver fights in life."

He paused, turned and saw that she was watching him curiously, and he looked away again. "I've never claimed to know whose side God might really be on in the war, but I felt the agony that Abraham Lincoln, the *man,* was feeling, and I felt his loss for his child—and his agony that children suffered at all. Well, we saw a little girl tonight who had been coached into being a truly frightening monster. Somewhere out there—or so Mary Lincoln believes—there is a little Confederate drummer boy. He's been turned into a monster, surely, but his soul is crying out for peace. Mary Lincoln's son comes to her in dreams, and he has told her as much. I'm going to find the little drummer boy. *We're* going to find the little drummer boy," he amended. "We're going to stop this."

Megan stood, feeling a new surge of commitment, a sense of real purpose and a need to stand by him. He hadn't left her; he'd been angry, but not angry enough to leave her.

She walked over to him and stood on her toes, brushing his lips with a kiss. "We have to be at the general's now," she said huskily.

He nodded, touching her cheek. "Do you think there's a prayer you'll ever listen to me?"

"Yes," she said, searching out his eyes. "But, it would help if you would listen to me, too."

"I was right, though," he told her, though softly.

"But the way it turned out, I wasn't wrong. Daniel—Daniel fought the ravenous hunger of what he might have become. He has incredible strength, Cole. And those creatures attacked at the school—what happened today would have killed Daniel and the father if we weren't there."

He shook his head. "I believe that the attack on the church came *because* you were there."

"*What?* Why? Why would anyone be attacking me? And, for the sake of the argument, we'll leave my father out of this. Why would anyone be trying to destroy me, particularly?"

"Maybe because you are unique. When your strength is at its greatest, they can rip and tear at you, but you'll heal. You have the power of the vampire, but not its bestial side. I don't know. Maybe I'm wrong. I'm guessing. But someone attacked you in the chapel in D.C., and now here, when they could have easily had Trudy instead," Cole said.

"We're seventy miles away, almost," Megan said, but something about his words made sense to her.

"Listen to me enough to stay close from here on out, please?" Cole asked her. He looked down at her with tenderness in his gaze, and with a husky passion in the lilt of his words.

She moved closer to him, and his arms came around her, pulling her close. He held her there for a moment, her head against his chest, his chin on her head. Then he murmured, "We need to go, before you reply—because trying to convince each other that we're right could become lengthy discussion!"

She nodded, and he eased away from her. She decided not to argue anymore, and he took her hand and they started down the stairs.

Sergeant Newcomb and his men were playing poker at their parlor area table. They waved and bade them a good evening, interested in little but their game.

And yet Megan knew that Newcomb rose and came to the door and then the walk to watch them down the few steps to the general's lodgings.

General Bickford was pleased to see them. He had his aide-de-camp at his side, and while they sat immediately to dine—a very quiet Trudy and a hard-as-nails Lisette with them, once again—Bickford had Dickens read off a list of necessary considerations to defend against a full-scale attack. "Bows and arrows—archery practice to continue. All deceased to be decapitated and buried with Christian rights. Stakes to be carried by all soldiers in the vicinity. Each man to be supplied with several vials of holy water. Instructions given that all wounded undead must be thoroughly dispatched immediately—no prisoners to be taken among these types of assailants."

"Yes," Cole agreed, when the aide-de-camp finished. Megan watched as Cole set down his fork and leaned forward. "Your men now know the basics, but there's more that you must be on guard against. When a being has managed to remain in existence as the undead for a period of time, it can become incredibly clever."

Bickford nodded. "Yes, Miss Annalise told us about the events with the child. We're aware that we must keep a careful guard against even our friends and fellows in the military—and, for some, even their wives, children, mothers and fathers."

"It's easy to be taken in," Megan said.

Lisette Annalise rolled her eyes and sighed impatiently. "Not if one uses a modicum of sense!"

Megan ignored her. "Trust me, General, it's easy to be deceived. Sometimes the diseased are simply maddened, and strike with the bite and rip of a tiger. And sometimes, the infected come, usually at night, but not always, to feed slowly and infect a person bit by bit. When the infected become weak, and then 'die' after a time, they will gain renewed strength as the infection rules the body. Only they will be more cunning than their wild counterparts."

"There were those in Victory, sir, and we never suspected. There was a clan out there with a leader who had taught his pack how to hunt. The leader can be very dangerous. He lets his minions take the risks, create the havoc—and clear the path for him to feed at his leisure."

Bickford nodded sternly. "There's an old local graveyard across the river on Maryland Heights. Some soldiers, returning from the battles wounded and dying, have met their final resting places there. If you're hunting beyond the town, I'd think that might be an area where these *things* might hide out. There's an abandoned, deconsecrated church on the edge of the cemetery, and there is a forest that would afford fine protection for such a monstrous hunter to leap upon its prey—the unwary horseman who might be using the old trail to the bridge. I've studied the terrain, and if there is a place where one of these *clans* might be forming, as you say, I believe this would be it. Dickens knows the terrain, as well. He will guide you well."

"Then that's where we'll begin," Cole said. He hesitated a moment, "I know that you've held a number of captives here. Tell me about the little Confederate drummer boy."

"Ah!" Bickford said, easing back in his chair. "So much has gone on here that I nearly forgot.... That... that was right when all this was starting, wasn't it? That's where it really seemed to begin...."

"The boy died?" Megan asked, but her words were really a statement.

"Yes, well, you've seen how the houses are built up on the hills, and in some there are entrances that rise high above the landscape to the rear." He paused and took a drink of water, slowly, as though lost in contemplation. "Billy! His name was Billy, though I do not remember his surname. In truth, the men loved the drummer boy. They did tease him sometimes, telling him that he needed to grow up and carry a gun rather than a drum if he was to fight *them*—good-natured soldierly jests. He lived with several of the men in the very lodgings where you're staying now, and he had become close to Corporal Nealy. When they were playing a rough game one night, someone pushed him too hard. He went out the back window and fell to the hard rock ground in the rear. He was pronounced dead and was buried. Nealy was inconsolable—he said that he hadn't gone to war to kill children. He began to tell his fellow soldiers that Billy came back to him at night, that he spoke to him—while he floated outside his bedroom window."

"Perhaps I could speak with Nealy before we go," Cole said.

Bickford shook his head. "You saw Nealy already. He was one of the seven killed prior to your arrival. Dickens reported that he has been decapitated and buried, with all due precaution."

"Where was the boy buried? I don't remember such a grave in the church cemetery, and I just went through the entire thing," Cole said.

"That's why I said that his death may be of extreme importance to you now," Bickford said. "He was buried in the old local cemetery across the river—the one where you might find a haven or sanctuary for the diseased. The one where you might find the mass infestation that seems to watch, lurk over Harpers Ferry now, watching—toying with us, perhaps, as cats toy with rats before honing in for the kill."

THE DAYS HAD been long, but Cole was restless when they returned to their lodgings. Bickford had seen to it that they were treated akin to royalty—or very special agents, at the least. There would be little for them to do in the morning except begin their ride out to the heights across the river. Their supplies and their horses would be waiting for them, and they would be given another three soldiers, in addition to Dickens, to make their party a group of ten, small enough to travel lightly and quickly, large enough to battle a fair number of the creatures.

Bickford was comfortable with the knowledge his men had been given. He was confident that his guards could protect themselves through the night—*and* keep an eye out for Confederate forces.

Telegraphs arrived every morning, and they would

head out as soon as the morning's news was received from Washington. Megan was anxious that they should know that everything was well with Cody, Alex, Brendan and Martha and her children.

When they returned, however, Cole started into Megan's room, but she stood still, staring at the doorway. His heart sank, as he wondered if she had decided that the night before had been a mistake.

"There's still a bit of—Betsy…in there," she said.

"Ah. Yes. We'll sleep in the other room."

She offered him a rueful smile. "And all I can see in *that* room is Lisette crudely humiliating poor little Trudy. I know—how ridiculous. We're in the midst of war on many levels, and I don't want to sleep in either bed."

Cole looked around. Newcomb and his fellows always kept their fire fed, and there was a nice expanse of hardwood flooring covered by a fine Persian rug in front of the fireplace. "I think I have a solution."

He set about his task, heading into his room first for the quilt and pillows and sheets there, and laying them down on the floor for a base. Megan saw his intent, and gathered more pillows and bedding herself. When they had finished, they had created a lovely little pallet in front of the hearth, with the fire casting a soft glow upon it.

"Will this do?" he inquired.

"Beautifully."

He stared across their newly made bed at her, and he felt again as if the world with all its horrors could just fade away. For a few minutes, or a few hours, it could be only the two of them, in this strange little haven.

He walked around to her, avoiding their bedding as if it were several feet high. He pulled her to him, entranced by the fire, and for a moment he kissed her, his lips gentle, just touching hers, and he savored the feel of her warmth, the supple feel of her body against his own, the heat from the fire that enveloped and cradled them. But the wonder of sex was still so new and fresh between them that a moment of tender intimacy was not one that could be long maintained, and his kiss went deep and wet and hard, entangling them together until their need ignited and soared.

They were heavily clad, so many articles of clothing to be shed. But that too became a strange art in the arena of lovemaking that night. His coat was quick to go, as was her jacket. And then the tiny buttons at the front of her dress, dainty little things that seemed to tease and taunt and win against the size of his fingers.

They wound up laughing breathlessly as they tried to help each other disrobe, and it soon seemed that their hands were everywhere—caught in a tangle of petticoats and stays, working at her delicate walking boots and his heavier pair. But eventually, clothing was disentangled and tossed aside, and they were on their knees before the fire, and he was certain he'd never seen anything as beautiful or desirable as the woman before him on the pallet of quits and sheets and pillows. They paused there, just touching one another's shoulders and backs in another moment of wonder and tenderness, then they kissed again, and the kiss brought them down into the bedding, and they made love far more wickedly to one another. He knew that he had to feel every inch of the sleekness of her flesh, and she in turn brought him to a rampaging state, nearly madness, with the brush of her fingers and her lips against his body. This was something that truly seemed of another world, a greater world, or a greater existence, as the red-and-gold cast of the flames played upon them, and then that world became vividly carnal and physical as he felt the draw on his body and his sex, as he felt the intimacy of her touch on him, as he returned it, as she rose above him that night, slowly coming down on him, moving and undulating with the fire creating a splendor of her damp skin and seeming to enter into her every movement, and his. The flames seemed to escalate before him and within, and he rose to climax in a wild extreme of need, everything within exploding amid a shattering moment of ecstasy that rippled the length of his body and left him trembling even as she collapsed against him and they lay still before the fire, cooling and still feeling the warmth, gasping, and yet even that sound, like a sweet music, drew them closer and closer. He smoothed her hair as she lay against him.

They dozed.

And they awoke.

And when they did, tangled together, it was easy to lay a simple touch on the other, and start the fires rising again.

Finally, when he awoke much, much later, the fire had died, and the sun was up, and it was time that they rose, and the day began.

THE HORSES AWAITED THEM just outside the home where they had lodged.

The night had been quiet, and, General Bickford assured Megan, the posts from Washington had been good: no activity there.

Megan couldn't help but feel that such might just be the calm before the storm.

Father Costello had come down from the church on the hill to wish them a safe journey, and to read them a blessing before they began, which seemed fine with their entire party, though Private Guilder was Jewish, Private Hanson was Lutheran and only Sergeant Newcomb and a few of the others were actually Catholic. For once, no one seemed to notice the differences between their choices of worship.

Megan had a chance to whisper to Father Costello and ask about Daniel. He assured her Daniel was doing extremely well; it almost appeared that he had never been sick. The two of them, had, however, taken to sleeping in the sanctuary of the church itself.

At last they rode out, with Dickens leading the way, Cole following him, she behind Cole, the others behind her and Sergeant Newcomb, almost a veteran of this action, as he told her jokingly, taking up the rear.

They rode for several hours, crossing the river, then following a winding path that led them deep into forests that managed to remain verdant on the mount despite the endless shelling from various battles. It was midday when they arrived at the plateau where the dead of the area had been buried since the first settlers found rich land in the hills and valleys. The cemetery didn't seem big, but it appeared to have been neglected for years. While dead soldiers might have been sent home to be buried, their loved ones were no longer near enough, nor had the time, to tend to their graves. Weeds and flowers mingled wildly through the headstones and the occasional pieces of funerary art.

The chapel sat at the far edge of the cemetery, where the path ended, the grave sites stretching out beyond it to nearly the edge of the mount. The little chapel seemed forlorn beneath the afternoon sun. The paint was peeling, the windowpanes were cracked and broken, and the front door hung lopsided from one hinge.

The breeze stirred as the riders reined in at the copse of barren land before the chapel and looked at the sad structure and the expanse of graveyard beyond.

Ragged grasses grew in clumps here and there. The entire scene felt eerily lonely and forgotten. As she dismounted, something grabbed Megan's peripheral vision.

She turned quickly to the chapel, and saw nothing.

But cold fingers still crept along her spine.

There had been *something.* A trick of the afternoon light playing with the darkness that hovered in the depths of the surrounding trees?

Or a dark shadow, something that had watched them come?

Something that had been *waiting* for them to come?

CHAPTER SIXTEEN

COLE DECIDED TO make the deconsecrated chapel their camp, and they spent their first thirty minutes or so unpacking supplies, finding a suitable tethering anchor for their horses and setting up. He spoke to the men then, telling him that they knew their business so he wouldn't be giving much in the way of orders. He just wanted them to be certain that they were ready at every minute to fend off a potential attack.

The men were all solemn. They nodded mutely at Cole's words.

And then they set out to explore the graves in the cemetery.

Beneath the jungle of wild grass, wildflowers and weeds, they found a number of graves with loose dirt. Dirt that seemed to have exploded upward from beneath the ground.

The men split into three divisions, the better to move through the cemetery. Though Megan was ready and willing to assist in the digging—and disposal—they insisted that she was best utilized keeping an eye on the forests that surrounded them.

And so she did.

The day was uneventful. Many corpses, appearing fresh, were dispatched according to Cole's prescription. Dickens let out a cry once, certain he had happened upon a vampire. Megan followed Cole to the grave and they stared at the body of a young man in a coffin, one who appeared as if he might open his eyes and speak.

"We'll do our usual, but I don't believe that this fellow has turned," Cole had said.

"Look at him!" Dickens had protested.

Cole had nodded. "I believe that's the work of a talented embalmer."

Newcomb was standing by them, as well. "Aye, lads! Some boys don't make it home, and in other cases… well, it is the embalmers and morticians who are making out like bandits. Every poor mother wants to look one last time on the countenance of her son, and the embalmers across this great country—or countries, as it may still prove to be—have worked endlessly to preserve those sons for their mother's eyes. Yes, see, on the coffin lid? *Tweesdale and Sons, Morticians, Gettysburg, Pennsylvania*."

They were all silent for a moment, then, looking at the soldier.

Then Newcomb had reached into the coffin and pulled out the body, shoving a stake through the heart.

"Never hurts to be certain," he'd said grimly.

"It never hurts," Cole had agreed.

The thing was, Megan wasn't so sure if Newcomb had staked the boy more for precaution, or more because he was irritated at the mortician's handiwork.

At dusk, the men built a cooking fire in the clearing before the chapel and brought out their mess. Megan had dined on hardtack and dried beef before, and she expected little other than sustenance. But one of the men, Wilson, had brought along a supply of herbs and seasoning, and he heated their meals with water, and the dried beef became more like a really edible, if not delicious, meal.

Newcomb carried a harmonica, and he played for a while as the men talked about their homes. They came from all over—New York, Massachusetts, New Hampshire, Maryland and Illinois. They were all fascinated by the West, and Cole told them what life was like out on the frontier. Then the conversation died away, and guard duty was divided for the night.

They'd arranged for Megan to have a little section for herself at the corner of the chapel, complete with a bedroll and a real blanket that they'd packed for her. She thanked them all for the courtesy, but when she lay down she realized that Cole wasn't in the chapel, and she rose, anxious to discover where he had gone.

She found him just outside, staring out over the graveyard.

He set an arm around her shoulder when she approached.

"We didn't find him," he said.

"Who?" she asked, thinking, despite all logic, that he might be referring to her father.

He turned to her and spoke softly. "Billy. We should have found him up here."

"We haven't finished yet," she told him.

He shook his head. "I'd hoped that we'd find him quickly and easily today, that he was seeking shelter here. But more and more I get the feeling that there is someone near us who started all this, someone who had an agenda. An agenda, of course, of death. They've been playing this almost like a military campaign. Create a disturbance in Washington, D.C. Gather a force of minions to attack, and if they're lost, so be it—men die in battles. This creature has loyalty only to itself, and doesn't care how many casualties of its own kind it creates. But it's smart enough to take a number of its victims under its wing, and teach them how to seduce and destroy targeted victims, if not much else. I think that Billy must be under that creature's power, and that he killed the ones who loved him most, first."

"We'll find him," she assured him gently. She hesitated then. "Cole, I thought I saw something when we first got here today."

"What?" he asked, turning to her.

"A shadow," she said.

He nodded, pulling her close. "Every time we dig up a recent corpse, we are thinning the numbers. But you're right. They're still out there." He tightened his hold around her. "Come on. Let's go and try to get some rest. Newcomb is on guard with three others now, and Dickens and I will take the hours closer to morning's light."

"They attack by day, too," she reminded him.

"But they can attack more freely at night. They can be one with the darkness."

She knew he was right. They walked back into the chapel together. Half of the men were sleeping, or resting, at least. Cole would have gone to lie beside them, on the bedroll laid out for him, but Megan held tight to his hand. "We can at least rest together," she said softly.

He hesitated.

"I really don't care in the least what anyone thinks," she told him.

He came with her, and they lay down on the mat on the hard floor together. She tried to rest, glad of his warmth and his presence at her side, and of his arm around her.

But she lay awake, listening. She heard the cries of night birds, and in the far distance, the lonely screech of a bobcat.

Hours passed, and she thought that morning might come without incident.

That was when the vampires struck.

COLE JUMPED TO HIS FEET, instantly alert. He'd heard Newcomb's shout, and had been half-awake anyway, so it was only seconds later that he snatched up a bow and a quiver of arrows and rushed out the door of the church.

Newcomb and his men were defending admirably.

The things had come like winged harpies in the night, joining with the darkness of the sky. He watched as the massive shadows swooped down and was reminded of the battle they had fought at Victory. He realized that this wasn't really an attack—they had come on a scouting mission.

And still, they were deadly.

His days on the Texas plains had taught him the use of a bow, and he could string, aim and fire approximately twelve arrows in a minute. But aiming at flying creatures was difficult. Still, with his speed, they began to fall.

His Union soldiers were indeed battle ready and well trained. They formed an arc before the door to the chapel. The rest of the men spilled out of the church as well, each ready to fight. Bows and arrows, holy water, bowie knives and stakes—each was prepared.

Newcomb took it upon himself to finish off the beings as they fell to the earth, staking the wounded with swift accuracy. Dickens and Megan were busy creating smoking, writhing masses out of the fallen that had not yet been struck in the heart.

It was all a cacophony at first—a massive invasion of flapping noises. At times the things indeed appeared giant winged bats. The men shouted to one another words of warning, and in the first assault, it seemed that they worked as one, arrows bringing the creatures down, water pinning them and stakes finishing them off.

Then, suddenly, there was silence.

Newcomb let out a holler of victory. "We beat 'em back, boys! We beat 'em back!"

The others agreed, and Cole was reminded of the Rebel cry that had spilled across many a battlefield.

A shout that had too often ended in the gasp of death.

"*Hold it! Hold it!* That was just the first. Make sure you're rearmed. They'll be coming again."

The area was strewn with corpses. Some were little but bone and ash, and some appeared nearly as they had in life, as boys, dead boys, already abused by the brutality of war. All of them young, all of them some poor mother's son.

Cole looked over at Megan. She was just a few feet away, silent, still and listening.

"Is it over?" he asked her.

She shook her head. "It's just begun," she said softly.

They waited again, still and on the alert.

Cole could feel the men around them growing restless. "Steady," he said quietly.

Another few minutes passed.

Then Megan cried out, "I hear them—they're coming again! Be ready!"

This wave was larger than the last. But there were ten of the party arrayed in a semicircle, and they caught most of the creatures in the air. One landed and charged Newcomb, but the hardened sergeant was ready, thrusting his razor-honed stake deep into the chest of the vampire-soldier charging into him. The animal stopped, pinned on the stake, writhing. Newcomb shoved harder and it fell.

But more and more of them were reaching the ground. Cole drew out his knife, slashing with all his might against the throat of a Union artilleryman. The head fell to the side at an awkward angle.

"Cole!" Megan cried, and he spun around as the artilleryman fell, only to discover a Confederate cavalryman about to pounce on his back. He reached for a vial of holy water with a split second to spare and threw the contents of the vial into the man's face. It let loose with a horrible scream, writhed and shook and began to steam and smoke, and fell to the ground.

It had become all hand-to-hand battle.

Cole slashed through another several men, approaching one who had pinned a terrified Dickens to the ground. Cole ripped his throat out by grabbing his hair, pulling back his head and slicing viciously. The man fell and Dickens crawled out from beneath him.

He turned to see that Megan was surrounded—and drew another arrow through the bow he whipped off his shoulder, taking down one and then the next. Megan had the last, and, as they fell, she sprinkled more and more of the holy water on them until it seemed that the ground was nothing but a pool of viscous, smoky oil. A cry from Dickens and a sense that someone was behind him gave Cole fair warning; he didn't turn, just used both hands to shove a stake backward in a savage motion. He hadn't taken the creature in the heart, but he wounded it enough to turn and jab the stake in properly.

He rose, looking around, ready for the next combatant.

But there was none. The clearing was quiet again.

The men were silent, alert, twitching—ready for the next assault.

"Is everyone all right?" Cole asked. His voice seemed loud and harsh in the darkness and the sudden silence that surrounded them.

"Sound off!" Newcomb commanded, and the men did so.

They were all accounted for. They still stood, waiting. But nothing else happened. Nothing else came at them.

There were at least thirty creatures that had come for them, thirty that now were dead in truth. Thirty—and all of them soldiers, from the North and from the South. Cole thought drily that Maryland, Virginia, and now West Virginia, were all border lands, so it was natural that men of both loyalties should lie dead upon the soil.

He removed the last head and looked to the sky. The first light of morning was beginning to appear from the east.

It had been a long night.

He surveyed the dead and fallen again.

Still, there was no drummer boy among them.

THE MEN WERE COURTEOUS to a fault. They accepted the fact that Megan was good at what she did; she could defend herself with the best of them. But they were still men, and she was still a lady in their eyes, and they wouldn't accept her help in the final dispatch, or in hauling the remnants of the bodies out to the cemetery.

As morning dawned fully, Newcomb and his fellows

built a great bonfire, throwing full corpses, and what remained of other corpses, into the blaze. And though they might have been destroyed as *something else,* the smell of the burning flesh was sickening—human—and Megan found herself remembering the Battle of the Wilderness, where it all seemed to have begun.

Cole stood with his hands on his hips, watching the blaze, and she stood beside him. Finally, she had to turn away.

They spent the rest of the afternoon walking the graveyard again, searching through the dead. But that afternoon the corpses they dug up had been long gone, and were in such serious stages of decay that there was no possibility they could rise by night.

Later that day, Megan realized that she couldn't stand the stench any longer—it seemed to linger on her. Dickens told her of a creek nearby, a freshwater creek that eventually flowed into the river below them.

"We can't split up," Cole said, frowning when Dickens noted that he could lead Megan to some privacy at the creek.

"Well, sir, I'd say that we're all beginning to be a bit—disgusting," Dickens said, looking at his hands. "It's not the dirt, though. It's—it's the bits of body clinging to me and the smell from the fire."

"Well, then, we'll all go together," Cole said.

Megan looked at him and arched a brow.

"We can find a bit of privacy for you—where we're all still within an easy holler," he said.

She smiled. Even in the midst of battlefields, she'd never been in a situation where men had to travel en masse to bathe.

"We could split up," Newcomb suggested.

"I don't like us being apart," Cole told him.

Megan touched Cole on the arm and said quietly, "Perhaps Sergeant Newcomb is right. I'm not sure we should leave our supplies untended."

He nodded, smiling slowly. "You're right."

She grinned in return. "Why, thank you."

It was decided. Newcomb, Hodges, and the three newcomers would stay behind while Dickens, Cole, Megan, and Banter and Briar made their way to the creek. It wasn't far—just a hundred yards downhill and through the trees.

The creek, splashing over rocks and falling downward toward the river, was beautiful. The water was cool and refreshing, and the air was clean. They set up a little area with a four-foot pool for Megan to have to herself while the men were upstream but a few yards, though divided by a slight bend in the creek and a thatch of trees.

She could hear them laughing as she enjoyed the brilliant blue of the water herself, and it made her smile. She scrubbed her hair with the bit of soap she'd been given, scrubbed her body and dipped low into the shallow water, shivering at the chill of it but delighted at the cleanliness it allowed her to feel.

She rose, smoothing back her wet hair, and opened her eyes.

There was a *whooshing* noise from above her. She ducked again instantly, and rose just as swiftly, looking around herself.

There were shadows. Shadows in the air, despite the sunlight. They were moving together toward the trees, and they seemed to be tumbling together as they disappeared into the canopy of the branches.

She blinked, and the sight was gone.

She blinked again, and the heavy sense of unease remained with her. She was facing the trees, and she could have sworn, again, that she saw something, heard something, and that there was movement in the forest.

"Cole!"

She shouted his name, running from the water, heedless of the rocks and pebbles beneath her bare feet. She reached the shore and didn't bother to dry herself, but scrambled into her man's shirt and breeches, staring up at the trees.

Cole, with nothing but a shirt wrapped around his waist, came running around the soggy bank, nearly crashing into her. "What? Where?" he demanded quickly as he took her into his arms.

"There—there's something in the trees right there. Something that has been watching us!"

She stumbled back into her boots as the men—in their breeches and with their knives at the ready—came in Cole's wake.

"Let's get back to the embankment on the other side, get ourselves well armed," Cole said, drawing her with him.

Dickens stood protectively next to Megan while Cole gathered the rest of his clothing. "Stick together!" Cole ordered, heading into the woods with Megan at his side.

"What did you see, exactly?" he asked her.

"A shadow," she told him.

They walked in formation. That way, one of them looked in each direction. Cole paused suddenly, studying a branch that was newly broken, the green of the stem showing them that it hadn't been exposed long.

Megan looked around. "There! Just there, ahead!"

She'd seen it again. The shadow. Only it had flowed strangely. It had been real.... It had been substance.... It had been hiding in the trees. And when it moved, it had done so with a swish, as if it had moved...as if it wore shirttails that flowed behind it.

She ran forward, heedless of the others, but when she reached the location, Cole at her heels, there was nothing there.

"Megan!" he called. "Don't do it—don't go ahead like that! There's safety in numbers!"

"I'm sorry, Cole," she said. "I didn't mean to rush ahead so far."

He nodded. "I know you can handle yourself. But we all need help now and then, especially during the kind of onslaught we faced last night."

"Of course."

The others joined them. They started forward again, winding through the trees back toward the chapel rather than taking the established path.

A startled cry behind them caused them to spin around. Dickens and Newcomb's man, Hodges, remained.

The other soldier was gone.

Dickens shouted, "Henry, Henry, where are you?"

There was silence. The breeze didn't even ruffle a leaf.

"What in the name of Lucifer—he was here, he was right behind me, I could almost feel his breath on my neck!" Dickens said. "He cried out, and now he's gone! Vanished, as if into thin air."

"Tighten up, and don't split up!" Cole commanded. He looked at Megan. "Listen to me now, I beg of you—listen to me!"

She nodded, her heart heavy. The shadow had taken Henry.

They turned back and searched for the man. Almost arm in arm, they stayed that close, but they found no sign of Henry or any creature lurking in the woods. After what must have been hours, they headed back to the chapel with heavy hearts. They had to explain to Newcomb and his men.

"Maybe he'll make his way back," Dickens said hopefully.

"It was a mistake," Cole said flatly as they spoke with Newcomb, still on guard at the door to the chapel. "We've had a man picked off, and we never saw what happened, what took him. We searched—and he's gone."

"It was Henry," Dickens said mournfully. He hunched down, looking ill. "It was Henry. His wife just had a baby. A baby boy."

They were all silent.

"Well, then," Newcomb said at last. "I guess the rest of us will just stay dirty." He looked at Cole. "We need more men."

"It's too late to head down for reinforcements now," Cole said. "It'll be dark in another hour. It's time to shore up for the night. I think we're going to take a different approach. Megan, we need a seal of holy water around the chapel, maybe additionally around the windowsills, too, just in case. We're not going to fight them in the open. If they come tonight, we're going to shoot them out of the sky from within, and clean up when the major onslaught is over—when the light comes in the morning. They can be up and about in the light, but they're not as strong as they are in the night, not the wild ones.... Maybe, though, they'll all just let us get some rest tonight instead."

Megan nodded, and went into the chapel for the holy water. She started carefully, as they needed to guard their supply, but did her job thoroughly as she trailed a tiny stream of water around the circumference of the chapel.

She wanted to talk to Cole, but he was working with the men, setting up guard stations at the window and at the door. Eventually he pronounced them as ready as they would ever be, and that it was time for mess.

That's when she realized that she was starving.

The fire was lit again just outside the chapel door, and the men set about preparing a meal, though far more quietly than they had the night before. Given her cup of mushy hardtack and seasoned meat, Megan sat beside Cole and spoke softly.

"Cole, I saw it again today—there were two shadows. Two of them. One was coming for me. The other was trying to protect me."

He looked at her, and he set an arm around her shoulders. "Megan, your father could have caught a ship to Europe by now, for all you know."

"But he hasn't. I can feel it. But—"

"Megan, when they attack, we can't just stop and ask them all if they might happen to be your and Cody's father."

"I know that, Cole. But if one of them is my father, he *won't be* attacking us," she implored him to understand.

He didn't answer. He pulled her a little closer. He looked at her and smiled. "Your hair smells good."

She smiled in return. "And you smell delicious."

"Good enough to eat?"

"Of course."

He didn't allow himself much of a moment of tenderness. He eased from her and rose, gathering her all-purpose bowl and his own to their small wash bucket to rinse out. When he was done, he addressed the others. "We'll feed the fire now and let it burn as long as it will. They don't like fire."

The men rose, gathering bracken and branches to keep the fire going as the darkness of the coming night settled down upon them in earnest.

Megan caught Cole's hand as he surveyed the night sky and waited for the soldiers to finish their task.

"There's something more, Cole."

He gazed down at her, his forehead wrinkling into a frown. "What?"

"I saw a skirt."

He stared at her, truly puzzled. "What?"

"When I ran ahead today…when I'd seen something in the trees directly in front of us, I saw a long fabric trailing the shadow. I think it was a skirt. Cole, our evil creature could be a woman."

He sighed, grimacing. "Megan, you don't like Lisette. I understand that. I don't like many of her ways myself. But to accuse her of being the mastermind of all vampires is stretching the imagination a bit, don't you think?"

"First, I didn't accuse Lisette. And secondly, if she's old and practiced at her existence, she could very well have fooled us all. But I wasn't implying that it was Lisette. I'm simply telling you."

He nodded in agreement, but she thought that he doubted her words. Then a curious cast came to his eyes and she almost backed away.

Yes, it could be a woman. She was a woman, and he knew the truth about her.

She turned away and walked into the chapel, taking up a position at one of the windows. They were down to nine. The chapel had ten windows, two in front, two in the back and three on each side. She watched as the men boarded up the rear, hacking up pieces of broken pews to nail across the windows. They determined to leave the front unbarricaded, should they need to flee amid fighting, but also as a lure, where they could focus their firepower on the horde if it came through all at once.

It seemed, as the last nail drove home, that the lanterns inside did nothing to ease the cast of darkness and shadow now upon them. The men took up stances at the windows, vials of holy water toyed with in some of their hands.

Hours passed. Cody gave alternate men leave to doze at their posts.

More time passed.

And then, it came. The attack.

But it wasn't as it had been the night before.

They heard a cry from the copse outside the chapel door.

Dickens was guarding at one of the front windows.

"It's Henry!" he cried with delight. He started for the door.

Cole caught him by the shoulders, swinging him around. "Dickens—it's not Henry. Listen to me, and listen well. It's not Henry—not the Henry you knew anymore!"

Megan came to look out the window, and she saw that Henry was standing there, indeed, just as Dickens had said. He stood casually by the remnants of fire, where only the embers still glowed red. He set his hands on his hips and called out to them.

"Hey! What's the matter with you all? I was lost, you idiots, and you left me out there. But I've found my way back and you've barricaded the place against me! Hey, come on, you asses! Open the door, let me in!"

Cole picked up his bow, slinging a quiver over his shoulder. He took out one of his specially hewn arrows and set his sights on Henry.

"Stop!" Dickens begged. "What if it *is* Henry? What if he really was lost."

"Dickens, it can take several bites for a man to become a vampire, or a good strike can turn him immediately, and he's been gone now a while. We have to…to do what we have to do."

"But he sounds just like Henry!" Dickens said.

"It's not Henry, son," Sergeant Newcomb said.

Cole was about to fire.

But none of them was quick enough to stop Dickens. He threw the door open and ran heedlessly to his comrade.

What happened then happened so quickly that Megan wasn't sure of what she saw herself. Dickens nearly reached Henry. Henry opened his mouth and let out a cry like a wolf, and he looked at Dickens with fangs exposed and saliva dripping. He lifted off the ground and started toward the hapless soldier.

But Cole had been ready.

His arrow flew, catching Henry dead center in the heart.

Henry seemingly froze in midair for a minute, and then dropped to the ground.

"Get the hell in here, now, Dickens!" Newcomb bellowed, and the young corporal, frozen in shock, his jaw agape, didn't even blink.

"Now!" Newcomb shouted.

Cole burst past Newcomb, going for the young man. He grabbed him by the cuff of his shirt and jerked him back, dragging him to the chapel door. Just as they reached it, a flurry of noises arose from the trees and everything seemed to come at them at once—flopping, massive-winged shadows.

Cole nearly threw Dickens inside and turned just in time to fend off one of the shades. Megan backed from the window, her heart in her throat as she lobbed vial after vial of holy water. The men had sprung to, as well, and they used their stakes and axes against the onslaught of wings.

The area at the door began to smoke, sizzle and steam. Cole came back in and slammed the door in his wake; they could no longer afford to keep an opening. All their own fire would have to be through the windows. Hodges understood the situation immediately; he hurriedly dragged one of the remaining pews to set against the door.

The fluttering suddenly came to a dead stop.

Dickens was on the floor, but he quickly stood up, his stance tall.

"For the love of God, forgive me!" he said. "So help me God, I will not fail or falter again, or be caught off guard."

"Get back to your post. They're coming again," was all Cole said.

The men ran to their window posts, ready when the siege began.

The horde struck the left side of the chapel, and Megan raced to join the men there, a quiver of arrows over her shoulder and a sack of holy-water vials in hand.

"To the right!" Newcomb cried.

"Hold your posts. Let Megan be the reinforcement," Cole ordered.

"Watch it!"

"There, there! Right there!"

"Steady boys…steady…"

And so they fought, and so the voices went on for the next thirty minutes. They had realized quickly any weakened position would be targeted, and that none could be left unmanned for too long. Megan moved from position to position, throwing herself past Hodges when she saw that one had gotten partway through the window. She felt the scrape of a fang against her arm, but she knew it would do her little harm; she merely prayed that Hodges, or the other men, hadn't seen it.

When it ended, she was exhausted. And yet they had to maintain their vigilance, for another attack could commence at any minute.

"How long until daylight?" one of the soldiers asked wearily.

"Just another hour, son, just another hour," Newcomb said.

They waited.

But once again, they would find the mode of attack had changed.

Megan heard it first. A beat. A drumbeat. She saw Cody stiffen, and they all listened to the steady rat-tat-tat-tat of a drummer boy's drum, the beat that led men as they marched into war.

The sound came right up to the chapel door.

And then it stopped.

CHAPTER SEVENTEEN

COLE HEARD THE drumbeat, and he knew that he had been right.

The drummer boy hadn't perished in the fall. He had been found by whatever vampire or vampires had been pulling the strings since the Battle of the Wilderness. He had been assumed dead, buried alive and revived by the effects of the vampire's bite.

Cole felt Megan at his side, and he knew that her gentle touch was a warning that they were all susceptible to their emotions, and that he couldn't afford to be fooled by this.

But he didn't intend to make any mistakes. He had never promised that he would find the boy and return him to the loving arms of his parents. He had vowed that he would find the boy, yes, and then allow him to lie in peace, in the arms of God or whatever great power ruled over them all, yes. But not to live.

He looked out the window, and there was the boy. He was in the tattered remnants of his regiment's uniform, his kepi in place over dusty brown hair. He showed his youth as he just stood there, picking up a beat once again. Rat-tat. Rat-tat-tat. Stop.

He smiled, a boyish grin.

"You've been looking for me!" he called out. "I'm here. You fools. I've been looking out for you, although

I did think about a bit of revenge. I mean, you all would deserve it, you know? I was a prisoner, and you teased me, and you made me cry, which was hard. I'm twelve. I wanted to be a man, and you made me cry. I wanted to be a man, and I was only a boy."

He waited, and then drummed out a beat once again.

"Come out! Look at me! I'm not broken to bits anymore. I've healed. I'm much, much better."

He looked so much like a regular child to Cole.

"Listen. This is the truth! I should have smothered, the way you all buried me so quickly. But I got out of that louse-infested shroud and dug free. Oh, come on out now. You teased me, but you liked me. I'm a good kid. I just wanted to go home to my mother. Please…come on. I'm just a kid."

Cole found himself mesmerized for a moment, watching the boy. He looked like a kid. Just like any kid. Just like dozens of boys who had been nothing but *children,* and yet had been drawn into the whoop and holler of the war effort, drawn to dreams of valiant victory.

A kid. He didn't even have a hint of growth of a beard on his cheeks.

"Cole," Megan whispered softly at his side.

He nodded.

The boy grinned and started tapping on his drum again.

"Come on, fellows. You said that no one could keep a beat like me. I want to be your friend again. I want to sit around while you drink your whiskey and tell your tall tales. Please, I'm well, but I'm lonely, and I'm afraid out here. There are monsters in the night, you know. Terrible monsters. I've tried so hard to hide from them."

Newcomb groaned softly.

Megan's touch on Cole tightened.

He exhaled and drew an arrow from his quiver.

He took slow and careful aim.

And he fired.

And caught the boy dead in the heart.

The boy didn't fall. He let out an unholy screeching sound and began to shake where he stood, the hands holding the drumsticks then causing an erratic and horrible beat. A pale miasma of ash and shadow formed around him.

"Jesus!" Newcomb said, and crossed himself.

Only after all that did the boy fall, and it seemed as if Cole heard a collective sigh from all those within the chapel.

There was silence then, broken at last when Dickens asked, "Should we go and get him, make sure that it's finished?"

Cole shook his head slowly. "No. They might still be there, trying to draw us out. It's almost daylight. We'll wait until then."

They eased back down at their positions. Megan slunk low next to Cole. She took his hand and smiled sadly as she looked at him. "You fulfilled your promise," she told him.

He nodded glumly.

"We'll get Father Costello over here," she said, "and he can say a service for all of the men, and it won't matter what their faith was."

He looked at her then, reached out and cradled her cheek. He wondered that she could have the blood of such monsters running in her veins, and be so deeply concerned for the well-being of others, so gentle and so tender in her outlook at life...*beneath* the surface, he reminded himself. And he almost smiled, thinking of the very ferocious young woman he had first met. But Cody had fought his inner demons by going to medical school—Megan had followed men onto the field of battle, not to kill, but to try to heal when she could.

But he knew then that he had uncovered much more than just her softer side. He wasn't sure how it had happened. Lust could exist at first sight, but not love. He had never known anything as sexually glorious and satisfying as sleeping with her. And he knew he loved her then. As they sat in the poor, abandoned chapel with death all around them, he knew that it had been something that had grown bit by bit, when they talked, when he had watched her move, when he had seen the beauty within her heart and her soul.

He touched her cheek, ready to say so—

"Thank God!" Newcomb's gruff voice suddenly boomed through everything, even Cole's thoughts. "The daylight is here at last. Men, we've got to divide, catch a few hours' sleep. Those things don't need rest to stay alert, but we do."

Cole squeezed Megan's hand and rose. "Quick catnaps, fellows. We're heading back down to Harpers Ferry. We haven't the manpower to fight night after night—we're going to get reinforcements. We'll catch two hours of sleep, divide up and one hour per man. Then we'll be ready to ride on down."

He walked to the door and opened it. Morning had come quickly.

He walked over to the body of the drummer boy, and he knelt down.

And he did what had to be done.

MEGAN DARED TO catch the first hour's rest, and she was surprised to wake and discover that she had slept soundly, through the entire two hours. She rose quickly, noting that Newcomb had the men packing in a manner that allowed each man to easily access certain supplies. She hurried out to find Cole.

He was standing by the horses, looking puzzled.

"What is it?" she asked him.

"The horses," he said.

"What about them?" she asked.

"All those hungry vampires out there—but they didn't attack the horses. A horse would be one really nice supply of blood."

"We're meant to take the horses," she said. "They've been left on purpose, so that we can ride out through the trails, supposedly."

He nodded. He looked back at the chapel. "When we leave here, we'll definitely be under attack in the open. But if we stay…we'll run low on supplies, low on food and low on manpower, because even if our fellows are hardened and battle weary, they'll have to have some real sleep."

She hesitated. "I can go," she told him.

He smiled, but took her by the shoulders. He brushed her lips lightly with his own, a kiss that wasn't passionate, just brief and tender. "Megan, you can't ride down by yourself. I know that you are amazing in your abilities, and I even know that a single strike wouldn't hurt you much. But they'll attack en masse, and there's no way even you could protect yourself from a horde falling upon you—none of us could."

She stiffened her shoulders, loath to point out the differences between them, and yet knowing that he was right and something must be done.

"Cole," she said quietly, earnestly, "I can move as they move. I can become shadow, and I can—I can be there before they've known that I've gone."

He winced, lowering his head.

Yes, in essence I am one of them, she thought.

He looked at her with his grimace set, and still, somehow, it seemed to catch at her throat and her heart, and hurt to the core. She didn't want to leave—she definitely didn't want to leave his side. She was so afraid that when she did so, she would never find her way back again. In fact, she realized that since she'd met Cole she hadn't even shifted out of her human form, so secretly scared she'd been—deep under the surface—that such a change would stop her return to this intriguing, wonderful man. But now that she was certain that she was more than just a physical challenge, or even a physical plaything, to him, the prospect of taking another form wasn't as terrifying.

"Cole, it's really our only hope," she told him.

He shook his head. "You have eight other men in that little chapel who would never dream of letting you go."

She turned around to head for the chapel.

"Hey, where are you going?" he called after her.

"To tell them the truth!" she yelled back over her shoulder.

"No!" He came running after her, catching her by the shoulders. "I've taught them not to give in to women or children, Megan. If they think that you're—what you are, they may fall upon you and kill you, thinking they're doing the only right thing!"

She hesitated. He had a point.

"Cole, we have to have reinforcements, or more will die," she told him.

"No. I will think of something else," he said. "I've got the men aware that our formation must be tight, and that we probably will be attacked. We'll make it," he said firmly.

"You know I'm your only chance," she whispered.

He drew her into his arms.

"Then I'll die happy with you." He released her and headed back to the chapel.

She watched him go, and it seemed that her heart had already been torn in pieces.

But it didn't matter. It couldn't matter. This time, she knew she was right.

She took her horse quickly. She had to have taken her mount, or the men would be suspicious.

She rode down the trail, listening, aware. But the attackers were watching the chapel.

Waiting for the men to move.

She left her mount near the foot of the main hill, gave the mare a slap to head her on in the direction of town, and paused, concentrating, summoning forth those feelings she'd neglected for a little while now, willing the change to take place.

When it did, she flew, and with all speed.

THE LAST OF THE SUPPLIES were gathered, with the men having checked and double-checked the position of the bows, quivers, stakes and holy water they all carried on their bodies. The packhorse was being loaded, and they were nearly ready.

That was when Cole called out for Megan, and she didn't answer.

He hurried over to Newcomb. "Where's Megan?"

Newcomb frowned, his grizzled face caught in a mask of concern and consternation. "She was with you, Cole. Last I saw her, she had awoken and was heading out to you."

Cole marched out to the burial ground, now little more than a field of dug-out dirt, hacked-up coffins and the remnants of the cremation pyre they had ignited.

"Megan!" he cried, and his voice carried on the wind, but there was no answer.

And he knew.

His fists tightened at his sides and he fell to his knees. He wasn't angry.

He was frightened.

He heard Newcomb running up behind him. "Sir! Her horse is gone."

He nodded.

"Tell the men to get back into the chapel, Terry. Megan has gone for reinforcements."

"What? She'll never make it, sir! We've got to go after her!"

"No, Terry, she's with us because she's so good. We have to give her a chance. We have to be prepared to end this thing, here, tonight."

SHE DIDN'T HEAD FOR the town itself straightaway. Instead, she went to the graveyard and landed as shadow. It was lonely and desolate: the perfect place to find her form again. There she willed herself back to look like what she had always sworn she really was.

She paused for a moment, finding her strength, because it had been a long, hard, speeding journey, especially since she hadn't fed or slept much.

But she couldn't tarry long, so she headed to the church and found Daniel making repairs to the roof with Father Costello.

Daniel saw her first, and there might have been something in the way she was walking that alarmed him. From up on the ladder he cried out and quickly came down to her. He caught her as she swooned to fall. Father Costello rushed forward, as well. They led her into the church and sat her down on a pew. "Megan! What's happened…the men, Cole…is all lost?" he queried desperately.

She shook her head. "No, no…one man is lost. And the others will be. They need reinforcements. It's a full-fledged war up there, Father, and our men are starting to run out of supplies."

"There's blood left in the cellar," Daniel told Father Costello. "I'll get it."

He left her with Father Costello. "I've done what you asked—we have a healthy supply of holy water here, and there are stakes and hammers, hatchets, swords, mallets, down with the Union garrison. We'll get word to General Bickford. It's been completely quiet since you've been gone, so he'll readily set out another troop.… But how did you get here?"

She looked into his deep, concerned eyes. "You don't want to know," she told him.

He smiled at her. "You've been safe in my church, Megan. There is nothing that will ever convince me that you are not one of the most beloved creatures of our Father."

Daniel came with a large canteen filled with blood. She drank deeply. Pig's blood. Not her favorite, but it was filled with whatever need she had for the substance.

"There's no time to waste," she said. Father Costello

helped her to her feet and started to escort her on her own out the door.

"Wait!" Daniel called.

They both turned. "Daniel, they might take you as a Southern prisoner," the priest warned.

Daniel shook his head. "I'm just a mountain boy, Father. Megan found me on her way here, and I helped her to the town. It makes sense."

As the three of them went down Church Street, one of the general's aides saw them coming and rushed into the headquarters. Before they even reached the door, General Bickford was in the street, walking toward her.

"Megan! How are you here—alone?"

"I ran out, General, because I'm familiar with this type of terrain, and because, frankly, we all know the men wouldn't concede on their own to let me come. This is Daniel, from the mountain. He helped get me here." She took a moment to catch her breath. "Please, sir, it's imperative that we get men up to the heights immediately. The troop has done well, but the—the *nest,* the core of the clan, the real monsters—*are* up on the heights. They have to have help."

General Bickford looked at her gravely for just a split second before calling out an order. "Do it! We'll take twenty men—Company A—armed and out of here in a hour!" He looked at his aide. "Get Lieutenant Dawson, and get it done!"

"Yes, sir!" the man replied, and ran off to do as bidden.

"Daniel, eh?" Bickford said, looking at the young man accompanying Megan and the priest.

"Daniel Whitehall, sir, at service in this battle," Daniel said.

Megan noted that he didn't say "at *your* service." Bickford noted it, too, probably.

"And you know the terrain, eh?" Bickford asked.

"Like the back of my hand, sir!"

"Fine. You'll lead. You, young lady, will get into my quarters and get some rest. We'll handle it from here."

"No, please, I have to go back," she told him. "General, this is what I do!"

"Inside and upstairs, young lady, and there are no two ways about it. I'm the general, and you will take orders."

She thought about arguing; it would be useless.

She looked at Daniel, and she knew that he was aware she could easily slip out when she chose and beat them all there.

"I'll take a wagon up the road for the holy water," he said. "Father Costello has been filling vials nightly."

"Do it, son," Bickford said, and Daniel turned with Father Costello to carry out the task.

Megan left them and went to the general's quarters and up the stairs, figuring she would have to escape Lisette Annalise and Trudy Malcolm.

But neither woman was there.

She paced restlessly, watching the preparations from the window, and waiting. At last, the multitude of men, heavily armed with the unique weapons, rode out of town. She watched them go, and restlessly, she waited.

She wondered again where Lisette might be, hoping she wouldn't reappear at a most inopportune time.

Then she remembered her dream. Her dream of Lisette Annalise walking toward Cole.

And she knew that she had to hurry.

BOTH HENRY AND THE DRUMMER BOY had been removed from the clearing in front of the chapel. They rested now, a true rest, in the graveyard—albeit it in pieces.

As the first hours of the morning went by, Cole ordered the men to eat and rest the best they could. With Megan gone for reinforcements, he had taken the supplies they were going to need in from the packhorse, but filled the bags and boxes the horse carried with various pieces of ripped-up lumber from the chapel, so that whoever—or whatever—watched them would think that the troop was still preparing to move.

"When will it come, Cole?" Sergeant Newcomb asked him.

"Not for a while, I don't believe. They'll wait a few hours, thinking that we're still preparing to get down the mountain. Rest. Get all the rest that you can."

Newcomb shook his head. "Megan," he said mournfully. "She'll never make it."

"Yes, she might."

"Why did she go? Why did she risk herself so?" Newcomb demanded.

Cole answered him quietly, but with conviction. "She felt that she had to, Sergeant. She felt that she had to. And she might have been right."

The sun rose to its zenith. Noon came, and went. As it did, the men were weary enough to rest and doze at their positions.

"Anytime now," Cole began to warn them. "They'll realize that we're not leaving and there's not enough daylight left to get down the mountain. They'll come at any time."

The words were barely out of his mouth before

Gerald Banter let out a cry. "From the west, from the west—they're coming!"

Megan wasn't with them to reinforce the alternate sides of the church as she had before. Cole had to trust Newcomb to take the front and hurry from window to window as the attacks came at them in swift fury. Cole used arrows as long as he could, but the enemy was coming at him far too quickly and managing to get far too close for them to suffice, no matter how swiftly he shot. He was forced to cast down the weapon, and take up with a bayonet, striking savagely and furiously again and again, all while keeping his distance. His arms ached; the bayonet attacks wounded, but didn't kill, and he had to keep both arms and hands moving at immense speeds as he plunged and cut and then made strategic use of the holy water.

The dead piled up at the windows. Others continued to use their arrows. Sometimes their arrows struck but didn't kill, and the beings would rise again and head for the windows. Sometimes Cole dared reach out to stake them, and sometimes he did not. Sometimes he used precious holy water, and sometimes he was able to stab savagely through their hearts and then quickly retreat before a counterattack came.

One flew through a window at Cole—its arm was quickly hacked off as Newcomb brought down his ax head. Cody impaled another flying creature hovering just outside the window with a stake from his right hand, and managed to catch a wounded one with a vial of holy water from the other.

After a few more tense moments, the attack ceased.

All was quiet.

"Hold, boys. Hold—and be ready," Cole said.

Another hour passed. The men were tiring, the tension of waiting adding to their exhaustion.

Newcomb gripped his arm and looked at Cole. "If they take me, if I'm…injured, you'll do what needs to be done?"

"They're not going to take you, Newcomb. We have to believe. Have faith."

Newcomb grimaced. "If you're first, I'll do you the same courtesy."

Then, he was stunned by the plaintive sound of a feminine voice at the door. "Hello! Cole, Newcomb—Dickens! What is going on here? Where is everyone?"

Cole quickly moved to look out the window. To his utter amazement, Lisette Annalise, beautiful in her riding outfit, sidesaddle atop a fine mount, was in the clearing before the chapel, her assistant, the ever-suffering Trudy Malcolm, just beyond her on a far less pretentious steed.

"Jesus, save me!" Newcomb muttered. "In the midst of all this, that woman makes it up to the mount? Is she insane?"

Newcomb started toward the door. Cole caught his arm. The other men were rising, Dickens among them. He came forward quickly. "Sir, we've got to get her in here, quickly! Those things could come back at any time. And she can shoot—I've seen her. She's here now, we've got to get her in and tell her the score!"

"No, stop! I'll go out to cover them, and if anything happens, you men get the door shut and barred again, and pray that more men get here!" Cole commanded.

Newcomb pulled the pew-bolt from the door and Cole

opened it. He waited for Lisette to dismount and come to the door.

"Cole Granger, what is the matter with you? I've come up here, and you don't even come out to assist a lady? Good Lord, you boys need all the smart help you can get, and this is how you behave?"

Cole didn't answer. He pulled a vial of holy water from his inner coat pocket and threw it into Lisette's face.

IT HAD SEEMED a greater effort to *change* again, but it was an even greater effort to move through the air. But Megan was determined, and desperate.

The men had all been warned. *Cole* had been warned. And yet they all knew Lisette well, and that she had come at the command of the Pinkerton Agency—and Pinkerton often worked directly through the White House—so they would never have suspected that she could be the demon moving so easily among them.

Megan was exhausted. She could barely will herself through the air, barely concentrate to create the shadow wings needed to propel herself faster. She didn't see the troops, and she didn't know how long the journey was taking her now, only that the landscape was moving by far too slowly.

At last, she passed the troops making their way in haste.

And after what felt like an eternity later, she saw the chapel before her.

She might be too late.

NOTHING HAPPENED.

At least, nothing that he expected happened.

Lisette stood there, sputtering, staring at Cole with incredulous indignation. "Cole Granger, what on earth is the matter with you? You may be a sheriff in Texas, but I swear, I'll see your ears pinned to your head in D.C.! Lord Almighty, what are men coming to?" she demanded belligerently.

Cole stared at her blankly.

Dickens went running by him, ready to make amends. "Miss Annalise, forgive him, we've just been through hell up here—hell, I do mean *hell!*" he told her. "You come right on in and I'll get you a cloth to dry your face, dear lady. Oh, Miss Malcolm, you come right in, too, please!"

"Cole Granger!" Lisette said furiously. She had dismounted and stood near the door. Trudy was still on her horse, shocked and waiting.

"Something is not right," Cole said, staring at her.

"You idiot bastard!" she said. "Trudy, get down here and let's get in. I don't believe this! Cole Granger, I'm warning you—"

"We've got to get in!" Dickens warned. "This isn't the time. Please, please, all of you! Trudy, come, please!"

"Something is not right," Cole said again.

"Dickens is right, damn it, move!" Lisette ordered haughtily.

But Cole stood there, wary, still staring at Lisette, and Lisette staring back at him with indignation and fury.

"Hurry!" Dickens urged. "Trudy, please, come!"

Trudy dismounted, clearly made meek and disturbed by the situation as she moved to join them. She looked uneasily from Cole to Lisette.

"All right, yes, let's get in!" Lisette said.

Dickens started toward Trudy, wanting to hurriedly get her inside while Cole dealt with the wrathful Lisette.

But it was then—as Cole stood, jaw locked, his peripheral vision on the sky as he wondered how he could be wrong—that the truth began to dawn on him.

"No!" he said, turning to catch Trudy Malcolm.

She'd been with the vampire child, Betsy, alone, and the child hadn't hurt her but gone straight for Megan. Lisette had searched her assistant, but she wouldn't have shown signs of a bite—because Trudy had been bitten long, long ago.

It was amazing how the woman could change so quickly, and so entirely. Suddenly, she wasn't stooped. She wasn't frumpy, and she wasn't downtrodden. She was tall and her eyes bore a malicious light of pleasure, cruelty and brutality.

Cole couldn't stop her. Trudy burst past Lisette, slamming Newcomb with a backhanded swipe that sent him flying across the chapel.

"Trudy, how *dare* you!" Lisette cried. "Oh!" she gasped, seeing the true picture in a moment of sick realization. The chapel door was open, and the sky came alight then with winged shadow creatures, all of them trying to force their way into the small church.

"Get down!" Cole shouted to Lisette, and she dropped to the ground, covering her head, as though that might help when the hungry came for her.

Trudy Malcolm, having worn the best mask possible, was now in the chapel in her true form—powerful and potent and clearing the way for more of the creatures to enter. Cole took up a position at the doorway, trying to stop the onslaught. One of the dark animals nearly landed on Lisette, but he was able to stop the creature with holy water. He raced to the horses, grabbing a cavalry sword from a saddle holster, and raced back into the fray, believing that slicing through the frenzy around him would stop the onslaught enough to give the others a chance.

But, apparently, Trudy Malcolm was set on bringing him down first. She burst out of the chapel in a cloud of black-winged fury, and she lit on the ground just feet away from him. "Ah, there he is! The great Texas lawman, dabbling his feet in Union waters. It's a pity I can't just let someone hang you as a traitor."

"Are you *fighting for the South?*" Cole asked her, weighing his chances as they circled one another.

"Me? Not particularly. Smart boy—I was pretty sure you had it all figured out. But you seemed to think it had something to do with Megan, that pathetic creature. I saw how your mind was working. No, no, you've missed what I would think is obvious. The country is busy killing itself. I'm just adding to the death toll, letting the fevered feed on the fevered, that's all. Eventually, it will be all one country again—my country."

"That's insane. What do you want with a country?" he asked her.

"The history of all empires is building a feeding ground," she said. "You killed the girl, and the little drummer boy. They were the beginning of my family, but that's all right, you see. I'll just pick and choose better and create the world I want to live in. It will still take some time, Cole, but I'm up to the task. And in the meanwhile I'll be—I've *been*—so amused, watching the way men kill men. Seriously, how can you think of *me* as a beast?"

"Because the men who die believe in a greater cause,

Trudy. It's tragic, but they fight for what they believe in. You kill for yourself," Cole told her.

"Oh, you are going to be delicious!" She paused for a moment, pouting. "Where is your delightful little girlfriend, Cole? I had imagined pinning her down first, and letting her see how a real woman handles a real man!" She laughed.

"Megan isn't here. You can't touch her."

"No matter. I'll just let her see the remains of what I can do!"

She lifted off the ground, fangs bared, ready for him. He splashed a vial of holy water at her, giving her pause—but just pause. "I'm stronger than that, big boy!" she said, though her face had been punctuated by some pockmarks. "But you really are making me angry, Cole. And when I'm angry, I can make it very slow and very painful!"

She pounced again. This time he raised his sword, not at all sure if even injuring her would suffice, but ready to fight until his last breath.

But she never reached him.

Something burst from the sky and caught Trudy Malcolm midair. They flew several feet together and then landed as a clump of rolling bodies just feet away from him. Dust rose, and for a just moment Cole couldn't see a thing.

But he knew Megan had come back. Megan had taken Trudy and was rolling with her in a death grip. When Trudy's jaws opened impossibly wide and he saw the length of the fangs she lowered toward Megan, he burst into a run, wrenching Trudy from her with all his strength and tossing her a good five feet off. Megan, weakened, staggered up.

Trudy herself rose, a cry of fury escaping her mouth to shake the very trees. She looked from him to Megan, and decided to finish Megan first.

There was no choice: Cole flew on top of Megan, forcing them both into a roll. Trudy hit the dirt just feet away from them but swiftly recovered. This time, her pocked face was covered with dirt, and with her spitting and screaming again—a sound more terrible than that of a banshee in the night, or the howl of a thousand wolves. Trudy was a terrifying sight to behold.

For an instant, Cole caught Megan's eyes. Saw the way she looked at him. And he whispered swiftly, "I love you."

Then he braced his core, because Trudy was coming again, and he didn't know if their combined strength or the vial of holy water he uncorked with his teeth could even give her pause in light of her torrid frenzy. He braced…

But the vampire never touched them. Something, a greater shadow, huge and winged and somehow beautiful, came and swept the woman away. The two conjoined shadows blew past then and went tumbling into a mound of ash in the cemetery.

Something else swept by him; the battle was still on. Yet more creatures emerged from the trees, though perhaps less than in previous waves. From his prone position, Cole launched the holy water vial at the creature nearest him and watched it go down in whirl of screams and cinders. He jumped to his feet, reaching down for Megan, drawing her behind his back and pulling out his cavalry sword all in one continuous motion.

But nothing else came at them.

Newcomb staggered from the chapel. He leaned

heavily against the door frame. "It's done. I think it's done."

"No, no, be on guard, there will be more!" Cole cried to him. Megan had moved from behind him. He turned to see that she was staring at the graveyard. A winged shadow was rising from the ash.

It didn't turn toward them. Instead, it soared high into the sky and disappeared over the trees.

Megan started running toward the ash. Cole ran after her. When she slowed to a stop he came around by her side.

What remained of Trudy Malcolm lay at their feet. Her head had been wrenched from her body and lay at an awkward angle. Her limbs were still twitching, but as they did so, they seemed to ooze and then blacken, and the flesh turned to powder, which the breeze picked up and blew into the distance. Soon they were staring at nothing but disarticulated bones.

He heard the sound of hoofbeats. General Bickford and his reinforcements had arrived and their fresh bows launched arrows into what was left of the straggling, frenzied creatures still flying about.

IN THE AFTERMATH, the world consisted entirely of silence.

Then General Bickford dismounted, shouting orders. Cleanup had begun, and Cole knew that neither he nor Megan were required to do anything more. She slumped into his arms, and he lifted her off her feet, cradling her against him. They had done what they needed to.

She looked up, her eyes wide, a curious smile on her lips. "It was my father, Cole. I know it was my father."

He didn't want to argue with her. *God knows, she might be right.*

"Maybe," he said.

Her smile deepened, and then she frowned. "What did you say to me?" she asked him.

"I said 'maybe.'"

"Before that."

He arched an eyebrow. He felt a grin tugging at his lips. "Oh, before."

"Yes, before."

"I said, *I love you*."

"Really?"

"Yes, really," he told her gravely.

She found the strength to thread her fingers through his hair and pull his head down.

And kiss him.

TELEGRAPH WIRES SENT an official report to Washington that the strange "guerilla" attacks on Harpers Ferry had been put down.

Cole made sure that it carried the information that a certain drummer boy, a Confederate drummer boy, had been laid to his rest and had received full burial rights.

Megan stood at the window in their lodging house, watching the street and waiting for Cole's return. He and a number of officers—and Lisette Annalise—had been sequestered with General Bickford while the goings-on of the episode were completely reported.

She looked at her hand, and she marveled at the plain gold ring on her finger. Cole hadn't had diamonds or jewels, but she hadn't wanted them. She still couldn't believe that he loved her so deeply, no matter what she was, no matter what her background, no matter the lives they had led or all that they had been through. It was humbling to think of how she was loved, and how deeply she loved in return.

Their ceremony at the church had been very simple, presided over by Father Costello, with Mary-Anne Weatherly standing by as her witness and Sergeant Newcomb standing by Cole. They had toyed with the idea of waiting until Cody and Alex could have been with them, but they knew that the two would understand.

They were living in perilous times. A time of war, and in such a world, every moment of peace was precious.

Her eye drawn back to the street below, she noticed a man on the sidewalk. He wore a handsome top hat, a long coat and carried a smart walking stick. She was curious, thinking that she hadn't noticed him in the town before.

He looked up. His face was caught in the moonlight, and she held her breath, staring back down at him.

It was Cody, but it wasn't Cody.

It was Cody as he might look in another ten or twenty years.

It was her father.

She froze there; she wanted to run down the stairs and into his arms.

He lifted a hand, and he blew her a kiss.

She turned from the window and raced across the hall, then down the stairs and out onto the street. She searched up and down, but he wasn't there.

Turning, she crashed into Cole.

"What are you doing?" he asked her.

"He was here, he was here! My father. It was my father. I saw his face. He's like Cody, Cole, so much like him, just older. Cole, I swear it was him."

Cole looked around them. "He's gone now."

"Why? Why did he see me and leave?" she whispered.

Cole lifted her chin. "Maybe he'll come to you when the time is right, Megan. When war is over. Or maybe he still feels that he has his own war to fight. God knows, maybe we've taken but one monster here, while others still wreak havoc elsewhere."

She looked at him and nodded at last.

"I really wanted to see that man," she said.

"Will this man do?" he asked her, a slow grin curving into his features.

"If he's mine for the night."

He swept her off her feet. "He's all yours. For the night, and forever," he told her.

"You've already carried me over the threshold. And I'm feeling quite well and strong."

"I hope so," he said.

"I don't want you huffing and puffing once we're up the stairs," she told him.

To his credit, he managed not to huff or puff a bit as he stood her up before the hearth—and their bed that remained a pile of pillows and sheets and quilts on the floor.

They looked at each other and smiled. And then they were in one another's arms, and clothing was flying and ripping, and they laughed all the while.

Soon they were down on the floor, and they made love tenderly, feverishly and tenderly again. And then, when they lay together, just looking at one another, she said, "You saved my life."

"You saved my life," he told her.

"No, you saved mine."

"You saved mine."

She laughed, remembering when the argument had gone the other way.

She touched his cheek tenderly.

"But you saved my soul," she told him. "Beat that!"

"You *are* my soul," he told her, and he kissed her again.

* * * * *